MIDLIFE IS THE CAT'S MEOW

MIDLIFE IS THE CAT'S MEOW
MY SO-CALLED HEXED MIDLIFE
BOOK ONE

T.B. MARKINSON
MIRANDA MACLEOD

Copyright © 2023 by T.B. Markinson and Miranda MacLeod

Cover Design by Victoria Cooper

Edited by Kelly Hathaway

This book is copyrighted and licensed for your personal enjoyment only. All rights reserved. No part of this publication may be reproduced, stored in a retrieval system, or transmitted in any forms or by any means without the prior permission of the copyright owner. The moral rights of the authors have been asserted.

This book is a work of fiction. Names, characters, businesses, places, events, and incidents are the product of the authors' imagination or are used fictitiously. Any resemblance to actual persons, living or dead, events, or locales is entirely coincidental.

Some of the contents of this book are based on characters and situations originally contained in the Witches of Pinecroft Cove series of paranormal cozy mystery books, which Miranda MacLeod and T.B. Markinson wrote and published under the pen name Nicole St. Claire. The plot, characters, and themes have been completely reimagined and rewritten as the first book in a sapphic paranormal women's fiction series. However, readers of the original series may recognize common elements between the two.

A NOTE FROM THE AUTHORS

This series was inspired by the characters and mysteries in the Witches of Pinecroft Cove cozy mystery series, which the authors published under the pen name Nicole St Claire in 2019-2021.

The books have been entirely reworked to transform them into a fresh, new sapphic paranormal women's fiction mystery series. However, if you have read the other series, certain circumstances may feel familiar.

You are not losing your marbles.

CHAPTER ONE

"What did you expect would happen, marrying a non-magical?"

My mother's voice rang loudly in my ears, the memory of her words so clear I snapped my eyes to the rearview mirror. Despite knowing that even for witches, teleportation only happened in movies, I was convinced I would find her seated in the back of my rickety station wagon.

Instead, I saw only my daughters, twelve-year-old Tabitha and nine-year-old Sabrina, dozing with their curly red heads pressed against the windows as the setting sun turned the sky behind them a million shades of pink and orange.

I continued driving east, my heart as heavy as my lead foot.

At forty-three years old, after spending more than a decade as a stay-at-home mom and full-time wife in an upper-middle class suburb in Ohio, I was newly divorced, completely broke, and heading to a place I hadn't called home for over half my life—a place filled with memories too painful to think about.

What had I expected when I'd married Phil seventeen years ago? Definitely not this.

As I approached the ferry terminal, the evening air along the seacoast was as thick and foul-smelling as a bowl of New England fish chowder left out in the sun for hours. A seagull cawed from the top of a post, and a shaggy black cat prowled the rocky shoreline, probably searching for an unsuspecting critter to have for dinner. I pulled into the parking lot and followed the bright red painted stripe on the pavement to the waiting area for the boat to Goode Harbor Island.

Stopping the engine, I rolled down the windows, my hair turning into a halo of bright red frizz around my head. I was exhausted and more than a little cranky, but I couldn't give up now. I held out hope for something, anything, to make the temperature bearable. Instead, it grew even more oppressive. I'd never missed magic more than I did right then, unable so much as to conjure a light cooling breeze.

I cursed the day the Shadow Council had taken it from me.

"Are we there yet?" Sabrina demanded with a sleepy croak, stirring in the back seat.

"Not yet but soon, sweetheart," I soothed, even though my stomach tightened. There were more cars ahead of us than I'd expected. I did a quick mental calculation of how many vehicles could fit on a ferry, disheartened by the answer. We'd be lucky to make it on board. And lately, luck had been sorely lacking, at least the good kind.

When you can't work magic, the vagaries of fortune are all you have to rely on.

A worker in a bright yellow reflective vest unlatched the safety gate, allowing it to swing wide open. I turned on the engine and inched up closer to the edge of the dock as the cars ahead of us rolled onto the ferry. Sure enough, just as I reached the ramp, the worker waved his arms, signaling me to stop.

"All full," he said with a shake of his head. "There's another boat tomorrow morning, 7:00 a.m. sharp."

As I caught sight of my girls in the mirror again, my shoulders slumped. After so many hours on the road, only a few miles of water separated us from cozy beds and a good night's sleep. But without a spot on the ferry, it might as well have been a thousand. I grabbed my phone and texted a quick status update to my mom, sweat dripping down my nose as I typed out the bad news.

"Do you happen to know of a place to stay nearby?" I called out to the ferry worker, who was busy waving off the handful of cars behind me. "Preferably under a hundred bucks?" I added, inwardly cringing at my bank account's depleted state. Finding a job on the island would be priority number one.

"For that price, I suggest the parking lot," the man said with a laugh as he returned to my car. "You won't find many vacancies, and if you do, it'll cost you two or three times as much. Shoulda called ahead for one of the reserved spots on the ferry."

No shit, Sherlock, I managed not to say out loud. "I tried," I said instead with an extra spoonful of sweetness, "but I was told they're completely booked until the middle of July."

He nodded, not looking surprised. "The big literary festival is this weekend. Plus, Goode Harbor's become a popular tourist destination since the condos started going in."

"Condos?" I was taken aback. "I had no idea Doris Greene had died, but if they're building condos, it's gotta be over her dead body."

Doris had been the president of the historical society since God was a child, and she was known to have opinions on everything from appropriate paint colors to how bright the light bulbs should be in the streetlamps. She was much too proud of the island's genteel heritage to allow something as tawdry as condominiums to be built without raising hell about it.

"Sounds like you know the island pretty well." As the man let out a hearty guffaw, a spark of recognition tickled my memory.

"Brett?" I inquired, maybe seventy percent certain of my guess.

His eyes grew round and then narrowed to a squint as he inspected my face more closely. "Tallie Shipton? Is that you?"

"In the flesh." I shook my head, struggling to square this middle-aged man with ruddy cheeks and a slight belly with the boy who had been captain of the football team my senior year. "Brett, my goodness."

"Why, I haven't seen you since..."

Since Maya's funeral.

The answer hung in the air between us, unsaid, as Brett shifted uncomfortably, and the air around me turned icy for a bat of an eyelash. Or maybe it was my imagination.

"It's been a long time," I finally said because someone needed to break the awkward silence.

In fact, it had been twenty-five years since my older sister had drowned when a freak squall swept her from the deck of her boat. I'd started college a month later, retreating as far from the shining waters of Crescent Cove as I could, never venturing back.

Until now.

"You here for the literary festival or the reunion?" Brett asked.

"Reunion?" My heart turned to an inanimate lump in my chest.

"It's the 150th anniversary of the founding of Chesterton Academy," he prompted, the sparkle returning to his eyes. "We're holding an all-alumni reunion in July. You should have gotten a flyer about it sent to your last known mailing address back in early May."

I probably had, but since the house occupying that address had been in the process of being seized by the FBI around that time—thanks, Phil—I'd forwarded the mail service to my mother. I assumed the reunion invitation would be waiting on her kitchen table for my arrival, along with a dozen other things I'd rather not deal with.

Brett glanced back at the ferry, which had yet to depart from the dock, possibly because he hadn't actually finished shutting the gate and raising the ramp. "You're the only car left in the line. Everyone else gave up. Tell you what. Give me a minute. I think I can squeeze you on."

"For real?" I flashed him a grateful smile. I might have been resigned to sleeping in the parking lot with two cranky kids, but I hadn't exactly been looking forward to it. After weeks of rotten luck, finally something was going my way. "That's really kind of you."

Brett hurried back to the ferry, and I watched as one by one, the last row of cars backed off the boat, traveled partway down the ramp, and then pulled back onto the deck in a tighter configuration. Sure enough, by the time the last car was in place, there was room for one more.

Just like magic. Almost.

"Thank you again," I called through the open

window as I slowed to a crawl and maneuvered my overloaded station wagon into the narrow spot.

"See you at the reunion," he called back, touching his forehead in salute.

Not if I can help it, I muttered under my breath as I waved.

Even if I hadn't been returning home a total failure, a reunion was the last place I would've wanted to go. I'd never completely fit in, even before my carrot orange hair had become a favorite target for Chad Kenworthy, the school bully.

The details of how it all started were hazy after so many years, but suffice to say that *carrot* rhymes with *parrot,* and somehow by the end of seventh grade, half the school was calling me Polly. As in *Polly wanna cracker?* Chad used to squawk at me from across the hallway, the sound echoing off the lockers as it blended with the cruel laughter of my classmates. The stupid name stuck all the way until graduation, and to this day, the sight of a parrot, or crackers, for that matter, made my blood run cold.

Willingly subjecting myself to a high school reunion? Not for a million bucks.

I tried texting my mom as soon as we were on board the ferry, but I couldn't get enough service bars for it to go through.

The crossing from the mainland was smooth, the water calm. As the girls continued to sleep, I opened the sunroof, tilted my seat back, and watched the changing colors of the sky. Closing my eyes, I dozed briefly, but it was a restless sleep filled with snippets of memories I preferred not to relive.

I opened my eyes again and continued to watch the sky.

THE LAST STREAKS OF PURPLE HAD FADED, and a scattering of stars were twinkling as the ferry approached the Goode Harbor dock. After adjusting my seat and starting the engine, I maneuvered my car down the ramp.

The minute I'd crossed onto solid land, I pulled over and tried to call the house, but it was no use. This time, my phone had no bars at all. Belatedly, I recalled my mom mentioning how spotty the phone service on the island could be without magic to give it a boost. I wouldn't know firsthand. The last time I'd been here, iPhones hadn't been invented yet.

I wondered if she was already in bed. Both she and Isodora—or Izzy, as we'd always called my great aunt, who lived with my mom and helped to run the bed-and-breakfast that now operated out of our old family home—were getting up there in years. I assumed they'd joined the ranks of the *early to bed and early to rise* crowd quite some time ago.

Guilt over my poor planning needled me. The girls

and I were already causing a disruption by coming to stay, but there was nothing that could be done about it. My felonious husband had left me with precious few options. I resolved that we would at least do our best to slip in quietly and let them sleep.

As I drove along Main Street through Goode Harbor's nineteenth century downtown, it looked unchanged from how I'd last seen it, yet somehow nicer, too. The vaudeville-era theater had a newly restored neon billboard twinkling out front, the carousel horses outside the old-fashioned soda fountain had been freshly painted, and dozens of quaint shops and cafés had opened where there had been only empty storefronts twenty-five years before. People walked dogs across the lush green grass that carpeted the town square, and inside a whitewashed gazebo, a jazz band was playing a summer concert in the park. The town appeared to be enjoying a significant renaissance.

The road forked just beyond the main drag, which came as a surprise since it had always gone straight through. To the right, I saw a whole section of cookie-cutter buildings I'd never seen before. I wished I wasn't seeing them now. That was how ugly they were. Soulless and cheap. I was hardly what anyone would consider a local anymore, but even so, I was offended by their very existence. Maybe I owed Doris Greene an apology. A large sign announced more condos and vacation units coming soon from none other than the Kenworthy Real Estate Corporation.

I should've guessed.

Whether my former bully was involved in the company bearing his family name, I didn't know. It didn't matter. Pretty much every member of that family was a real piece of work. The only one who had been worth anything was old Doc Kenworthy, the island physician. It struck me how funny it was that the word *worthy* was a part of their last name. Their family tree bore nothing but rotten apples as far as I could tell. Not a worthy one in the bunch.

The crowds of vacationers thinned rapidly as I approached the edge of town, where the island's stone church with its imposing bell and steeple stood like a watch tower. Behind it was a graveyard filled with crooked and crumbling monuments, the final resting place of generations of the island's founding families. A chill crept along my spine as I passed, just as it always did. Plenty of Shiptons were buried there, though not my sister. It wasn't possible to bury someone if the sea refused to give back the body.

My foot sat heavily on the brake as I rolled to a stop at the corner. The moon was little more than a sliver in the sky, its light ineffective at chasing away the deep shadows cast by the giant mausoleum in the center of the cemetery. For a moment, I swore I saw a movement in the darkness and a faint blue glow of mist creeping along the ground like something out of a horror movie.

I blinked, and my vision returned to normal. I let out a low sigh. On top of everything else, I was overdue to have my eyes checked. I'd need to find a new optometrist and make an appointment. That reminded me that I needed a job with medical insurance.

Getting older while simultaneously starting over sucked sour lemon balls—and you can quote me on that.

I pressed my foot to the accelerator, grateful to put the church in all its creepiness behind me. Soon the last structures of Goode Harbor faded from view, and the winding road hugged the edge of a jagged cliff overlooking the sea. Even after twenty-five years, I could find my way home from here with my eyes shut.

Good thing, too. As soon as the lights from downtown faded, my already limited view of the road rapidly dissolved into inky darkness. Doris Greene and her historical society mavens considered the lack of proper lighting tasteful and authentic. If you asked me, it was an accident waiting to happen.

At last, a carved wooden sign with *Shipton Inn* written in gold lettering and illuminated with a single, historical-society approved, low-wattage bulb came into view, marking the entrance to the long driveway that led to the house. As I made the turn, I heard the familiar sound of crushed shell crunch beneath my tires. I slowed the car to a crawl, easing it the last few yards until the house came into view.

Confusion washed over me.

Beyond the tall trees at the end of the drive stood the same house I remembered from my childhood, with its gray cedar shingles and that wraparound porch where I had spent many a lazy afternoon curled up in a rocking chair with a good book.

But in the middle of the expansive front lawn burned a roaring fire. My mother and aunt Izzy—who were most definitely *not* in bed despite the late hour—chanted and swayed with an almost childlike abandon around it, floral wreaths encircling their heads like crowns.

"Mom?" Tabitha's voice came as a whisper from behind me. "Why are Grammy and Aunt Izzy naked in the front yard?"

CHAPTER TWO

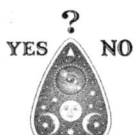

"Tallulah, you're here!" Breaking away from the fire, my mother hurried to greet me, long red hair flying every which way, her arms spread wide to give me a hug as I sprung from the car and slammed the door shut to keep what I was about to say from singeing the impressionable ears in the back seat.

"Mother, what has gotten into you?" I hissed, dodging her naked embrace with a withering glare that stopped my mom in her tracks.

"It's Litha, darling," she replied, using the traditional word for the summer solstice holiday. "Did you lose track of the days? There's still plenty of time to celebrate."

"You know I don't allow magic around the children."

Already my brain was whirling with possible explanations, none of them remotely plausible, for what my daughters were witnessing. They were both wide awake, of course, staring through the car windows with saucer eyes. Who could blame them? Too bad their crook of a dad had run off to Central America with all our money because they were going to need therapy for life after this.

"You only forbade magic because Phil didn't like it. Besides, you texted saying you weren't going to make it." My great aunt approached, walking slower than my mom had, but still sprightly for a woman in her eighties. Her hair was as unruly as my mother's but white through and through. Two cotton robes with clashing floral prints were draped over one arm. Inexplicably, it had not occurred to either one of them to use these handy garments to cover their nudity.

"No. I gave all this up a long time ago," I corrected, reciting the familiar half-truth. I stared pointedly from my naked relatives to the robes they were not wearing. I would have given anything for the ability to conjure clothing out of thin air right about then. Or blinders. "I don't want to expose Tabitha and Sabrina to any of this, and I'd appreciate you respecting my wishes."

A muscle in my mother's jaw twitched, almost imperceptible but enough for me to know I was teetering on the edge of trouble. "If you didn't want your girls to know they're witches, perhaps you shouldn't have brought them to live in a house with witches."

As if I'd had a choice.

She did have a valid point, though.

"I'm sorry, Mom," I backtracked, not completely out of remorse but because the last thing I needed after a full day of travel was to get into a war of wills with a naked, red-headed witch. "You surprised me, is all. I thought we had reached an understanding about the no magic thing when you last came to visit."

"In *Cleveland*, yes." The way my mother said it made it clear she considered Cleveland a place where magic didn't stand a chance, anyway. She wasn't wrong. That was the main reason I'd chosen to live there. "Now, are you going to let my grand babies out of the car so I can say a proper hello?"

"Are *you* planning to put on a robe?"

"You'll have to tell them," Aunt Izzy said as she handed one robe to my mom and slid the other over her sloping shoulders, tying it closed around her plump waist. "You don't want them to start getting their powers without knowing what to expect."

Her words evoked a sense of dread and revulsion in the core of my being. Explaining menstrual periods had been difficult enough. The mere thought of helping my girls make sense out of what I'd come to think of as the Shipton family curse drained every remaining ounce of energy from my spirit.

Living in Cleveland, far from anything remotely magical, I'd never expected I would need to. But we were back in Crescent Cove now, a community crawling with witches. The situation had drastically changed.

It'd become infinitely more dangerous.

"I know." I sighed, wearily. "But please, not tonight."

I entered the house in a daze, but not without noticing as we passed through the living room—or what we sometimes called a parlor when we were feeling fancy—that the antique cream-upholstered sofa and armchairs were still in the exact arrangement from twenty-five years before. I recognized the lace doily on the coffee table as the one my grandmother had crocheted. The crimson-and-blue Persian rug in the middle of the room was the one she and my grandfather had purchased on their honeymoon. The woodwork gleamed with a soft sheen, and the familiar smell of lemon and wax permeated the air. The overwhelming sense of returning home hit me like a blow to the sternum.

After climbing the wide curving staircase to the second floor, my mom opened the door that concealed the much narrower stairs leading to two small bedrooms that had been carved out of the third-floor attic. Mom stood beside the door to the room that had once belonged to my sister, ushering my daughters in with kisses to the tops of their heads. The room was freshly painted and outfitted with two twin beds topped with matching purple comforters.

Fresh nightgowns sat folded on the pillows, along

with toothbrushes, so we wouldn't have to unpack until morning. Mom and Aunt Izzy had even figured out the girls' favorite band—definitely the result of magic since I could never remember who they were despite hearing about them daily—and had tacked several of their posters to the walls.

"Home sweet home," I said with more cheer than I felt. "Bathroom's across the hall. Let's brush those teeth and climb into bed, sleepyheads. It's very late."

"I thought you'd want to decide what to do with yours," my mom said, motioning toward my childhood bedroom.

I paused in the doorway to catch my breath, taking in the room's familiar whitewashed dresser and nightstand with matching blue-and-white fringed scarves on top. The twin-size wrought iron bed, also painted white, occupied the same space I'd expected it to be, and the bright floral quilt my grandmother had stitched by hand still covered its top. It was a space frozen in time. There was a nightgown for me and a toothbrush, too. For a second time that night, an unexpectedly sweet sense of nostalgia washed over me, along with deep and genuine gratitude.

"Thank you, Mom."

She paused at the top of the stairs and gave me a thoughtful look. "We'll have a good, long talk in the morning," she said, although I felt anything but reassured by it.

The last thing I wanted to do was chat about how

everything I thought and knew about my life and the man I'd chosen to share it with were based on lies.

I changed and washed up as quickly as I could in the small bathroom. After kissing the children goodnight, I returned to my bedroom, but all the exhaustion I'd felt only moments ago evaporated the moment I turned off the light and placed my head on the pillow. Instead of winding down, my brain hummed like I'd chugged a pot of espresso.

My room was so dark that even with my eyes open, I hallucinated spots of light to make up for not being able to see a thing. I'd forgotten how intense the nights could be on the island without the brightness of a full moon. But as my eyes began to adjust, a beam of illumination swept across my window, sending my pupils into momentary shock.

I crawled back out of bed and crossed to the window, pulling aside a gauzy white curtain. The back lawn stretched out for some distance, cloaked in shadows, before merging with the rocky shore and rippling water of Crescent Cove. For the briefest moment, the trees on either side of the house seemed to radiate a faint blue glow, but it disappeared as soon as I rubbed my eyes.

Just what I needed, more proof my vision was failing me.

Far in the distance, on the other side of the cove, the roofline of Chesterton Manor—one of the island's most iconic landmarks—was dark and imposing. There had been at least a dozen Gilded Age mansions on the island in its heyday, but through fire, natural disaster, or general neglect, only this one remained. It had been empty as long as I could remember, its heavy iron gate locked but powerless to keep the weeds and vines from reclaiming its once stately gardens.

The flash of light swept past again, and this time, I could tell it was coming from the lighthouse that stood beyond Chesterton Manor. Had its beacon always been so bright? Or had I been better at sleeping through it when I was younger? These days, between my anger at Phil and worry over the future, it seemed I rarely slept at all and never well.

Letting the curtain fall against my back, I rested my forehead against the cold glass, my eyes fixed on the cove. I couldn't see it in the darkness, but the details were etched in my memory. Not its beauty on a calm day, sadly. All I could remember was the fierceness of the storm, the churning waves, and the tiny white sail of Maya's boat slipping out of sight.

I shivered as a sudden gust disturbed the still air. I turned from the window, my heart racing as sheer white fabric billowed all around me like a spectral being. As quickly as it had come, the wind was gone. The curtain settled around my face like a cobweb, and I clawed at it as I fought back a rising panic that threatened to squeeze my airways shut.

As soon as I'd freed myself, I raced back to my bed and pulled the covers over my head. I stayed that way until finally plunging into a fitful sleep, filled with snippets of Maya, her boat, and the faces of the Shadow Council as they rendered their judgment and banished me from my island home.

All memories best left in the past.

The next time I opened my eyes, I was immediately aware of two things. First, bright sunshine was streaming through the open window, along with a light morning breeze that brought with it a whiff of the wild roses that grew in the woods.

Second, sometime during the night, a twenty-pound weight had been deposited on my chest as I slept. I cracked one eye open. A pair of green eyes stared back at me, unblinking, surrounded by a profusion of black fur. I struggled to sit up, but the enormous cat on my torso held me down.

"Hey!" I groused as I wiggled my shoulders from side to side. "Go on, now."

I may have been born a witch, but there was nothing in my DNA that predisposed me to like cats. Especially black ones. As if knowing this, the cat let out a mournful bawl, mocking me, and didn't move an inch even as I gave the covers a jiggle.

"Listen, cat," I warned. He shook his head like a lion shaking its mane, and the fur billowed out wildly all around him. The twinkle of a brass name tag that hung from a collar around his neck caught my eye. I squinted at the letters engraved on it. "Buster. Is that your name?" He meowed loudly, which I took as a yes.

I gathered all my strength and propelled myself upward. Buster rolled off my chest and landed at the foot of the bed. He promptly began licking his hind leg as if that was exactly what he'd had in mind to do all along.

"Let's get this straight," I informed him as I rose and smoothed the covers back into place. "This may be your house, but it's my bed, and I don't like to share. Especially not with a flea-bitten thing like you."

The look he gave me as I left the room made it perfectly clear he had understood everything I said and simply had no intention of dignifying my accusation with a response.

Tabitha and Sabrina were sound asleep, and a quick check of the clock revealed why. It was barely six in the morning. When had I become this person who bounded out of bed with the sun? I missed the blissful days of youth when I could lounge in bed until noon, but it was no use. Even if a random cat hadn't accosted me first thing, I doubted I would have slept any longer. The day I'd hit forty, my bladder had shrunk to the size of a pea.

As I wandered across the second-floor landing, the mouthwatering scent of cinnamon permeated the air. The clattering of pots and pans told me I'd find Mom and Aunt Izzy in the kitchen, so I headed directly there by way of the back stairs. By the time I hit the first floor, the smell of sweet-potato waffles was so thick in the air I could taste them when I breathed in.

"Good morning, Tallie," my aunt greeted me, turning from her spot at the stove. The whorl of snowy curls had been tamed into a bun, and a large apron covered her generous hips. In her right hand she held what could have been mistaken for an ordinary wooden spoon, except for the sparkles emanating from it.

"Morning," I mumbled, looking away from the magical utensil that served the same function as a wand when placed in the hands of a skilled kitchen witch.

That was what my aunt was, and my mother, too. All my Shipton ancestors had been, as far as I knew. I, on the other hand, was better off not touching ordinary kitchen implements, let alone enchanted ones. My lack of culinary skills was a secret I'd never shared with either of them. Shiptons were kitchen witches, after all. Except, apparently, for me.

I'd had all sorts of odd abilities in my youth. Conjuring rain clouds. Controlling the wind. In other words, I'd excelled at any number of things good, respectable witches didn't do. Maya had covered for me as best she could. In the end, it had cost her everything. Sometimes, the guilt threatened to cut me in two from the inside out.

"You're up early," my mom commented, not missing a beat as she prepared the largest bowl of waffle batter I'd ever seen. At least it was an ordinary whisk in her hand and not something that could put me under an enchantment. "Waffles?"

"Yes, please," I said, although there was hardly a need since in the time it had taken me to answer, she'd already finished preparing my plate. I followed her to the dining room and took a seat at the long table. After tucking a cloth napkin into the lacy neckline of my granny nightgown—I really needed to unpack so I could find the sweats and old T-shirts that were my preferred sleeping attire—I grabbed the jug of real maple syrup from the table and gave it a liberal pour.

My mom sat beside me, angling her chair to face me. "Well?" she asked as I took my first bite.

"Mmm, so good," I assured her, my mouth too full to say more. It was an old family recipe, and every bite brought back a memory as sweet as the syrup on top. Finally, I swallowed the last morsels. Recalling the gallons of batter my mom had been mixing, I asked, "Do you need me to help with cleaning up this morning?"

Mom waved her hand. "Thanks for the offer, but there's no need. Alice will come by later to do all that."

"Alice?" I frowned, unable to match the name to a face.

"The housekeeper we've hired to help for the summer season."

"I thought that was Helen." Honestly, though I would never admit it to my mother, the witches of her generation tended to blend together in my mind. She'd insisted on informing me of all the island gossip over the years, but I could never keep them straight.

"No, Helen moved to Florida after that bad winter we had. But the last of Alice's kids moved out recently, and she was looking for something to keep herself busy. You remember Alice," my mother pressed when I didn't answer, though I'd certainly given no indication this was the case. "Alice Crenshaw."

"Oh, you mean *Mrs.* Crenshaw," I said, unable to bring myself to use her first name, like it was against some cosmic rule. I had to stop myself from laughing at the ridiculousness of it. Here I was, a woman in my forties, uneasy about calling another adult by their given name because she'd once been a teacher's aid in my kindergarten class. "Of course, I remember Mrs. Crenshaw. How many kids did she have, anyway?"

"No idea. A lot," my mom said with a soft chuckle. "All foster kids, too. She took in so many over the years, and her a single woman, you know. If you ask me, she's a saint."

I nodded in agreement. I was so overwhelmed by my own two I couldn't imagine voluntarily taking in anyone else's. "I should've asked before. Are there guests staying in the inn this morning?"

"No, and it will be quiet for a while, with only one couple staying with us until after the literary festival."

"Has business been bad?" My nerves jangled in a way that was becoming familiar as I feared my family's finances might be little better than my own. "What can I do to help?"

"Business has been fine," my mother reassured me. "We'll only have two guests, but they've booked all five rooms for the next several weeks. Something about needing privacy. As for last night, you know we never host guests when we're performing holiday rituals. Unless they're witches, too, of course."

There it was. It had taken my mom mere minutes to introduce the first of several topics I'd been hoping to avoid.

"I think it's time to bring the luggage in from the car." I scooted my chair from the table, poised to run, but Mom stopped me in place, not with a spell but with a withering look of motherly disapproval I would have given anything to have perfected with my own daughters.

"Tabitha will be thirteen on her next birthday." She didn't say more and didn't need to. I knew as well as she did that thirteen was the age a natural born witch got her powers. The sand was running out of the hourglass much faster than I would have liked.

Once my mother found out what I'd done, there would be a reckoning.

"It might not even happen," I said. "She might take after her father."

"Let's hope not." From the way my mother's nose wrinkled, I didn't think she was limiting her statement to my ex-husband's lack of magical abilities. "She needs to be prepared, Tallulah. Izzy and I—"

"I can handle it, Mom. She's my daughter." Beneath the knee-jerk annoyance brought on by my mother's meddling, unease needled my insides. Having either of my daughters inherit magic like I'd had was one of my greatest fears.

"You think you'll be prepared to teach her?" Mom scoffed. "You probably need a tutor yourself after all these years."

"I most certainly do not." I straightened in my chair. "My magical abilities are the same as they were twenty-five years ago."

This was a lie. Or if it was true, it was only because I knew something no one else did. After my sister's death, the Shadow Council—that aptly named shadowy group of witches who served as the enforcers of magical law throughout the world—had slithered into town under the cover of darkness to conduct a top-secret inquiry. Their magical powers must've been out of this world because they even escaped detection by our island's overactive rumor mill. I wouldn't have known a thing about it if they hadn't shown up in my college dorm room that fall.

The council had never opened a public investigation, nor even so much as declared a crime had taken place. That hadn't stopped them from making it clear they considered me their prime suspect in whatever it was they thought had gone down with my sister's death. They told me I was a danger, that back in the good old days, witches like me would have been locked away. But they couldn't tell me why, and they never offered a single shred of proof that would've held up in any court, magical or otherwise.

Even so, I'd agreed to their deal in the end just to make it all go away. After swearing me to secrecy, they'd bound my powers, and the powers of any of my descendants. Not only that, but I was exiled from my home forever.

My family could never know what I'd allowed the Shadow Council to do.

And the Shadow Council could never know I'd returned.

CHAPTER THREE

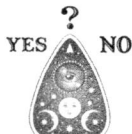

The pounding on the front door rattled my teeth. It was just after lunch, and I'd taken refuge in the parlor as my girls launched into yet another episode of *Bewitched*, a television show about a witch who marries a mortal, of all things. My mother's idea. The woman has never been accused of being subtle.

My heart raced as the god-awful racket continued, dredging up memories of that early morning raid that had been my first clue that good ol' Phil had been up to no good. I may have come from a family of kitchen witches, but it was the mild-mannered accountant I'd married who had excelled at cooking the company books.

Only it wouldn't be the FBI coming for me here.

Dread nailed the soles of my slippers to the floor.

Was it possible the Shadow Council had already discovered my presence on the island? I knew it was a risk, but it wasn't like I was wearing an ankle monitor or they had the island encircled in a magical forcefield or something.

Despite the fact they possessed magic, they were still a bureaucracy with all the usual staffing and budget shortfalls, all the same disgruntled pencil-pushers of any similar agency in the non-magical world. Besides which, their closest field office was hundreds of miles away in Boston. Believe me, I'd checked. I'd truly believed I would have more than one good night's sleep before I had to worry about them finding me.

"Coming," Aunt Izzy called out as she made her way toward the source of the incessant knocking, not noticing my frozen and distraught state.

The knocking didn't let up, even after this reassurance, and I saw my aunt's shoulder's tense, an unmistakable expression of annoyance settling over her features. Her white hair and grandmotherly appearance might not have seemed particularly scary to a casual observer, but I knew how powerful of a witch she could be when the need arose. Still, the pounding continued.

Aunt Izzy cracked the door open just wide enough to peek through. I half expected the person or people on the other side to come barging in, wands blazing.

When that didn't happen, I walked to a better vantage point, still out of view but enough to get a glimpse of who was outside.

I'm not sure what I was looking for. It wasn't like members of the Shadow Council wore uniforms. They wouldn't show up in flowing robes and pointy hats, pounding on our front door like it was a drum. In fact, they likely wouldn't announce their presence at all, until it was too late to run. Even so, every muscle in my body readied in case I needed to leg it to the back door to escape their detection.

"Can I help you?" My aunt's tone lacked its usual warmth as she opened the door a sliver more, though not enough to let the visitors in.

From what I was able to see, a well-dressed man in his fifties and a woman who appeared to be a decade or more his junior, stood amidst a towering pile of expensive looking luggage. The man was red in the face, but for some reason, though he clutched a single leather satchel close to his chest, I got the impression it was the younger woman beside him who had done most of the lifting and carrying.

"Didn't you tell them we were arriving early?" the man said, his flush cheeks intensifying to an alarming shade of eggplant that made me want to check his blood pressure. He looked like he might expire right then and there. At first, I thought he was yelling at my aunt, but then he turned to confront his companion, who withered visibly at the attention. "I specifically told you to arrange for that, Celia. Useless. Utterly useless."

My hands balled into fists at my sides, spurred by the man's casually condescending cruelty. My immediate concerns over the Shadow Council had subsided, but the leftover adrenaline in my system left me itching for a fight. Especially with a thoughtless cad. I'd had about enough of men who thought they were better than everyone else and used the women in their lives—wives and daughters, for instance—as little more than stepping stones to raise themselves higher.

"Is there a problem?" my mother asked as she joined my aunt at the door, speaking in that calming tone she used to employ on me when I was little and on the verge of throwing a tantrum. Given this dude's age, I doubted the trick would work. Then again, his behavior was infantile, so I couldn't be sure.

"Alexander Tate," he announced with the air of someone who expected his name to open any and every door.

It must have come as quite a shock when my mom and aunt didn't budge, keeping the door half shut in a way that barred his entrance. The man shifted on his feet, his facial color getting stormier.

"And, who are you?" Mom's attention turned to his companion, her demeanor thawing noticeably as kindness filled her words. Mom didn't abide rudeness, and if this man hadn't bothered to introduce his companion, she seemed determined to make it happen herself.

"Celia Lopez," the woman said after a moment or two of silence had passed, during which she seemed to consider whether or not my mother truly wanted to know her name. Like she wasn't used to being seen. Though her bone structure and shining brown eyes suggested she was pretty, she'd done just about everything possible to draw attention away from this fact. Her clothing was plain, her straight black hair styled in a no-nonsense ponytail, and not even a swipe of clear lip gloss had touched her skin.

"My fiancée," the man grumbled, adding this tidbit of information with the same enthusiasm he might have shown when requesting a roll of antacids at the pharmacy.

My aunt and mother exchanged a knowing look, and suddenly I wondered if they'd ever had cause to do the same when they'd first met Phil. Had I, too, been this blind?

I was overcome with the need to pull this poor woman aside and tell her to make a run for it. Perhaps it was my own recent experience talking, but this whole scenario was no good. It had taken Phil seventeen years to reveal himself to me as an ass. Meanwhile, this Tate guy was already intolerable, and he hadn't even put a wedding ring on her yet.

By habit, I swiped my left thumb along the inside

of my ring finger, still startled to find the skin bare. It was a strange, disconcerting feeling. I glanced down at an indentation of silvery-white flesh, the ghost of where my wedding band had been. Seventeen years would leave a mark on anyone. It was too late for me, but there was still time for Celia Lopez to escape her fate mostly unscathed.

"I take it you want your room now, despite being three hours early?" my mother inquired languidly, neither she nor Aunt Izzy budging even though it was clear their lack of movement was steadily driving our guest to the edge of an emotional cliff.

"Yes. That was supposed to be arranged." He tossed another scorching glance toward his victim—er, I mean fiancée.

"It can be now," my mother said sweetly. "You just have to say please."

He must have really wanted to be let in because he actually did as she suggested. The word seemed to stick in his mouth, barely squeezing through his lips, and from the look on his face, it killed part of his soul in the process.

Score one for Mom.

"Let me check in with housekeeping to see how quickly we can get everything set," she chirped, allowing the door to swing open so the guests could come in. "Izzy, can you give me a hand?"

As my mom and aunt disappeared upstairs, I had to

stifle a chuckle. I knew the room had already been prepared hours ago. Mrs. Crenshaw had arrived after breakfast, and though she was at least fifteen years older than I was, she'd performed all her cleaning tasks with the startling speed and efficiency of a woman who had more than a little magic mixed in with her cleaning supplies. Despite this, I could hear her in the upstairs hallway, playing along with the ruse to make our rude new guest sweat.

Word to the wise: don't mess with witches.

I stood a little way from the foyer, studying this man and wondering how someone like him had become such a bore. Born wealthy? That was my best guess. He acted like the world owed him and lacked the can-do attitude of someone who rolled up their sleeves to earn every penny they made. Even Phil, who had technically embezzled what he made, had done it with a certain grit and determination. His midwestern roots had encouraged my ex to embrace that good ol' Protestant work ethic, minus the part where stealing is frowned upon.

Not this guy, though. Not that working hard for a living made it hunky-dory to be an ass, but I might have had a smidge more respect if Alex What's-his-name had some dirt under his fingernails. Or if he hadn't lifted the satchel strap from his shoulder and, rather than setting it on the floor beside him, shoved it into his fiancée's arms without a word as if it was her problem to deal with.

Jerk.

"Your room is ready," Mom called downstairs.

"We asked for two *separate* bedrooms." This was said in an extra surly way, as if to make up for being forced to say please before. "And we've bought out all the others until after the literary festival is over. I have work to do and can't be disturbed. I hope that information managed to get through."

"I'm sure you can have your pick," I told him before he complained loudly enough for my mother to hear and got himself into even more hot water. All the while, I couldn't help wondering how his desire for privacy could possibly be worth the expense of booking five rooms for several weeks in a seaside inn during peak season. And, why the separate bedrooms for an engaged couple?

Then again, I doubted his fiancée minded the arrangement. If it were up to me, Mr. Big Shot could be sleeping in a refrigerator box under a bridge for the duration of his stay on the island. I really hoped that was her plan. A small victory for female kind.

"Up the stairs, to your right," I directed.

He immediately made a move for the staircase, and I looked with sympathy at his companion, who had been left to gather up the bags. The woman's face crumpled, and for a moment I was terrified she was going to cry. But she pulled herself together quickly in what seemed to be a practiced way.

"He has a deadline looming, and he's nervous

about the festival," she explained with a weak smile, still holding tightly to the satchel. This was certainly not the first time in her life she'd apologized on this man's behalf. Heck, it probably wasn't even the first time on this trip. With a fuse as short as his, he likely exploded several times a day, like a town canon going off to mark the hour.

"Oh?" I asked because it seemed the polite thing to do. "Is he an author or something?"

She laughed like she thought I was joking, so I laughed along.

"I guess I can't blame him for being on edge," she said. "It's one thing for a debut novel to spend fourteen weeks on the New York Times bestseller list, but he's never been shortlisted for a major literary award before."

Perhaps I was wrong, but I didn't discern the glow of pride in her demeanor that I would've expected to accompany such an amazing achievement by someone you loved. Meanwhile, I had my doubts that his attitude would improve with the addition of an award, so hopefully she wasn't counting on that.

"How nice for him," I started to say, but my words were drowned out as a motorcycle roared past the house, its revving engine grating on my last intact nerve. It wasn't the typical tourist moped that could be rented by the hour near the docks. This was bigger and so much louder. I could only imagine it belonged to a man in the middle of a midlife crisis. I assumed Phil probably had one like it by now, in whichever extradition-free country he was currently calling home.

"Will that happen a lot?" Celia asked, a deep furrow creasing her brow.

"I don't think so," I said, though I was tempted to say it would to see if Mr. Fancy Pants upstairs would fork over some money to the town to close the road for a few weeks. That would be fun to see.

The housekeeper, who had definitely been upstairs a moment ago, emerged from the door to the kitchen as if by magic, except I knew it wasn't anything mystical, just the back staircase that had been built in the house from the days when servants weren't supposed to be seen.

"Can I make you some tea?" Aunt Izzy asked Celia, emerging from the same door Mrs. Crenshaw had come through a moment before. I wanted to answer yes on Celia's behalf. Her defeated demeanor inspired me to help, and tea would calm my nerves, as well.

"That would be so lovely," Celia responded with a contented sigh, a bit of color returning to her cheeks to brighten her sallow complexion. "Thank you."

"Sugar?" Aunt Izzy asked.

"None for me, but Alex likes honey, if you have some."

"Very well. I'll send up a pot and two mugs when it's ready." My aunt disappeared into the kitchen.

"Please, let me take that heavy bag from you," Mrs. Crenshaw offered, gesturing toward the satchel.

Celia hesitated. "I'm not sure. Alex doesn't like to let his work out of his sight."

Mrs. Crenshaw shrugged as she curled her hand around the handle of the largest suitcase. I was about to protest—after all, I was much younger than she was—but she lifted it with such ease I changed my mind. Whether it was magic or a better physical fitness routine, there was no question this woman was significantly stronger than I was.

"I'll come back for the rest," Mrs. Crenshaw said when she'd loaded herself up. Were all witches this strong? I felt like a ninety-pound weakling by comparison. Without any powers, the other witches my age were likely to kick sand in my face. "Tallie, I think your aunt would like a word with you in the kitchen."

For a moment, I thought she was using some sort of mental telepathy to discern this, but then I spotted Aunt Izzy near the kitchen door, waving her arms at me like mad. I went to join her, and as soon as I felt secure enough of not being overheard, I whispered, "Are all the guests like this?"

"Not usually. Fortunately, we have our ways of managing the difficult ones. Let me show you." As she said this, Aunt Izzy opened a cupboard to reveal an assortment of hand labeled jars. They looked like the spices you would find in any kitchen, but I recognized them for what they were: ingredients for a potion.

My throat went dry. If my aunt wanted my help with this, what could I say? There was no way I could fake my way through an entire magic potion without revealing my utter lack of powers. My goose was cooked. Not that I knew how to cook a goose—another fact my aunt didn't know.

"Planning to transform him into a toad?" I joked as my stomach tried to turn itself inside out.

"Too messy," Aunt Izzy said with a laugh. "Can you put the kettle on?"

I breathed a sigh of relief. Putting the kettle on was something that required neither magic nor culinary abilities. I was in the clear.

I grabbed the teakettle from the stove and crossed to the sink to fill it with water from the tap. My aunt reached for a plain white porcelain pot and a tin of looseleaf English Breakfast tea, which she set right next to a bottle of dried chamomile flowers and several other items she'd pulled from the shelves of the cupboard.

"Oh, dear. We're low on honey," she said, holding up a jar that was no more than a quarter full. "I'll have to ask Alice to bring some. She keeps bees, you know."

"As you and Mom keep saying, she's a marvel." I studied the array of ingredients my aunt had laid out, my limited knowledge of medicinal herbs returning with much more clarity than I would have thought possible. "I know chamomile and lavender reduce anxiety, and St. John's wort elevates mood, but what is the celandine for?"

"Well..." My aunt's eyes shifted guiltily to the

ingredients. "Technically, it's a treatment for hemorrhoids, but I think the man has made himself a big enough pain in my rear end it can't hurt to see what happens."

At my aunt's revelation, I let out a cackle that was worthy of any witch.

CHAPTER FOUR

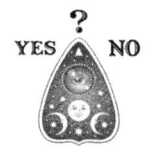

"Sabrina!" I called up the back stairs in what my daughters frequently referred to as my mom screech but what I liked to think of as my very low-tech intercom system. "We're leaving for the library in five minutes."

It was Saturday morning, and while I knew enough not to start hollering with paying guests in the house —especially ones with the prickly temperament of our illustrious author and his beleaguered bride-to-be— they had both gone out for a walk about thirty minutes prior. The change in the inn's atmosphere was palpable. Maybe Alexander What's-his-name would slip and fall off a cliff into the ocean.

One could always dream.

Tabitha went out the front door to find bicycles for us in the shed. Meanwhile, I went to the kitchen and found Aunt Izzy standing silently at the stove, slowly stirring a large cauldron with her magic spoon. There was no mistaking the fact that the steam rising from the pot was glowing a bright and mystical blue. The hair on the back of my neck stood up, and I thanked my lucky stars the girls hadn't followed me into the kitchen to witness this spectacle.

Hiding the presence of magic in this house was going to be even more of a challenge than hiding the sound of me unwrapping the candy I'd stolen from their plastic trick-or-treating pumpkins on Halloween when they were little.

I cleared my throat loudly to announce my presence, but my aunt continued the rhythmic circles while staring blankly at the wall. Finally, after at least a minute had passed, she turned her head toward me, her eyes blinking rapidly as if coming out of a trance.

"Good morning, my dear," she said with a smile.

"Good morning, Aunt Izzy." I craned my head to see into the pot. I'm not sure what I had expected to see in there—a large batch of oatmeal or perhaps some soup? Instead, I was surprised to find a dark liquid topped with soap suds. "What are you up to?"

"Cleaning the house," she replied, tapping her spoon against the pot to shake off the water droplets. A single bubble that had clung to the spoon popped as she slipped it into the pocket of her apron.

"Is that what Mrs. Crenshaw uses to make the work go so fast?" I half expected the next step involved handing me some rags, filling a spray bottle with the contents of the cauldron, and telling me to get to work. Not that I would've minded. It was high time I started earning my keep.

"Oh, no dear," my aunt surprised me by saying. "The cleaning's done."

"Are you...?" But as I looked around, I realized she was right. The kitchen was immaculately clean, every surface shining. I poked my head into the dining room and saw that it was the same. "The whole house?"

She nodded. "My grandmother's cleaning spell. It took me years to perfect, but now that I have, I can get all three stories sparkling clean in the time it takes to boil the water."

"That's amazing," I said then frowned. "If that's the case, why do you have Mrs. Crenshaw upstairs right now changing the sheets on all the beds?"

"Nothing beats the sunny smell of line-dried sheets," she replied. "Besides, I've never been able to perfect the spell so that it produces a sharp hospital corner. Even the best witches need to know their limitations."

"Speaking of limitation, I'm reaching the end of my patience with a certain salty nine-year-old." Even without checking the time, I knew more than the five minutes I'd allotted had passed. "Where is that kid?"

As if summoned by my question, Sabrina came into the kitchen, her arms folded in defiance. "I'm staying here. Libraries are dumb."

I mirrored her combative stance. "You're the one

who's going to look dumb if you show up to the first day at your new school this fall and you didn't finish any of the books on your summer reading list."

"Summer just started. And no one likes reading." Sabrina added an Elvis-worthy lip snarl. If she weren't my kid and giving me attitude, I might have given her some points on overall presentation. If she was this good at looking menacing at age nine, I could only imagine how she might perfect it by the time she was a teenager.

I was screwed.

"Too bad, kid. Summer reading is a requirement at your new school. It's island law."

"This is the worst place to live ever!" Sabrina stomped a foot, her tone rising in pitch until I could imagine dogs barking all around the cove. "I hate this place. All of my friends are in Cleveland! This is your fault!"

She stomped several more times on her way out of the room, prompting me to wonder how sturdy the floors were in this old house. The last thing I needed was to have to hire a structural engineer.

Instead of being horrified, Aunt Izzy laughed. "Island law? That's what you went with?"

"It was the best I could come up with on short notice," I said with a shrug.

"Ice cream," Aunt Izzy said solemnly, as if imparting the secret of the universe to me. "Promise her ice cream."

"I don't have the cabbage for that," I snapped.

"Cabbage?"

"Yeah. You know, spinach. Sugar. Kale. Lettuce. Dough." Frustration bubbled in my chest. Why didn't she understand what I was saying?

"You mean money?" My aunt's expression was unreadable.

"That's what I said." I frowned, suddenly not knowing what, exactly, I *had* said. I'd meant to say money, so where had all those other words come from? "Sorry, Aunt Izzy. I didn't mean to get testy. I just don't have a lot of cash to spare until I figure out my job situation."

Without saying a word, my aunt fished a ten-dollar bill from her apron pocket. Before I could argue, she'd pressed it into my palm.

"Get a scoop of the rum raisin for yourself," she counseled, a twinkle in her eyes. "It's made with real booze."

"Now that's the berries," I remarked as I slipped the money into my wallet.

My aunt gave her snowy white head a bemused shake. "I guess it's true what they say. Everything old is new again."

I paused on my way to the door, turning back to face her. "What do you mean?"

"I don't think anyone's used slang like that since my mother was young."

"Why couldn't we drive here again?" Sabrina asked for the three hundred and twelfth time as she slammed her bike into the rack outside the library.

I'd discovered on the ride from the house that asking a nine-year-old to provide her own foot power for transportation was akin to sending her to a forced labor camp. Who knew?

"If we're having ice cream later—though the chances aren't looking so good with your current attitude—it wouldn't hurt any of us to get some exercise," I said, lowering my voice to a whisper as we entered the library. I refrained from mentioning how high gas prices were on an island, or the fact that a rattling noise had started up in my car's engine right as we left Ohio.

My head swiveled toward Tabitha, bracing myself to deal with whatever complaint she was preparing to lob my way, but her attention had been captured by a tall boy with bronze skin and curly black hair who stood in front of the young adult fantasy section. Despite his height, he appeared to be roughly her age. He flipped through a book and did his best to ignore the little girl next to him, who was wearing nearly the same Disney princess T-shirt as Sabrina, her hair in several dozen intricate braids.

At that moment, if Tabitha had been a cartoon character, her eyes would have turned into hearts and bugged six feet out of her head while steam billowed from her ears. When had my little girl reached the boy crazy stage? On top of everything else, I feared this might be the straw that broke me.

"Come on, Sabrina. Let's get some books!" Tabitha was way too enthusiastic as she said this, and one more glance at the way she still had her eyes locked on the boy confirmed that we were definitely entering the hormonal teenage years. From what I could tell, she was even prepared to use her little sister as her wingman.

Goddess, give me strength.

As I made my way alone to the circulation desk to inquire about summer reading, I spotted a female librarian behind the desk with her back to me. The moment she turned, the shock of recognition sent adrenaline pumping through me. Though it had been twenty-five years since we'd seen each other, or even spoken, I would've recognized my childhood best friend anywhere.

"Dana?" I croaked through a rapidly thickening throat.

"Yes. May I help—Tallie?" As soon as she realized it was me, Dana came out from behind the desk, throwing her arms around me with a squeeze a boa constrictor would've envied. "Is that really you?"

I was too choked up by now to say a word. I closed

my eyes and leaned into the hug, feeling slightly silly at how totally overwhelmed I was. What kind of grown woman is reduced to tears by a hug?

One who had desperately missed her friend while on the verge of a nervous breakdown. That's what kind.

"It's been so long." Dana held me at arm's length to get a look at me, all the while keeping a hand firmly on each of my shoulder's as if she feared I'd run off again and not return for another quarter century.

There wasn't any admonishment in Dana's expression, but guilt spooled inside me anyway. In the painful aftermath of Maya's death, with the Shadow Council breathing down my neck and making life a living hell for everyone around me, cutting off communication with all my friends and loved ones had seemed like the best, or maybe the only, way to keep them out of the fray.

Not that I'd ever explained this to anyone. No doubt they all thought I was a heartless jerk who didn't care about them.

"Are those your girls?" Dana asked as she looked toward the stacks where my daughters were choosing books.

"They are," I confirmed, my heart bursting with pride despite the hellish bike ride they'd just put me through. "The older one is Tabitha, and the younger is Sabrina. I'd introduce you, but for the first time in weeks, they're actually not complaining. The silence is golden."

Dana laughed. "It's difficult being that age. Feeling awkward about everything and not understanding half of what's going on, all the while convinced you know everything."

"I remember."

Standing there in front of this friend I'd abandoned so long ago and uncertain how to make it right, I was acutely aware I might never have left my awkward stage behind me. I still didn't understand things, people most of all. How hadn't I realized what Phil was doing sooner? But I'd wasted too much of my life on such a loser already. The last thing I wanted to do now was give him any more of my headspace.

"What brings you into the library today?" Dana asked, always the one to know how to smooth things over.

"Actually, I'm trying to get the girls started on their summer reading. Do you happen to have the lists?"

"I do." Dana reached for her tablet, tapping on the screen. "Let's see. I'm guessing Tabitha will be starting sixth grade, and is Sabrina going into fourth?"

"That's uncanny. You didn't use any, you know—" I put my finger on the tip of my nose and gave it a wiggle, Samantha Stevens style, the universal sign for witchcraft.

"No need, or have you forgotten you can't scratch your butt in Goode Harbor without everyone knowing about it?" As Dana retrieved a couple sheets of paper from the printer, I tried not to think about how vulnerable this made me when it came to the Shadow Council learning of my return. The one saving grace was that, as much as locals loved to gossip, absolutely no one wanted outsiders getting involved in island business. Not even magical outsiders. "Here ya go! Two summer reading lists."

I scanned the titles with a sinking in my chest. *"The Crucible?* Are they serious?"

Dana shrugged. "It's a classic."

Just what my girls needed. More witchy stuff. It was like everyone on the island wanted to remind me that I still hadn't had that all-important talk with the girls. When the time inevitably arrived for me to come clean, would it be harder to admit I'd lied about magic being make-believe or that I'd robbed them of their birthrights before they'd even been born?

"So, what happened, Tallie?" Dana leaned against the circulation desk. "Not that I'm complaining, but why on earth did you leave the big city to come back here?"

I gave her a quick rundown of my life over the past several months, not bothering to censor myself the way I did when the kids were around. I let it all out like pus from an infected wound, a painful but necessary release.

"Now Phil is in Nicaragua, or maybe Venezuela, and I'm the one left to pick up the pieces." I vibrated with anger. "I can't shake this feeling. What's going to happen next?"

"I'm not one to dismiss premonitions," Dana said, her expression one of compassion, "but in this case, maybe it's nothing bad. You need to figure out what the universe is telling you."

The internal vibration I'd experienced while talking about Phil intensified, morphing into something else entirely. It was a feeling I knew well but hadn't experienced in years. It was the unmistakable crackle that occurred when an unknown witch was nearby, a sensation that started off like a finger in an electrical socket but lessened over time until you really couldn't feel it at all. I'd assumed I'd lost the ability to sense other witches in this way after the Shadow Council bound my powers, but perhaps I'd been wrong. Maybe it was just that there hadn't been any other witches in Cleveland all these years.

But there was definitely one in the library now.

A woman approached the area where my daughters were browsing through books. Her style of dress was best described as boho, with a long flowing skirt and peasant blouse. Her appearance—tall with dark bronze skin and long wavy black hair—was similar enough to the boy and girl she was with that I immediately assumed she was their mother. If I hadn't already figured out she was a witch, the silver pentacle charm she wore on a ribbon around her neck would've been a big clue.

"Who is that?" I inquired of Dana, trying to keep the edge of panic out of my tone. When I was younger, I'd known every witch on this island. This woman was not familiar to me, and my muscles tensed at a terrifying possibility.

Could she be a member of the Shadow Council?

"Over there?" Dana seemed completely at ease, but that wasn't enough to soothe my fears, and I continued to stand with my hands clenched against my thighs. "That's Samira Scott. Marcus and Ruby, the kids your daughters are talking to, are hers. She's Betsey Scott's granddaughter."

"You mean Betsey the psychic who lives in that brightly colored house with the tower and the ornate gingerbread trim?" That figured. If Hollywood designed a witch's house, it would look exactly like that one, only with a little less technicolor.

"That's right," Dana confirmed. "Mira and her mom, Phoebe, moved to Virginia when she was little, but they both came back here a few years ago, along with Mira's little ones, after Mira's husband died unexpectedly."

"Oh, that's sad," I said, meaning it. Just because I sometimes wished Phil would drop dead didn't mean I would ever want that to happen to anyone else. "Sounds like you two are close friends."

"You could say that," Dana answered. "Actually, I'm part of a little group with Mira and another woman, Brigit, who moved here from Manhattan and opened a vintage clothing store on Main Street. She's about our age, too. You know, it might do you some good to join us sometime. We can always use a fourth."

Dana didn't call this group of hers a coven, but she didn't have to. I knew what she was saying, and that the fourth they were looking for wasn't to play a few hands of bridge. With four members, a coven could call the corners, invoking the elements of earth, air, fire, and water. There was great power with that many witches gathered in one space.

But even if I'd been able to, I wanted no part of it.

"Thanks, but I'm not really—"

"Tallie, you're home now," Dana said softly. "Maybe it's time to stop running from who you are."

"What do you know about it? You've never had to hide who you are from anyone." I snapped, wincing at the harshness of my tone and the way my volume was amplified in the quiet space. "I'm sorry. It's just, with the divorce, needing to rejoin the workforce, and trying to manage the girls, I don't think I can take on anything else right now."

"You don't know what I've had to do. But, I get it," Dana added, thankfully willing to drop the subject, at least for now. "Hey, speaking of the girls, we have a summer camp starting Monday. You should sign them up."

I frowned. When Dana said *we*, exactly who was she talking about?

"Is this some kind of witch camp?" I asked in a hoarse whisper.

To my surprise, Dana laughed. "Oh my God, Tallie-Wallie, you're too much. It's an arts and crafts camp run by the library, four days a week. They can make friends, and it'll give you some space. I imagine you haven't had much lately."

"True." I nibbled on my bottom lip as I weighed the benefits of summer camp and my own sanity against my pathetically limited funds. "How much does it cost?"

"That's the best part. It's a town program, so it's totally free."

"Free?" I was about to take Dana up on her offer, but I was interrupted as a motorcycle whizzed by. Despite being on the other side of a closed door, the engine was so loud it drowned out my words and set my teeth on edge. "What the hell is that? Is there a motorcycle gang in Goode Harbor? I've been hearing that racket every single day since I got here."

"That's Nora Kenworthy," Dana said, sucking her cheeks in to keep from laughing. I couldn't blame her. I knew I sounded like an old lady screaming at the kids to get off her lawn, but I didn't care. "She loves that motorcycle of hers more than just about anything."

"Kenworthy, you said?" My eyes narrowed and my jaw tightened, the very name raising my temperature to the boiling point. "I should have known. Someone should call the sheriff. She belongs in jail for disturbing the peace."

"Jail?" Dana laughed. "I'm not saying the sheriff wouldn't enjoy the opportunity."

"Why do you say that?" I asked, eager for any ammunition I could get on the miscreant who was terrorizing my neighborhood with noise pollution.

"No reason." Dana shrugged, but there was a funny look on her face that confused me. "Let's just say a lot of people love Nora."

"I don't." I crossed my arms, resolute.

"You never know. You might, once you get to know her." Dana's eyes twinkled with a hint of mischief. For the second time in as many minutes, I had the sense of not being in on a joke, and I didn't like it one bit.

"Not a chance." I slapped my hand onto the desk for emphasis, trying not to wince as pain radiated up my arm. It made me madder and more determined. "She's loud, and a Kenworthy. That's two strikes against her!"

"Three strikes and she's out?" Dana teased.

"This isn't baseball. Two strikes is plenty. But, I'd better go round up the kids," I said, giving my friend a hug. "It's time for ice cream."

"Nothing soothes what's ailing you better than a scoop of ice cream," Dana said.

"Except maybe meeting up for coffee with a friend?" I replied, lifting my eyebrows like a question mark at the end of my sentence.

"I can't think of anything I'd rather do," Dana assured me with a smile. "And Tallie? I think once you get used to it, you're going to love being back in Crescent Cove."

It was possible my friend was right, but that still didn't mean I would change my mind where the Kenworthys were concerned.

CHAPTER FIVE

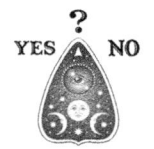

The inn was unusually silent, my mother having taken the girls into town to watch a Fourth of July concert at the park, which was probably why the sound of a gentle cough as I helped Aunt Izzy with the breakfast dishes nearly made me jump out of my skin. I glanced up from the sudsy sink to see the award-winning author's beleaguered fiancée at the edge of the kitchen, looking like she'd been sent to meet her executioner. Actually, the way her shoulders were bent, I had a quick thought she might have preferred such a fate to her own. There was something to be said for a quick chop rather than the death by a thousand cuts he was forcing her to endure with his terrible mood swings and surliness.

"I'm so sorry to trouble you," she said, "and I'm well aware this request will sound utterly ridiculous, but Alex is demanding extra blankets for his bed. He claims he's cold, that there's a draft or something in his room, although I've felt nothing of the sort in mine. Not that I'm complaining. But is there any chance—"

"No trouble at all," my aunt said before the woman could finish. She was already reaching for the teakettle, something that had become a habit over the past several days. Alexander Tate had gone through more of my aunt's special brew of calming tea than I'd thought humanly possible. His temperament had improved, but that wasn't saying much considering how far he still had to go to reach the level of basic human decency. Luckily for us, he mostly kept to his room, when he wasn't on one of his walks. "Tallie, would you mind running up to the attic to retrieve a few of the winter quilts?"

"Of course not," I said, stifling a giggle as my aunt added another heaping scoop of the hemorrhoid herb to her brew. I couldn't blame her. This guy was like a boil on the butt of humanity.

"Now, where's that sugar?" my aunt muttered, searching the cupboard.

"Honey, actually," Celia reminded her gently. "He prefers honey."

"Yes, of course." Aunt Izzy blinked a few times, shaking her head like she was trying to knock a loose wire back into place. "I must be losing my marbles with all this heat."

"It's terrible, isn't it? Warmest July Fourth on

record, or so I heard on the radio earlier." Celia inched her way toward the open cupboard. "I can't believe Alex thinks he'll need a blanket tonight. But there's no talking sense into him when he's trying to write."

"Is he making progress?" I asked, not that I cared personally, but I knew she probably did.

"Not as much as he'd like." Coming up beside my aunt, Celia reached into the cupboard and pulled out a jar of honey, deep and red. "This is the one your housekeeper brought in the other day. Alex says it's the best honey he's ever had."

"Oh, yes. Our Alice is a real bee charmer." My aunt shook her head again, and my insides squeezed with the sudden fear that her memory was starting to go. I would need to remember to ask my mother if this forgetfulness happened a lot. It killed me to see her so out of sorts.

"Is there anything we can get *you* to make your stay more enjoyable?" I asked, stepping in quickly to fill my aunt's shoes as best I could.

Like a sharp ax and a solid alibi? I couldn't help thinking, even though I probably lost a few hostess points because of it.

"I'm all set," Celia assured me with a smile, almost seeming overwhelmed at having been asked a single thing about herself. A rare occurrence, I was sure, considering the man she was marrying. "Thank you all so much for your hospitality."

To avoid setting off the terrible guest yet again, I didn't waste time getting the quilt.

The attic door was just down from my bedroom, at the end of the hall. I paused before I turned the knob, a patch of cold sweat beading on the back of my neck despite the oppressive heat that engulfed the third floor. I wasn't sure how or why it happened. As spooky attics went, I would rate ours maybe a six out of ten at the worst.

On the one hand, it was filled to the brim with all your basic Hollywood horror movie props: dusty steamer trunks, wicker baby carriages, and at least one dress form that, if you saw it out of the corner of your eye, looked like a floating body with no head.

On the other hand, the space had a light, and it wasn't one of those bare light bulbs with a dangling cord hanging from it but a proper switch that controlled an overhead lamp.

Plus, all the newer items that had been stored there, including the quilt I'd been sent to find, were in clear plastic bins close to the door. There's nothing scary about that. Also, there were none of those disturbing porcelain dolls that look like they've been possessed by a demon. You know the ones I mean. I wouldn't opt to sleep in the attic overnight, but I shouldn't have been breaking into a cold sweat being there, either.

It took no more than a few seconds to spot the bin I needed. Aunt Izzy must have been feeling particularly well organized when she'd stored the quilts after winter, because each bin was clearly labeled on all four sides and the top as well. I could have left right then, except after I'd pushed the quilts into the hallway, but before I'd turned off the light, I heard a sound like a rolling or a scraping coming from the far end of the cavernous space.

This is the part where, if I had been watching it in a movie, I would've started yelling at the character to run for their life.

Of course, I didn't run. I did what all the dumb heroines do and took a few steps in the direction of the noise. So next time you watch one of those films and smugly think you'd be smarter, trust me; you wouldn't be.

Just like they said, curiosity killed the cat. Luckily, I wasn't one. It might have been good if I were, because I had a sneaking suspicion I knew what was causing the scraping and rolling I'd heard.

Forget ghosts and chainsaw killers. There was about a ninety-percent chance it was coming from a mouse.

An infestation of mice was bad news. If that was happening, we needed to know. My mom and aunt depended on this inn for their livelihoods, and until I could find other employment, I did, too. Where would the girls and I go if the inn was shut down by the health department?

I had taken no more than three steps when I

detected the scent of roses, stronger than was natural and much more concentrated. That was odd as it was an enclosed area with no open windows, and I couldn't figure out where it was coming from.

Curious, I went deeper into the shadowed space. I was about halfway to the other end when it occurred to me for the second time what a terrible idea this was.

Was I really chasing after mice? I hated mice!

I shuddered and turned toward the door, but a black shadow stopped me in my path. My heart pumped like mad as my blood turned to icy sludge in my veins. That was no mouse.

"Meow," said the shadow.

"Buster?" I gave a shaky laugh as two shining green eyes peeked out from behind a trunk. "You nearly gave me a heart attack, you bad cat." Remember when I said I had no interest in owning a cat? Now you know why. Nothing but trouble! From what I could tell, this one came and went as he pleased, like he owned the place.

I walked toward him, moving to scoop him up and carry him out, but he was too quick for me and ran toward the door. Instead of following, I went to investigate the trunk where he'd been hiding and quickly discovered the source of the rose scent. The trunk lid was open, and an old perfume bottle had been knocked over. The last few drops of its highly fragrant contents had dribbled down the side of the trunk. If I had to find the culprit for this accident, my money was on Buster.

I removed the upset bottle, set it on the floor, and peered into the trunk. It was filled with clothing, hats, and accessories. With mild curiosity, I pulled out the top piece, my breath catching as I held it up. It was a black silk dress, sleeveless, like something you'd wear to a fancy evening party, with intricate silver beading all down the front. From what I could tell, it seemed almost exactly my size.

While I didn't know much about vintage styles, it looked like something a flapper in the 1920s might have worn but almost brand new for something a century old. It was very high quality even to my amateur eye. I longed to pull out the rest and see what it all looked like, but I hesitated. Some of the fabrics looked delicate, and I was uncertain if touching them would be harmful.

With a sigh, I pulled my hand back and closed the lid of the trunk very carefully to keep the dust off. I would have to ask Aunt Izzy later if she knew anything about them. For as many times as Maya and I had played in the attic as children, I couldn't recall ever coming across this particular trunk before. The attic was large, though, and packed to the rooftop with stuff. It could easily have been missed by two preoccupied young girls.

As my eyes were drawn along the oily trail the perfume had left along the trunk's outer edge, my gaze came to rest on the spot where the bottle's glass stopper had fallen onto the rough pine floor. Next to the stopper, and partially obscured beneath the trunk, was a flicker of dull silver metal.

At first, I thought it might be a coin or religious medal, but when I grabbed hold of it, I realized it was a ring. Though old and tarnished, the overall design was beautiful, with an intricate filigree and small stone that sparkled in the middle.

My left thumb brushed across the empty space where my wedding ring had been. The absence of it was driving me nuts, not for any sentimental reason, but because every time I came across the emptiness where that ring should have been, I was hit once more with the disaster my life had become.

And I was tired of it.

On impulse, I slid the ring I'd found onto my finger. It was a perfect fit. Did I worry for a moment that I might start hunching my back and hissing *my precious* all over the place? I'd be lying if I said no. But I didn't turn invisible—at least, I didn't think I had—and I didn't feel suddenly possessed or anything, so I left it on my finger. After closing the attic door, I scooped up the quilt and headed down the stairs.

"Good morning, Tallie," my mother said when I strolled into the dining room on Wednesday morning. She frowned as my response was cut short by a loud yawn. "Didn't you sleep?"

"The noise from the fireworks kept me up late," I told her. It was partially true. That and the dreams. They'd become stranger and more disjointed since returning home, but I could never seem to remember any details for more than a minute or two after waking.

"Darling, you're not wearing your wedding band, are you?" My mother's lips puckered like she'd sucked on a lemon as her eyes glued themselves to my left hand.

I held it up to my face so I could see and laughed. "Not a chance. I'd melt that thing down if I didn't think I might need to pawn it someday. As a matter of fact, I'd been meaning to ask you about this ring."

"What would I know about it? You're the one wearing it."

"Yes, but it came from your attic," I said, holding out my hand for her to see. "I found it yesterday when I went up to look for blankets."

"Blankets?" My mother frowned. "In this weather?"

"Long story. But there was an old steamer trunk with the lid open, and when I went to close it, I found this ring peeking out from under it." I tilted my hand back and forth. Despite the layers of grime, the small center stone glinted in the light. "I put it on and forgot it was there."

"It's lovely," she said, "but I can't say as I've ever seen it before. You said it was in a steamer trunk?"

"What was in a steamer trunk?" my aunt asked, joining us at the table and setting a strong coffee in front of me.

"Bless you," I said, cupping my hands around the steaming mug.

"Tallie says she found that ring she's wearing in one of the steamer trunks in the attic," Mom explained.

"More like under it," I corrected.

"Must've been one of Agatha's," my aunt said, referring to my grandmother, who had been her older sister. "She brought them with her when she—"

My aunt stopped suddenly, she and my mother exchanging nervous looks.

"When she what?" I prompted, my curiosity piqued. What was it they didn't want me to know? It was clear there was something going on. The longer the silence stretched between them, the tighter my chest became.

"I guess we've never told you this," Aunt Izzy began.

"There was never a reason," my mother interjected. "It hardly makes a difference now."

"That's true," Aunt Izzy said with a vigorous nod of her head. "It makes no difference at all. It never did."

"Is someone going to tell me what the hell is going on?" I demanded, my heart pounding. It was like watching a comedy duo with these two, only I didn't find it remotely funny. Something was going on, and whatever it was, I could already tell I wasn't going to like it.

"It's just, you see, while your grandmother was like a sister in every way," Aunt Izzy said slowly, "the truth is, she was adopted. My parents took her in as a toddler, years before I was born. She arrived from England, where she'd been in a home for orphaned witches, along with two steamer trunks. Those trunks and their contents were all that was left of her history."

"You mean, she wasn't a Shipton?" My eyes widened as the full truth sank in, my throat growing tight. "You mean, we're not Shiptons? Then, who are we? Mother, who *are* we?"

My mother put her hand over mine. "Now, dear, this is why we never said anything before. There's no reason to get worked up. It doesn't change anything at all. We're Shiptons through and through."

I snatched my hand away, running it through my tangled curls as my head spun from this unexpected revelation. All those times I'd struggled to keep myself from causing the wind to blow or the clouds to pour down rain, was it this unknown magical heritage that was to blame?

"I have to know more," I gasped. "I have to know

everything. Mom, you have to tell me everything you know."

But despite my begging, she didn't answer.

My mother—perfectly fine a moment before—sat with her hand pressed to her head, her eyes staring blankly ahead.

Before I could react, my aunt had dropped to her knees, cupping my mother's face in her gnarled hands. The familiarity of the movement was unsettling—like something that had occurred many times before. "Diana? Oh, honey. Is this another one of your episodes?"

"Episodes?" I shrieked. "Since when does Mom have *episodes*?"

"Dr. Kenworthy has a fancy name for them, but I can't remember it." Aunt Izzy put her hand on my mom's shoulder and gave her a gentle shake. "Basically, they're mini strokes."

"My grandmother was adopted, and no one told me? My mother has had a *stroke*, and nobody told me?" My anger and panic fed off one another, kicking my nerves into a higher gear. Mom was now the same age her own mother had been when she'd died. Of a stroke, no less. I'd be damned if the same thing was going to happen to her. Here I'd been worried about Aunt Izzy just the day before. Seems like I had a whole hell of a lot to worry about these days.

"Mini strokes. Not a big one," Aunt Izzy said, making me feel not a single iota better. "But Dr.

Kenworthy did say we should call if it happened again."

I was already halfway to the phone—an ancient landline that hung from the kitchen wall. "I'll call 911."

"Try Rosie's Diner," my aunt suggested. "The number's above the phone."

"I need a doctor, not takeout," I shot back.

"This time of morning, odds are good you'll find the doc there. Rosie makes the best biscuits and gravy on the island."

I shook my head as I started to dial—a rotary telephone, no less, possibly the last one still in operation on the planet. Dr. Kenworthy was no spring chicken, with dietary habits that were frankly questionable on the part of a medical professional. Seriously, who partook of biscuits and gravy on a regular basis these days? It made me wonder whether I shouldn't maybe give 911 a call after all.

"Rosie's Diner," a woman's voice on the other end of the phone said before I had the chance to change my mind and hang up.

"Is Dr. Kenworthy there?" I gasped, nearly breathless as the urgency of the situation hit me. "I think my mother's having a stroke."

"Who's your mother, dear?"

"Diana Shipton," I managed to say, my hand shaking so badly I could barely hold the receiver to my ear. "I'm at—"

"Oh, yes. I know the Shipton place," the woman said, because, of course, she did. On an island as small as this one, she probably would have known the color of my socks, if I'd been wearing any. "I'll send the doc right over."

After hanging up the phone, I paced the dining room as the seconds ticked by. Whatever had been plaguing my mother was starting to reverse itself, at least a little. Her eyes regained focus, and her lips began moving deliberately to form words, even if her lack of volume made them impossible to hear. Still, when the bell rang, I raced to the door like my feet were on fire, never more eager to see a gray-haired old geezer in my life.

I swung it open and gaped.

Instead of the old doctor, a woman stood on the porch. She was gorgeous in a bad girl kind of way, though the fine creases around her eyes put her at roughly my age or a few years older. Clad in head-to-toe leather, her long, dark hair was wild and wind-blown. I would never have recognized her had it not been for the motorcycle helmet tucked under one arm.

Nora Kenworthy, Chad's juvenile delinquent cousin. She'd been two grades ahead of me in school, so we hadn't interacted much, but I knew her well enough by reputation, and by the motorcycle that had been damaging my eardrums since the day I'd arrived. That bad girl persona she was rocking wasn't just about fashion. Frankly, from the stories I'd heard in my youth, I was surprised she wasn't in jail.

I gritted my teeth. "Where's your dad?"

"Somewhere around the ninth hole at Pebble Beach, I'd assume," she replied with a wicked grin that brought out a dimple in each cheek. I found myself staring, riveted. "He retired years ago, after I took over the practice."

"You're the island doctor now?" I was pretty sure if my eyes bulged any more, they'd fall out of the sockets and plop onto the foyer floor.

"Nora Kenworthy, MD." She swapped the helmet to her other side to free up her right hand, offering it in greeting. Her brow furrowed when I failed to respond, and she studied me for a moment, her front teeth biting into her lower lip. "Polly, isn't it?"

I balled my hands into fists, wanting nothing more than to land one of them right in the middle of her plump pink lips. Was that how she planned to play this? Hell no.

"It's Tallie," I growled.

"Is it?" She shrugged as if expecting me to believe the use of that horrible moniker her cousin had tormented me with was nothing but an innocent mistake. "I'd better see to my patient now."

With that, Nora Kenworthy, *MD*, stepped across the threshold, brushing past me as she entered my house without so much as a please or thank you.

CHAPTER SIX

"Transient ischemic attacks." Sitting behind the oversized desk in her office at the clinic an hour later, Nora Kenworthy repeated the medical term once more. She said it slower this time, allowing me to catch all the tongue-twisting syllables. "They don't cause permanent damage, but one in three people who experience them will go on to have a stroke, often within a year."

I nodded silently, finding it even more difficult to reply than to wrap my head around the fact this woman was really a doctor. Even after watching her perform a thorough exam on my mother—with admittedly a lot more care and patience than I'd been prepared to give her credit for—I still had my doubts. "I think we should get a second opinion."

"I absolutely agree with you," Nora said with only the slightest raise of one eyebrow to indicate she'd caught the underlying hostility in my tone. "In fact, I've been urging your mother for several months now to go to Portland for tests, but she won't listen to me."

"Mother!" I looked accusingly first to my mother, who was seated in the chair beside me, and then to Aunt Izzy, who sat two chairs away. I treated them both to my most menacing scowl.

"Who has time to go to Portland?" my mother argued in her own defense. "The inn doesn't run itself, you know."

"People who want to stay alive, that's who. You can't run the inn if you're dead." I gripped the armrests of my chair, ready to do battle if I had to. I knew my mother would put up one hell of a fuss. What I wasn't expecting was the laughter that emanated from the good doctor, whether at my mother's stubbornness or my fighting stance, I wasn't sure.

What surprised me even more was the way my insides did a belly flop, filling me with all the palm-sweating anxiety I hadn't suffered since my teenage years. Was I still so concerned about what others thought of me that a little laughter could turn me inside out? I wanted to believe I'd matured, but the evidence wasn't on my side. What else could explain the sudden, overwhelming self-consciousness I experienced the moment Nora Kenworthy so much as glanced in my direction?

Now was hardly the time to dwell on it. I had a mule of a mother who needed to go to the hospital. I decided to weaponize all the guilt I had in my possession to make that happen.

"I don't want to lose my mother. Not when I need her the most." Calling on every school play I'd ever been in, along with the fact that I truly believed what I was saying, my eyes started to glisten with tears.

My mother's brow furrowed, uncertainty overtaking her. It would have made me feel terrible if it wasn't the exact effect I'd been going for. "Honey, it's not—"

I sliced the air with a hand, landing it against my open palm. "You're going." I whipped my head toward Nora with a determination that would leave her no choice but to back me up. "How soon can you get her in?"

"Let me see what I can do." With that, she left her office, phone in hand. But before she did that, she winked.

My heart sent out a flurry of staccato taps, like an urgent message over a telegraph wire. If I had to guess, my erratic pulse was signaling SOS. Was I going crazy, or had a Kenworthy just winked at me? I didn't even know what that meant! Were we in cahoots now? Was she going to shank me when my back was turned? The uncertainty stirred up all kinds of turmoil in my insides.

What kind of legitimate medical doctor went around winking at people? And, why was I reacting in such a weird way? I'd heard that coming home again could make you regress to childhood, but I hadn't expected all the drama and angst of my teen years to come at me so fast.

"But the inn, Tallie," my mother pleaded, not ready to give in.

"The last thing the inn needs is a ghost. I need you alive, okay? So do Tabitha and Sabrina. End of conversation." To prove I was no longer the adult I'd believed myself to be when I woke up that morning, I stomped my foot and crossed my arms in exactly the same way I used to when my mom told me I couldn't stay out late on a school night.

My mom's mouth flew open to argue some more, but my aunt wagged a finger at her niece. "Tallie's right. I should have insisted months ago."

Finally, the only true adult in the room was laying down the law. Thank the Goddess for Great Aunt Izzy.

Only she wasn't actually my great aunt, as I'd so recently learned. My gut went cold at the thought.

"Good news!" Nora breezed back into the room, sliding her phone into her back pocket. Her leather pants were so snug I was amazed there was room for anything bigger than a dime. I had to admit she wore them well. Too well, even. It took considerable effort to drag my gaze back up to her face before I got caught staring. "I've pulled a few strings and called in some favors. If you can leave on this afternoon's ferry and stay over in Portland tonight, you can be seen first thing in the morning."

"We have guests at the inn," my mother said, though none of us was paying much attention to her excuses anymore.

"You should be back by Friday afternoon," Nora said in a reassuring tone.

"Tallie, do you want to go with her?" Aunt Izzy's tone said the matter was settled. Mom was going to the hospital, and that was that.

"I suppose the girls wouldn't mind a trip to the big city," I started to say, but Nora was shaking her head.

"How old are your girls?" she asked.

"Twelve and nine," I replied cautiously, not sure why it would matter.

"I'm afraid the hospital doesn't allow visitors under the age of thirteen," Nora said.

"Oh." I chewed at my lip, my brain sputtering as I struggled to figure out a plan B.

"I could watch them," Aunt Izzy offered.

"I don't know. I feel like I can't leave them so soon after—" I was about to say their father skipped out on them, but remembering Nora was listening, I pivoted, ending with, "all the travel."

My aunt nodded, sadness weighing down her shoulders. "Can you do this on your own?" she asked my mom.

"No," I said quickly, determination strengthening my resolve. "You have to go with her."

"We can't leave you here by yourself," my aunt argued. "You haven't run the inn on your own."

"There are only two guests, and I'll have Mrs. Crenshaw to help me. I'm a grown woman and a mother of two. I'm sure I can take care of keeping things running until you get back," I insisted. "While Mr. What's-his-name is a pain in the ass, what's the worst that can happen?"

There was an important lesson to be learned here, though I didn't know it at the time. Never ask a question you don't want to find out the answer to.

"Time for bed, kids," I said, stretching my arms above my head to work out the kink that had formed in my neck.

With my mom and Aunt Izzy in Portland, the girls and I had gathered for the evening in the small sitting room off the kitchen where the inn's only television was hidden. Three empty snack bags of microwave popcorn sat on the coffee table in front of us, along with soda cans and the greasy box from the pizza I'd had delivered. I would need to make an effort at proper nutrition in the future, but as far as I was concerned, it could wait until my mother was there to witness and give me credit. Tonight was all about keeping my girls happy so they would forget their beloved grandmother was spending the night in the hospital.

"Can't we watch one more movie?" Tabitha begged,

unfurling her legs and bounding from the couch. She plucked at the selection of DVDs on the shelf, reading off the titles one by one. "There's *Bedknobs and Broomsticks… Hocus Pocus…*"

"Another time," I interrupted, holding up a hand. Inside, I was wondering exactly how many witch-themed movies and shows my mother had managed to procure before our arrival. She claimed it was because the internet was too spotty for reliable streaming, but it didn't take magic to spot her hidden agenda. If I wasn't ready to talk to the kids about our family heritage on my own, I would be forced into it through the power of Walt Disney.

"It's not even ten," Sabrina protested through a yawn.

"You know the rules. Off to bed." I pointed to the narrow back staircase that led to the second floor, recalling with a pang of sadness how Maya and I had explored all the house's hidden passageways when we were little.

Tabitha went instantly, and even Sabrina didn't put up much of a fight, rising from the couch and trudging to the stairs with little more than an exaggerated eye roll. I nearly told her that if she did that too much her eyeballs would fall out, but I decided not to poke the bear. From the very start, Sabrina had been a challenge. I'd foolishly thought Tabitha's easygoing nature was a result of my expert parenting. Sabrina's mission in life was to teach me how wrong I'd been about that.

After ten minutes, I popped upstairs to say goodnight to the girls. Both were zonked out. Meanwhile, the caffeine and sugar I'd consumed buzzed through my veins like an ill-mannered alarm clock. With how worried I was about my mom, no way was I ready to call it a night.

I went back downstairs to peruse the bookcase, relieved the options here included more than stories about witches. I grabbed a paperback romance and headed back upstairs to my room, tiptoeing past the bedroom door behind which the sound of fingers tapping on a keyboard were virtually unending. There were many things I could fault Alexander Tate for, but his work ethic wasn't one of them.

Settling into bed, I opened my book and forced myself to read as the anxiety in the pit of my stomach expanded.

The stillness was broken as a storm rolled in over the cove, one of those fierce summer types with whipping wind, blue flashes of lightning, and claps of thunder that could frighten the dead. The light on my nightstand flickered, sending a shiver down my body. Ever since the summer when my sister died, I'd been terrified of storms. They'd been non-stop that year, worse than anyone could remember.

I gripped the book tighter, trying in vain to focus on the words on the page.

My eyelids grew heavy.

The lights flickered again, and I shut my eyes

tightly to block my growing sense of dread. I switched off my bedside light and drifted into a fitful sleep, filled with disjointed dreams. I woke some hours later, disoriented, to the sound of scratching at my bedroom door. I stood in the dark and shuffled to the door. When I opened it, Buster came bounding in, meowing at me incessantly as he jumped onto the bed and spun himself in circles.

"Seriously?" I muttered as he settled into the nest he'd created and curled into a ball with his bushy tail tucked beneath his nose. "You woke me up in the middle of the night so you could steal my bed?" He didn't bother so much as to open an eye in response. Why my aunt kept him around, I couldn't imagine.

With a sigh, I started down the stairs. My throat was beyond dry, and a tall glass of ice water was too tempting not to pursue. As I reached the second-floor landing, I paused. The house should have been silent, but the faint sound of music coming from the direction of the living room tickled my ear.

I turned away from the back stairs and crept down the main staircase instead. The music grew louder, a classic jazz song, and I detected a tinny quality to the sound like it was a very old recording playing over a static-filled radio station. I frowned, wondering if either Alexander or Celia had been unable to sleep and had come downstairs and turned on the old stereo.

It had to have been early in the morning because a soft, gray light was filtering through the windows, making it possible for me to see the entirety of the living room as soon as my foot hit the bottom step.

The first thing I noticed was the absence of people, but this detail didn't matter much once I realized the room also looked nothing like the living room I'd expected to see. It was the same room, yes, but all the walls were covered in a garishly bright floral paper. I blinked rapidly, and as I did, the walls returned to white, but my pulse continued to race. The music was still going strong.

The cherry cabinet, which I knew from memory was stamped with the brand name "Victrola" but had always held a modern stereo inside it for as long as I could recall, stood in its usual place near one of the windows. I could see it clearly. The music was definitely coming from it, but as I walked closer, I realized the stereo I was expecting to see was gone. The lid was open, and a turntable sat inside, twirling rapidly while its heavy needle scratched its way across the black disc that spun on its surface.

I watched the spinning disc, mesmerized and breathless, until the song ended and the room filled with the sound of static. The needle reached the end of the record, and the arm raised itself and traveled back across the turntable until it came to rest on the other side.

Right when I was about to turn and leave, the large handle on its side began to crank all by itself. Then the needle lifted up from the cradle and started to play at the beginning of the record again. I gasped as something like an electrical current coursed through every nerve. I might not have known much about antique record players, but I knew enough to know they weren't supposed to do any of that. Not without help. Never mind that I had no idea where this one had come from, or why it was playing in an empty room before dawn. To be honest, I had no desire to find out.

I turned on my heel and raced upstairs, nearly taking out Alexander Tate, who was pacing the hallway, wringing his hands.

"I'm so sorry," he said.

I sucked in a breath. Had Mr. Rude apologized for something? Extra weird, considering I was the one to blame.

"It was my fault," I told him. "I wasn't watching where I was going and nearly knocked you down."

"So, so sorry," he sobbed, and I suspected he wasn't talking to me at all.

Had Celia kicked him out? I couldn't blame her if she had.

He tugged at his hair, muttering like a mad man. "I had no idea this would happen. You have to forgive me." He was mumbling, crying as he said what I thought was a name. Joe? George? I couldn't make it out.

"Are you okay?" I asked, reaching for the man's hand, shocked by how cold it was. Despite the storm, it was another warm night, yet his skin felt like ice. No wonder he'd been asking for extra blankets.

He started walking away from me, but then he pulled up short as if he'd seen a ghost. I was beginning to think there might be one.

I was on the verge of freaking out and preparing to —well, honestly, I didn't know what I was going to do. Run out of the house? Call the cops? Beg for my mother to come save me? Here I was meant to be the grown-up in the house. I had to pull it together. My girls were snug in their beds upstairs, and they needed me to keep everything under control, no matter how terrified I might be.

"Mr. Tate," I said sternly. "That's quite enough."

To my surprise, the author went still, as if all the animation had been drained from him. Without another word, he retreated to his room, quietly shutting the door.

What the hell had just happened?

Sleepwalking, I told myself.

That had to be the explanation. For one thing, had the man been fully awake and aware of his actions, he would have slammed the door behind him. In the days he'd been there, he'd never missed an opportunity to do so, rattling my nerves at every turn.

He'd had a bad dream. He was sleepwalking.

Hell, I'd probably had the same thing happen, come to think of it. The storm had made all of us restless.

I'd been half asleep, imagining things that weren't there. So had Alexander Tate. It was as simple as that.

Wasn't that what the experts always said? The simplest answer was usually the right one. So, that settled it. Because if that *wasn't* the explanation behind all this weirdness, I was all out of anything simple.

CHAPTER SEVEN

I checked Dana's text again, matching the address she'd provided for Goode Time Tea against the numbers on the front door of the shop. This was definitely the right place, even if the shop's pastel walls and doily-covered surfaces made it seem all wrong. I opened the door cautiously, as if expecting some sort of trick. But there was Dana, seated at one of a dozen floral-print draped tables, perusing a menu.

Good thing she'd gotten there ahead. Every seat was filled with people dressed in their Sunday best, eating delicate sandwiches and pastries from three-tiered serving trays. I glanced down at my simple sun dress, suddenly feeling out of place.

When I sat down in the chair across from Dana, she greeted me with a smile. "You found it okay?"

"Yes, but I'll admit when you said Samira Scott

owned a tearoom, and knowing she's a *you know what*," I lowered my voice so no one else could hear, "I pictured something else."

"Let me guess," Dana said with a laugh. "You thought of a dark, mystical sort of place with magical potion ingredients like eye of newt and dragon scales kept in bottles and jars on dusty shelves."

"Or maybe some of those big apothecary cabinets with all the tiny drawers." I grinned. "Naturally, I assumed we would be sent behind a beaded curtain at some point to get our palms read. I was not prepared for afternoon tea in Wonderland."

"I wasn't sure after all these years," Dana said, seeming uncharacteristically shy, "but from what I remember when we were younger, I thought this type of establishment would be right up your alley."

"You were one hundred percent correct," I assured her.

A few moments later, Mira came over to the table, wearing a frilly apron over the long, flowing skirt and peasant blouse that seemed to be her signature style. Her long black hair was braided in a single rope down her back, and she held a pad of paper in her hand to write down orders. Though her arrival still sent a crackling feeling through me, it had lessened significantly on account of having seen her several times at the library when I was dropping off or picking up the kids from summer camp.

"It's lovely to see you again," Mira said, offering a friendly smile.

"Likewise," I answered, wondering when I had become a person who said things like *likewise*. Was it the formality of the surroundings? Ever since coming back to this island, I wasn't quite myself.

"How are the kids?" Mira was clearly a pro at this. Asking another mom about her kids is a surefire way to break the ice.

"Loving summer break. As for me, I'm counting down the days until I can ship them back to school," I confessed. We laughed together in solidarity, as I'd figured we would, since every parent I knew felt the same way before July was halfway done.

"Speaking of restless kids," Mira began with a slight lengthening of her words that hinted at hesitation, "would your girls like to come over for a sleepover tomorrow night? I know we don't know each other very well yet, but I heard about your mom and aunt being away, and since the kids get along so well at camp, I thought it'd be fun."

My nerves zinged on high alert as I tried to ascertain if she was on the up and up, or if this was some sort of ruse to proselytize my children for a life of witchcraft. But I quickly relaxed as Mira's genuine smile reassured me. It would be good for my girls to have friends and fun this summer after everything their father had put us through.

"I'm sure they would love that," I answered, "if it isn't too much trouble."

"No trouble at all."

"Can I join the sleepover?" Dana asked. "I'm a little old, but I'd much rather watch movies than have to get up in front of hundreds of people tomorrow night and give out awards."

"Is that the literary festival?" I asked.

Dana sighed. "Ever since my mom's days, it's been tradition for the head librarian to introduce the finalists. But I'm terrified, and I can't even practice ahead of time to ease my nerves."

"Why not?" I asked.

"Because the identities of the finalists are kept hush-hush until the envelopes are opened on stage. Only the judges know who has been chosen," Dana explained. "And they guard the information like it's the nuclear codes. I'm certain I'll trip over one of the names and make a fool of myself. I keep telling Mom I'm going to make her get up there and do it. I don't care if she's retired or not."

"Is your mom going?" Mira asked.

"Every year," Dana said, the relief evident in her tone. "I'm not sure how I would handle it if I had to be there all by myself. No one becomes a librarian because they love public speaking."

"You'll do fine," Mira said, patting Dana on the shoulder. "Now, can I start you two off with some tea?"

"English breakfast for me," Dana said.

"Me, too," I added, glad I hadn't said *likewise* again.

"That was nice of her," Dana said when Mira had moved to another table. "It must be hard with your mom away. Is she coming home today?"

"No." My shoulders slumped as I delivered the news, which I had only just received. "Aunt Izzy said she needs to stay the weekend. I don't know what to think. I thought about asking Dr. Kenworthy, but the clinic's closed today."

I scanned the room, noting a surprisingly rowdy bunch at the far end that I could only describe as nerds. Although a few women's faces dotted the group, they were mostly men, and they looked dressed to sing in a barber shop quartet.

"What's up with them?" I asked.

"Those are the semi-finalists for the Chesterton Prize, which will be given out at the festival gala tomorrow night. It's tradition for all the authors who've made it this far to gather for afternoon tea."

"I have to be honest. I've had my fill of authors." I held my hand above my head to indicate how over them I was.

Dana cocked her head. "Why is that?"

"Didn't you hear? The guests who've been staying at the inn the past few weeks are an author and his fiancée."

"Which author?" Excitement kindled in Dana's eyes, which I should have expected given she was a librarian. "Is he one of the semifinalists? Point him out to me."

I scoped out the group and didn't see Alexander Tate, much to my relief. "That's funny. When they first arrived, his fiancée said he was here for an award, but I guess he didn't make it as far as he thought he would if he didn't get invited to the tea."

"Tallie, I'm a librarian. You can't say you have an author at the inn and not tell me every detail. Starting with his name."

"Honestly, I think he's a nobody, some jerk who's full of himself and putting on airs." At this point, the tea arrived, and I paused to fill two mismatched vintage china cups with the dark brew. "Do you still do milk and sugar in yours?"

"Tallie!" Dana was leaning forward, clearly at the end of her patience with me for not sharing the name of our guest already.

"Sorry." I slid her teacup toward her. "His name is Alexander Tate."

"You're pulling my leg." Dana's teaspoon dropped from her hand and clinked against the saucer. "Last I'd heard, he'd flat out told the committee he would be a no-show."

I frowned, unable to figure out Dana's reaction. "I don't get it. You mean, you do know him?"

"He's only one of the most famous authors on the planet," Dana spluttered. "Honestly, how have you not heard of him?"

"I guess with my life falling apart, I haven't had as much time for reading as I might like," I quipped. "Are you saying he was on the up and up about being here for the award after all?"

"If he's actually come to Goode Harbor, I'd say he must have it on good authority that he's won, or at least is a finalist. The judges aren't supposed to, but sometimes they'll tip someone off to entice them to attend, depending how famous they are." Dana shrugged. "I have nothing to do with that part of the event, so I couldn't say for sure."

Before I could reply, a man at the author table waved, calling out, "Dana! Just the woman I wanted to see!"

He got up from the table, and I stifled a laugh at the sweater vest and tweed newsboy cap he wore, despite the warm summer weather. I assumed the vest was to hide a protruding tummy and the cap was to cover a balding head, though his perfectly groomed handlebar mustache attempted to make up for whatever might be lacking up top.

"What's going on, David?" Dana asked sweetly.

"Would you say this outfit makes me look erudite?" David strutted in a circle, making him look more like a confused pigeon in my opinion, not that he'd asked me. For that matter, I wasn't sure he'd registered my existence.

"Very spiffy." Dana appeased the preening man.

"I bought it especially for the author tea today, and I'm doing a reading at the bookshop right after."

"Well, you look fabulous," Dana told him, her lips twitching just enough that I could tell she thought this much vanity in a middle-aged man was as ridiculous as I did.

"Tomorrow night's the big event. The Chesterton Prize." His chest puffed out even more than it already had, which I wouldn't have thought possible. "This is my year. I know it."

"You seem very certain." As a mother, I recognized Dana's subtle caution. It was the same way I'd sounded when Sabrina had her heart set on making the lead in the all-school play even though she was only in kindergarten. I suspected the recent revelation of our guest's identity may have had something to do with it.

"This time I have some important insider information. As of yesterday morning, my main nemesis isn't on the island." He flashed a smug smile. "I've been checking the ferry passenger lists myself for the past week."

"If you're nemesis is who I think it is, I have some bad news." Dana motioned to me. "Alexander Tate is staying at the Shipton Inn."

"He arrived over two weeks ago," I added.

"That can't be!" The color seemed to drain from David's face as his head swiveled toward me, noticing my presence for the first time. "Who are you? Wait.

It's Polly isn't it? I think I remember you from school."

"It's Tallulah," I said, making my best effort not to grind my teeth into dust.

"David was in the grade ahead of us at Chesterton Academy," Dana explained. "Tallie's recently returned after years living away."

"London?" he guessed.

"Cleveland." I watched the only spark of enthusiasm he'd shown for my existence fade from his eyes.

"Can you believe Tallie didn't know who Alexander Tate was?" Dana laughed in a good-natured way. "I mean, imagine. *Oceans of Glass* has sold almost as many copies as the Bible. They're making it into a TV series."

"They made mine into a movie," David spat out, his face turning the same eggplant color as Alexander Tate's did when riled up. "Cinema. Big screen. People are already talking Academy Awards, you know."

"Yes, I've heard." Dana stiffened slightly, and I got the impression she'd listened to this conversation several times before.

"Meanwhile this Tate joker tossed a couple of dragons into some fanfic, and everyone raves about it." David's arms flailed as he acted out people being bowled over by Tate's brilliance. At least I think that was what he was going for. I didn't know about his movie, but his own acting skills weren't exactly Oscar-worthy. "Dragons are not literary!"

As he had made this pronouncement loud enough for the entire tearoom to hear, Alexander Tate walked through the door, his fiancée a few steps behind.

"Got something to say to me, Spencer?" The author's eyes shot daggers, and it was clear he'd heard every one of his rival's insults.

"There's no way you're going to win tonight, Tate." David's face had turned an alarming shade of red. "Your daddy's big time publishing connections might have gotten your foot in the door, but you can't steal my award."

"Oh yeah? I've been informed I'm a lock for it." Alex's lip curled. "Why else would I come to this godforsaken little island of yours?"

As the men's voices increased in volume, Celia took a step back.

Alex looked David up and down, his expression dripping disdain. "Interesting outfit. Did you borrow it from your grandfather?"

David inched closer. "Say that again to my face."

"No one cares about your book." Alex tapped David's chest with a finger to punctuate each word. "I've seen suicide notes that were more cheerful."

"Happy endings are for chumps." A light spray of spit accompanied David's words.

"I fast forwarded that movie they made of it," Alex said, not reacting to the moisture that surely coated his nose. "Bleakest two minutes of my life."

"You wouldn't know literature if it bit you in the

ass." David put his hands on Alex's shoulders, giving them a push. Celia took another step back, her eyes wide.

"Says the man who's going to lose tonight." Alex returned the shove.

"None of the others think you're a real author!" David spat out, waving to his writing buddies at the table who were doing their best to pretend this scene wasn't playing out right before their eyes. "Come on, guys. Back me up."

"You see?" Alex's laugh lacked charity. "Not even your companions are on your side. Loser."

Reaching the end of his rope, David took a swing at the man, but Alex ducked right in time. Now the other authors were out of their seats, pulling the two men apart. Dana, Celia, and I looked on in horror, along with the rest of the people in the tearoom. I'd never seen such a stupid argument between two grown men escalate so quickly.

"You're a dead man, Alexander Tate!" David bellowed as his friends dragged him back. "You hear me? You're a dead man."

"Not if I see you first." Alex broke free from the two people holding him back. Thankfully, he did not lunge at David but made his way to the door, grabbing Celia's arm and dragging her along. "Not if I see you first."

Once his rival was gone, David skulked back to his side of the tearoom, his chest heaving up and down.

I had to force my jaw shut before asking, "Are literary festivals always this entertaining?"

But Dana wasn't listening. Instead, her eyes were on the door, which had clicked shut after Alex and Celia's departure.

"Who was that woman with Alexander Tate?" she asked, sounding slightly out of breath.

"His fiancée."

"What a shame."

I nodded my agreement. "Phil was no picnic, but he was nothing like that. If he had been, he wouldn't be on the lam right now. He'd be six feet under."

"Do you have your toothbrush?" I stood firm in my conviction that I had every right to ask this question as Sabrina let out a groan.

"You are so embarrassing," my younger daughter informed me with a roll of her eyes.

"She's kind of right, Mom," Tabitha added, casting a nervous glance at Mira's waiting minivan, as if trying to calculate the likelihood that Marcus had overheard my question from his spot in the front passenger's seat.

"Promise you'll be good," I said, raising my voice so there would be no doubt this time about whether anyone else could hear. I pulled them both into a group hug for good measure, giving each girl a kiss on their curly heads as their duffle bags whacked our legs. "No arguing, no talking back. And I want you to try to get some sleep, you understand?"

"We're going now," Sabrina announced, wriggling from my grasp as I stifled a laugh.

If I couldn't embarrass my own kids in front of their friends from time to time, what was the point of living?

I stood at the edge of the long driveway, waving, until Mira's car had pulled out of sight. When I made my way back inside the house, I immediately wished I hadn't. From the entryway, it was impossible not to overhear every word of the argument going on between our guests upstairs.

"This is all your fault!" A loud crash accompanied Alexander's screaming. "You're supposed to be helping me. I don't know why I keep you around. All of this is your responsibility!"

There was another crash, and I ducked instinctively, even though I was nowhere near the line of fire.

"My responsibility?" Celia shrieked, with more forcefulness than I'd ever dreamed she could muster. "You're the one who decided to head to an island right before a big deadline so you could accept an award we both know you don't deserve!"

"I don't. I don't deserve this award." There was a muffled sob, followed by several more. Was the man crying? "I should never have agreed to a two-book deal. I should have known I couldn't do it. I'm a fraud! A failure! I can't finish it, and now I'll be out millions."

"We both will be," came Celia's surprisingly cold response. "Which is why I'm not going to let you fail. You may not deserve this, but I do."

I flinched as another round of sobbing echoed through the house. I was still standing in the entry, the front door partially open, when Dana came up behind me. Her eyes widened with concern as she took in the scene, pointing upstairs with an expression of both alarm and confusion.

"It's Alexander Tate," I informed her, wondering if this would change her opinion of his brilliance. "He's been up there screaming and crying like a spoiled brat for at least fifteen minutes. Oh, and don't forget throwing things, too."

"Is his fiancée all right?" Dana seemed genuinely worried. "Do we need to go check on her? She might not be safe up there with him."

Just as I was trying to decide if Dana had a valid point, the man of the hour stomped down the staircase in a black tie, shaking the entire inn. Both Dana and I jumped out of the way to avoid being run over.

"I need some air!" he yelled at no one in particular before barreling out the door and slamming it behind him.

"I'm really starting to despise authors," I said,

exchanging a wary glance with Dana. "Insufferable people."

"What was he so upset about anyway?" Dana massaged her temples, looking shellshocked, as I did my best to summarize the fight. "Sounds like a bad case of imposter syndrome to me."

"What's that?"

"It happens to even the most famous, successful authors," she explained. "They start to doubt themselves, believe all the negative reviews, and basically talk themselves into serious writer's block."

"I can't wrap my head around why he was blaming poor Celia for this new book not going well," I remarked. "How is that her doing?"

Mrs. Crenshaw swooped into the room with a silver tray that contained a pot of tea, a mug, and a nearly empty jar of honey. "Has he left? I was going to see if some tea would calm him."

She didn't need to explain that she'd made a fresh batch of Aunt Izzy's potion for him. Dana and I were both witches. We understood.

"His fiancée might like some," Dana suggested, and it struck me how much more concern she was showing for the woman than her own fiancée seemed to have.

"I have a better idea," Mrs. Crenshaw said, already heading back to the kitchen with the tea. She stopped at the sink and poured it down the drain before I had the chance to say I might like a cup of it myself. "Would anyone like chocolate chip cookies, homemade today? I whipped up a batch for the girls earlier, and there are plenty left."

"There's nothing a cookie or two can't make better," Dana pointed out, showing remarkable wisdom.

I had to admit the thought alone soothed me more than any tea ever could. "Mrs. Crenshaw, you're a treasure."

I swiped a cookie after Dana took one, needing to settle my own nerves, when I spied Celia sneaking down the back stairs.

"Are you okay?" Dana asked, beating me to it.

Celia's face crumpled. "I'm so sorry you had to witness that."

"Don't you worry about that at all," Dana said. "Authors are volatile, and you're not responsible for his behavior."

"Dana's right," I added. My mom had something along those lines after the FBI kept giving me looks that implied they knew I was in on the scam as well.

"I know," Celia said sadly. "He's… struggling. Coming to this island was a terrible idea. I told him over and over. At first, he agreed and said he wouldn't come, but in the end, the lure of prestige was too enticing."

That didn't explain why he was blaming her, but I didn't want to press. "Can I get you something? Cookies, maybe?"

"I need a broom," she said, averting her eyes from mine. "There was an accident."

Right. Like her rage-fueled fiancé grabbing a bunch of breakables and chucking them at the wall, accidentally? I refrained from calling her out on this fib to save her from further embarrassment.

"Don't you need to be getting ready?" I asked instead, taking in the casual clothing she was wearing, contrasting it to the formal wear Alex had worn when he'd stormed past me. "I think Mr. Tate might already be on his way to the award gala. I can take care of the mess once you've gone."

"No way am I going." Celia crossed her arms, showing another hint of a backbone I hadn't been aware she had. It seemed she'd been pushed past her breaking point this time. "I think I'll stay in and head to bed early."

"Not a bad plan," I said kindly, handing her a broom and dustpan. "I might do the same."

"Actually," Dana said, drawing the word out so that it had way too many syllables. "I need to talk to you about that. Mom's feeling poorly and can't go tonight. Will you be my date? I tried calling but couldn't get through."

"I really wish I could," I said, even though this was a total lie. I didn't want to go at all, but I didn't think that was the right thing to say. "I can't leave the inn empty for the night. Celia might—"

"Don't you worry about me," Celia cut in. "I might

be planning to spend the evening wishing I didn't know Alexander Tate exists, but that's no reason you two shouldn't have a fun night."

"I don't have anything to wear," I argued when Celia had gone upstairs. "When I packed everything up in Cleveland, I didn't exactly grab any ball gowns."

"You don't need a gown. How can a grown woman not have a little black dress? I mean, even I do, and I'm not exactly the dresses and high heels type."

"Well, I don't. There's not a single thing in the house I could wear. Well, except—" I stopped suddenly, choking back the rest of the sentence. I had the perfect excuse. Why was I trying to ruin it?

"Except what?" Dana's eyes lit up like she knew I'd busted myself.

"There are some dresses in the attic, old ones. I found them in a trunk and then forgot about them because mom's episode happened right after. But I don't know if any of them would fit." I had a pretty good idea at least one of them would, that gorgeous black dress with the silver beads that had been at the very top.

"Could you try, please?" Dana begged.

"I don't know." But my resolve was softening like a stick of butter left on the counter.

"Don't you worry about the inn," Mrs. Crenshaw said, putting the final nail in my coffin. "I'll take care of everything before I head out. You should go and enjoy yourself."

I let out a long, tortured sigh that may have been slightly exaggerated for my own benefit. "Fine, I'll make you a deal. If the dress fits, I'll go."

With that, I headed to the attic, hoping the cookie I'd eaten might have added enough girth to my hips for the dress not to fit.

CHAPTER EIGHT

It took 512 steps to get from Dana's car to the front entrance of the Goode Harbor Orpheum Theatre. I know because I'd counted, each step more treacherous than the last in my borrowed high heels.

"These shoes are brutal," I whined, knowing I sounded like a brat. It had been nice of Celia to loan me a pair, even though I wished she'd gone in my place. Fancy shindigs were not my cup of tea.

"I'm so sorry." Dana held onto one of my arms, doing her best to keep me upright. "If it makes you feel better, I've never seen you look lovelier."

It did make me feel better, a little anyway. It had been a long time since someone complimented me on my appearance. "I can't remember the last time I had to get all dolled up."

"Dolled up?" Dana raised a quizzical brow. "Is that what the cool kids are saying these days?"

My cheeks tingled. I'd done it again, using a phrase that was probably out of fashion before Aunt Izzy was born. "You know, Phil and I stopped going out on dates years ago. Even when my mom would come to visit and offer to watch the kids at her hotel, he'd come up with something else to do. Like taxes."

"Like cooking the books, you mean." Dana's expression shifted. "Your mother stayed in a hotel when she came to visit?"

"I didn't allow magic in the house, what with Phil being non-magical, and she couldn't figure out how to make the coffee pot work without it."

"I get that. The coffee pot, that is. Phil being uncomfortable around magic should have been your first red flag." Dana flashed a cheery smile. "Good thing you're home now and don't have to suffer such non-magical indignities."

"Yeah, good thing."

My heart sank. Would I ever be able to reveal the truth? Phil hadn't been the one to forbid magic. He hadn't even known I was a witch. I'd only claimed he was against it because it made it easier to hide my own secret. Would I ever be able to be honest about my past?

Dana opened the door for me, and I stumbled into the theater lobby. I nearly wiped out completely, taking

Dana down with me, but she righted us both in the nick of time.

"Maybe I should get you a drink," Dana said, leading me to a cocktail table where I could steady myself properly.

While Dana headed to the glittering brass bar that stood at the far end of the room, I remained at the table and took in the scene with a curious eye. A bartender was mixing cocktails and pouring champagne for the evening's well-dressed guests. Despite my aching feet, I couldn't help but feel the thrill of excitement in the air for the evening's festivities.

While it was mostly used as a movie theater nowadays, the Orpheum had been built in the early 1900s as a live performance venue and still retained all the red-velvet-draped elegance of a bygone era. It was a far cry from the previous week when I'd taken the girls here for a matinée, and we'd trailed bits of buttered popcorn as we walked across the plush carpet in flip-flops. Dressed up the way I was, I felt like I truly belonged. It was an unusual feeling for me since my return home.

A new sensation replaced the general buzz of anticipation that coursed through me, one that made me immediately tense and wary. A crackle in the air forced my eyes to a woman who was headed my way, platinum blonde hair in a 1950s coif with a vintage gown to match. I knew at once she was a witch. An extremely stylish one at that. Did she spend her spare time on catwalks in Paris?

"That's a stunning dress," the witch said with open admiration.

"This old thing?" I laughed nervously. It was a cheesy line, but I couldn't help myself. It would probably be the only time in my life I could say it and have it be true.

"The word is vintage, darling. Like a fine wine." There was a slight hint of a foreign accent as she spoke. "It reminds me of a Jeanne Lavin *robe de style* from *l'hiver dix-neuf-cent-vingt-six* collection."

"That was all French to me." I chuckled self-consciously. Two corny jokes back-to-back? I was like butter. On a roll.

"Winter, 1926," she translated.

"You sound like you know what you're talking about."

"I don't think we've met. I'm Brigit Laveau." She held out her hand, which I was oddly delighted to discover was clothed in a white silk glove. "I'm the proprietor of Rags to Riches, the vintage clothing boutique on Main Street."

And the third member of Dana's coven.

"Tallie Shipton. Pleasure to meet you." I took her hand in mine, marveling at her effortless refinement. Anyone else might have said they owned a shop, but the way Brigit had phrased it made it sound like more than what it was. How did she do it?

"I'm a glamor witch," she said in a low voice, as if answering the question in my head. "And yes, I'm slightly clairvoyant, but don't worry. I don't make a habit of reading people's minds."

"Good to know." My eyes darted to the bar. Dana was nowhere near the front of the line, which was a shame. Brigit's revelation left me in serious need of a strong drink.

"Now you must tell me, wherever did you get that dress?"

"I found it in the attic in a trunk with a few others," I said.

Brigit eyed my garment like it was a steak and she was a dog who hadn't eaten in a year. "Are all of them this impressive?"

"I haven't gone through them yet," I admitted. "I'm usually more of a jeans and T-shirt kinda gal."

"If you'd ever like to bring them by the shop, I'd be more than happy to look them over and let you know what you have." Brigit's attention was caught by someone at another table. "Now, if you'll excuse me, I need to mingle."

Almost as quickly as she'd arrived, the witch was gone. The crackling in my veins had subsided when I spotted a newcomer who sent an odd burst of adrenaline zinging to my fingertips and toes. I almost didn't recognize her without all the black leather.

Catching my eye, Nora smiled and made her way to

my table. "I didn't expect to see you here. You look fantastic."

My lips flapped a few times, but I didn't know what to say. Everyone was complimenting me tonight. I couldn't remember the last time Phil had so much as looked in my direction.

"Er, you look nice, too," I finally managed to get out. It was true. Her sleek black pants suit was a perfect choice, feminine but professional. "Attending was a last-minute thing. I'm Dana Wardwell's date for the evening."

"Lucky lady." The way Nora said this, I wasn't sure which of us she considered the lucky one, me or Dana. Either way, there was a certain something in her expression that hadn't been there a moment before.

"Should I be concerned?" I blurted out, recalling that among other things, Nora was the island doctor. "They're keeping my mom longer than I thought they would."

"Come again?" Nora slanted her head, a blend of concern and confusion in her eyes.

"At the hospital." My voice trembled as I fought to hold back tears. "You said she'd be home yesterday, and now it looks like Monday at the earliest."

"Oh." Nora straightened up slightly, as if switching into her medical persona. "Most likely, there's nothing to worry about. It's a holiday this week, which I'd forgotten."

"Are you sure?" I hated how needy I sounded, but I

couldn't control it. After all the times I'd had to be strong since the day I'd found out what Phil had done, I'd reached my limit of what I could endure.

In response to my distress, Nora rested her hand on my shoulder, her surprisingly soft palm brushing my bare skin. The hairs on my arm stood up as if activated by static electricity.

There was a loud cough. Nora jumped, her hand falling to her side. A tall woman with short-cropped blonde hair and an athletic build had approached us, standing so close to Nora they were nearly touching. Her face, though rugged, was attractive, but the khaki polyester uniform she was wearing, along with a broad-brimmed hat she clutched in one hand, weren't doing her a lot of favors. A shiny brass badge identified her as the sheriff.

"Hey there, Doc." The sheriff gave Nora a playful nudge with her shoulder, eliciting a slight yelp that made me think the woman was even stronger than she appeared.

"Will you excuse me for a minute?" Nora asked, directing her question at both of us. "I need to check on something."

With Nora gone, the silence was deafening. The woman across from me showed no sign of talking, nor of moving on. My muscles started to twitch.

"You here to arrest someone?" I gave what could only be described as a guilty laugh. My earlier attempts at jokes had been funny, if I did say so myself. This one fell flat and made me sound like an idiot.

"Anyone in particular?" The sheriff didn't crack a smile, but there was a look in her eyes that suggested she was considering slapping handcuffs on me. I had no idea what I'd done to earn such instant animosity, unless she was the type to think bad comedy a crime.

"Not that I'm aware of," I babbled. "Although, I did hear David Spencer and Alexander Tate threaten each other's lives the other day. Over tea, no less. I had no idea these literary types were so competitive. Then there's Nora, disturbing the peace with that iron of hers."

"Iron?" The sheriff looked at me like I'd started speaking a foreign language. "A clothing iron?"

"What? No." I frowned. Had the woman never seen a motorcycle before? I mimicked the sound to the best of my ability, which wasn't that great if I had to be honest. "You know, a..." My frown deepened as I questioned the word I had used before. Since when did anyone call a motorcycle an iron? Yet I was certain that was what it meant. I had no idea why I knew it, or what had possessed me to say it.

Meanwhile, the sheriff drew in a breath, her nostrils flaring like an angry bull. Dear goddess, why couldn't I stop making an ass out of myself?

"You got a problem with motorcycles?" she growled.

"No. Of course not." I swallowed hard. Now she

thought I was anti-motorcycle, which was very bad news for me. She was a cop. She probably rode one for work every day. I might never recover from this blunder.

"Well, we generally frown upon arresting people without any reason around here, but if you get some evidence of a crime, please feel free to let me know." The sheriff's tone remained even, and it was impossible for me to tell whether she was finding any of this remotely funny, or if I was about to have my rights read to me and be hauled to the clink for pissing her off.

The awkward silence that descended between us threatened to stretch on endlessly. If I'd had any inclination to break the law during my time on the island, I would definitely have rethought it about now. This sheriff seemed like the type to murder a person and feed the body to the sharks simply because they'd been annoying.

This did not bode well for me.

"Good news," Nora said, saving us from more torment by her return. "I took the liberty of calling the hospital to put your mind at ease. Nothing from the first test revealed anything serious, but the doctor is being extra cautious. I've got a call in to the head of neurology to make sure."

"Uh, thanks," I grunted, the air thoroughly knocked out of me at how nice the doctor was being while the sheriff continued to size me up.

Instantly forgetting my existence, the sheriff turned to Nora. "In that case, maybe we could—?"

But Nora wasn't paying any attention. She was too busy pressing her fingers to my temples, studying my face. "Have you been sleeping okay? You look exhausted."

I raised an eyebrow, though I didn't move away from her touch. "That's what every woman wants to hear when out on the town."

"I'm sorry." Oddly, Nora's cheeks turned red, and her gaze shifted like she was suddenly too embarrassed to sustain eye contact. "I didn't mean it that way. You really do look lovely."

"As I was saying, Nora—" The sheriff was interrupted by Nora's ringing phone.

"Life of a doctor," Nora said by way of excusing herself.

While Nora went to the far corner to speak in privacy, the sheriff put on her hat and prepared to leave.

"It was nice to, uh, meet you," I said somewhat stupidly. It wasn't like the sheriff had done anything to indicate the feeling was mutual. Hell, she hadn't even told me her name. Which was why it came as such a shock when she stooped down and got right in my face.

"I don't know what your story is, and I don't really care," she added before I could act on any mistaken belief that she might be interested. "I know your type, and I don't want any trouble from you. You got that?"

"Yes," I croaked. "Er, yes, ma'am."

From what I could tell, she and I weren't too far apart in age, but all of a sudden, I'd been reduced to a teenager getting caught smoking behind the gym at lunch. I was getting a definite mob boss vibe from this woman that was turning my insides to jelly. I pictured an interrogation room in my future, one where the video cameras conveniently stopped working when the batons and tasers came out.

"I don't want you getting any ideas," she hissed, pausing to tug at her belt loops with her thumbs, an action that served to quadruple an intimidation factor that was already off the charts. "Nora Kenworthy is mine. You understand? The doc belongs to me."

What I understood with this unhinged woman towering over me was that I was about two seconds away from peeing myself in the middle of the theater lobby. Meanwhile, as the sheriff sauntered away, she looked back at the doc in question in a manner that suggested if she were a canine cop, she would've turned back around and pissed on Nora's leg, just to make sure her claims of possession were loud and clear.

I was still trembling when Nora returned. She gave no indication that she'd witnessed the sheriff—that is to say her *girlfriend*—behaving in such a menacing way toward me that I was contemplating sleeping with a knife under my pillow that night. Nora flashed one of her charming, sheepish grins, and it was everything I could do not to whip my head around to make sure the sheriff hadn't seen it.

"Where's Dana? Should we be going inside?" Nora didn't seem to be in a hurry to join the other guests. In fact, she seemed quite content where she was. Every so often, her eyes would flick down my neck and across my shoulders with an intensity I could almost feel physically along my skin.

It was a strangely pleasant sensation.

"She was supposed to be getting me a drink," I said, wishing she'd succeeded. Considering some of the inappropriate thoughts that were trying to race around in my addled noggin, I really needed one.

Since when did I notice how another woman was looking at me, let alone care?

I stumbled over a rough spot on the carpet in my ridiculous shoes, and Nora looped her arm through mine and led me to the bar. "Red, white, or something stronger?"

The fabric of her jacket brushed the inside of my elbow, and my internal temperature skyrocketed. Perspiration beaded on my brow. I attributed it to fear, specifically fear of what the sheriff might do if she spotted me walking with her girlfriend like this. Even if it was totally innocent, the good doctor doing her best to keep a damsel in high heels upright, I doubted it would go over well.

"Red, please," I managed to say, my head swiveling for any sign of Dana. I needed my friend to come over and knock some sense into my skull and possibly provide backup in case the sheriff came running over like a raging bull to force her woman to unhand me. "Where do you think she went?"

"Dana? I imagine she had official duties to take care of." As Nora handed over a wine glass, the house lights flashed to indicate it was time to take our seats. "Let's see if we can find her inside."

I took a step, wobbling, and Nora promptly held out her arm to help me. Another caress of silky fabric against my skin. Shivers all over, the good kind, and maybe not completely innocent. If the sheriff ever guessed what effect this walk was having on my insides, I probably wouldn't live to see the sunrise.

Inside the auditorium, Dana went racing past like a runaway locomotive. "Tallie, I'm so sorry! Bit of a last-minute emergency."

"That's okay," Nora called after her. "I'll make sure your date's taken care of."

"I appreciate it," Dana hollered back, nearly breaking into a run.

"I wonder what's going on," I said to no one in particular. The large room hummed with conversation, but no one aside from Dana seemed in much of a rush.

"Would you like to have lunch on Monday?" Nora asked once we took our seats. A few rows up, the sheriff was shining her flashlight into an aisle.

"Uh—" My heart clenched. This was going from bad to worse. Would the sheriff execute me on the spot if she overheard?

"Or we could do later in the afternoon, say 2:15? Unless mornings are better." Nora sounded a little flustered, or maybe that was me projecting my own fears.

"Huh?" I knew I had to look insane, staring with my mouth gaping and my eyes as big as saucers, but I didn't seem able to control it. If I kept this up, the doctor would have no choice but to shove chill pills down my throat. "What are we doing together Monday?"

"Setting up a time to discuss your mother's test results." Nora tilted her head to one side, perhaps hoping this change in perspective would make me seem more normal. From the continued look of confusion on her face, I don't think it worked.

Meanwhile, I didn't know what to do with the disappointment that had crushed my chest when I realized Nora's proposition was one hundred percent professional. Thankfully, I was saved from responding as the lights around us dimmed and the stage grew bright.

"Good evening, everyone. Welcome to the annual Goode Harbor Literary Festival Gala." Dana stood on the stage, smiling until the applause died down. She sounded confident, but I noticed her holding onto the sides of the podium like she wanted to stop herself from bolting. "In a moment, we'll announce the two finalists for this year's Chesterton Prize. But first, we're going to have some musical entertainment from the Goode Harbor Symphony Orchestra."

"That's odd." Nora flipped open the program she'd been handed as we came in. "They're going out of order. The music isn't supposed to come until after the finalists are announced."

"Maybe that's part of whatever emergency Dana had to deal with," I suggested. "Perhaps someone is sick."

"If that were the case, surely someone would have let me know." Nora closed the program, looking worried. "Maybe I should go see if they need my help."

"I'm sure if they needed help, they'd let you know." I nearly rested my hand on her arm but thought better of it, folding my fingers in my lap like a good girl instead.

It was possible Nora Kenworthy wasn't quite the ogre I'd made her out to be. I might even go so far as to say I liked her. A little bit. But in a thoroughly platonic sort of way.

That was all.

Besides, if I so much as waved hello to the woman, her crazy girlfriend was likely to rip my heart from my chest and dump my carcass into the sea.

The music ended, and Dana took up her position at the podium once more. She looked even more nervous than before. "I know everyone's been waiting for this big moment, so I guess we can't put it off any longer."

If that was the case, why did it look like that was the one thing Dana wanted desperately to do?

"Our first finalist is…" A drum roll began, and a man walked across the stage with an envelope in his hand. Dana took it from him and broke the seal, sliding a card from inside and holding it up to read. "David Spencer! Please come up on stage."

Applause began, and music played, but nothing happened. There was murmuring in the crowd, heads turning this way and that, but no David came into view.

"David? You out there?" Dana shielded her eyes from the lights.

"He's probably in the bathroom," someone called out from the audience, prompting a burst of collective laughter.

"You're probably right. When he comes back in, he'll join us." Dana was really gripping the podium now, but she had to pry her hands off as the man handed her a second envelope. "Let's give this another try. Alexander Tate!"

The applause started again, more music playing. Again, nothing happened. People began looking around.

"Alexander," Dana repeated, "would you be so kind to come up front? And David. Both of you, really."

The symphony launched into song for the third

time, but it was hardly enough to drown out the growing murmur from the audience, as everyone began to wonder out loud where Alexander and David were.

Dana laughed nervously into the mic. "Has anyone seen either of our authors this evening?"

Had that been the emergency? Neither of them had checked in with Dana?

"No, but I saw them in the tea shop yesterday," someone helpfully, or maybe not-so-helpfully, shouted.

"They got into a brawl!" another said.

"I heard that, too!" a third piped up, illustrating how quickly news travels on an island.

"Yes, but has anyone seen them in the theater?" Dana continued to hold up a hand, scouring the room, every second looking more deflated.

The murmuring built to a roar, but as the seconds ticked by, it died down, becoming a whole lot of silence that unnerved me.

"What's going on?" Nora whispered, tickling my ear. "Where could they be?"

"I have no idea." My shoulders moved up and down as a chill traveled along my spine. "It's a mystery."

CHAPTER NINE

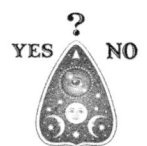

*I*t was an hour later when I stood on the inn's front porch, unwrapping my arms from around my torso long enough to try the doorknob. Locked. I wasn't sure if Celia had gone to bed early or no one was home, but either way was an issue since I didn't have a key.

"There's a spare under the flowerpot," Nora offered as she crossed to the railing to retrieve it.

"How do you know that?"

"Because it's Crescent Cove," she said with a chuckle. "Safest neighborhood on the island. Everyone here keeps their spare key under the flowerpot."

"Would you mind unlocking it?" I asked, my hands trembling. The wind had shifted, and I'd been cold ever since we'd finally left the theater an hour or so after the awards had come to an abrupt halt. "I think I had too much wine."

"You had one glass," Nora countered with a teasing laugh that made me feel tingly all the way to my toes.

"I don't need to tip a few to get zozzled." I frowned as the words ran through my head. What the hell was that supposed to mean?

Nora laughed so hard she nearly choked. "Spoken like a true flapper."

"You understood what I said?"

"I've kind of got a thing for the 1920s. It's my uncle's doing. He's a nut for the island's Prohibition history." She shrugged. "I guess it rubbed off on me."

"I didn't know the island had any Prohibition history."

"Sure. I mean, the ladies at the historical society like to focus on the Gilded Age, but there were also rumrunners, speakeasies, you name it." Nora's voice took on a wistful tone. "Must've been something."

"I bet." For some reason, a sudden sense of unease sent a chill through me, and a gust of wind whipped hair into my eyes.

"I'd better get this door open." Even after saying this, Nora held my gaze for a moment, not moving, an unreadable expression on her face. It sent chills of a totally different type running through me.

That settled it. I was a complete and utter fool.

Never in my life had I been interested in any woman before. Up until recently, I'd been convinced I would hate this particular woman with my dying breath, based only on her possession of the Kenworthy name. But now, just because I'd found out she was dating a woman, I was obsessed.

Just because she's into women, doesn't mean she's attracted to you, I reminded myself. And I didn't want her to be! Sure, I hated Phil, but one rotten husband didn't turn a person off men, right?

She was being nice, and I'd missed that. Surely, that was the only reason my heart fluttered as she turned the key and made a gallant gesture toward the open door.

"My lady," she said, but not before turning on the light in the entry so I could see, proving she knew the place well.

How many times had she been by to take care of my mother?

Before I could ask, Nora said, "Sleep well tonight, Tallie."

"You too," I replied, my whole body going up in flames.

Probably a hot flash.

I was shedding my heels as soon as my feet hit the hardwood floor. Now that Nora wasn't here to catch me if I fell, it was better to be safe than sorry.

My first order of business after that was to find a bandage for my feet. Second was to check the inn to see if Mr. Tate had come back. I'd given Dana my word that I would when I got back. After the debacle at the awards ceremony, Dana had been in tears, certain the literary society would somehow blame her for the mess. I'd never seen Dana so upset. Not since her date split his pants at the junior high dance when attempting to break dance.

This situation didn't seem to be a laughing matter, and my body tingled with dread. Upstairs, Celia was sound asleep in her room, but there wasn't a sign of the author anywhere. I checked every bedroom. Nothing.

Still in my gown and bare feet, I headed back downstairs, taking up watch in the living room, intent on waiting for Alexander Tate to return. I wasn't sure if I would read him the riot act for destroying Dana's ceremony first or wait until after thanking the Goddess he was still alive.

Surely, he was still alive.

I closed my eyes and rested my head against the back of the chair.

Waiting.

THE NEXT THING I KNEW, I WAS NOT IN MY chair but was standing in the center of the room, bright sunlight streaming through the windows. The furniture was mostly the same, but the wallpaper was an eye-popping green stripe with the gaudiest pink roses I'd ever seen.

I wore a dress made of black silk with elaborate beading. It was clearly new, the fabric crisp and pristine.

Jeanne Lavin robe de style, a voice with a slight French accent said in my head. *Winter, 1926.*

The sound of a woman's high heels retreating down the hallway echoed in my ears. The cloying scent of rose perfume singed the hairs in my nose.

"Thank goodness she's gone."

Startled to hear a voice in the empty room, I wheeled around only to discover the room wasn't empty at all. A young woman, perhaps in her early twenties, stood on the ottoman in a gown equally as splendid as mine, while another woman of roughly the same age, or perhaps a few years older, scurried around her hem with pins sticking out from her mouth.

A gasp caught in my throat as my eyes focused on the face of the woman in the dress. If I hadn't known better, I would have sworn it was Maya, looking every bit as beautiful and fresh-faced as the last time I'd seen her. Oh, how I wished this was my sister! With all that had happened these past several months, I needed my big sister like I needed air to breathe. But how could it be?

"Who's that, miss?" the kneeling woman inquired,

her teeth never losing their firm grip on the pins as she spoke. She reminded me of Aunt Izzy, but impossibly young, though my aunt was born in the 1940s while this woman wore her brown hair styled in the type of Marcel wave that was popular in the 1920s.

"Our mother," not-Maya replied.

I shivered at the response, feeling in my bones that this mother she referred to was someone to be feared.

The seamstress nodded as she put another pin in the hem, though she refrained from commenting, perhaps because it was likely the woman in the high heels and rose perfume was the one who would be paying the bill. "These are the finest dresses I've ever seen, if you don't mind me saying."

"Aren't they divine?" said the woman who wasn't Maya, though somehow, I couldn't shake the sense that she was meant to be my sister in whatever strange world I'd suddenly found myself in.

Her name was on the tip of my tongue.

"They're just dresses, Sarah," I heard my own voice saying. Sarah. That was her name.

"They're fit for queens." Sarah smiled dreamily. "That's what mother said."

"She should know," I muttered with a petulance I couldn't explain. "She's trying to become royalty, after all. American style, naturally, by marrying the richest man on the island and then selling us off to the highest bidders."

"That isn't fair," Sarah chided. "Roberta has far too many suitors and doesn't pay the slightest attention to any of them. I'll be quite happy to have my choice of them once we've taken our place in island society. There are some real swells."

"How thrilling," the seamstress said, the two women clearly sharing an excitement I didn't feel.

I shrugged, the strap of my gown bobbing on my shoulder. "Swells aren't really my type."

"Oh, but they're mine," Sarah said with a girlish giggle.

"Mine, too," the seamstress agreed. "What I wouldn't give to have someone rich and handsome to sweep me off my feet! Of course, your soon-to-be stepfather is the richest of them all."

"Yes. Mother says once they've married, all of our gowns will be made for us in Paris, not seconds, like these—" Sarah waved at her dress. "Come now, Sister. Don't you want your pick of rich, eligible bachelors?"

"What would I do with a husband? They're more trouble than their worth." Although I'd spoken without thinking, as if reciting lines from a play that had been written for me, I couldn't help but agree with myself on this one. After Phil, I'd had my fill of men.

"There you go, miss. All set." The seamstress straightened. "You can go change while I take care of your sister."

When Sarah had left the room, the seamstress

motioned expectantly at the ottoman, but the last thing I wanted was to stand around in a dress like some kind of mannequin. I hated the things. My only other dress fitting was for my wedding, and look how that had turned out.

"Say, wanna sneak outside for a ciggy?" I asked, my brow furrowing at the use of a word I'd surely never used before. And since when did I smoke?

She hesitated, but I could see the temptation in her eyes. "I don't know. It wouldn't be proper."

"I don't give a fig about proper," I told her, hiking up the too long dress.

I padded toward the door in my stocking-clad feet. When I paused by the front door, I looked in the mirror, and the face I saw wasn't exactly the one I'd been expecting. I was so young! My skin was as smooth as butter, my hair its familiar shade of Shipton red but styled in a similar fashion as what the other woman wore and with not so much as a single streak of gray. I couldn't be more than sixteen, if that.

Was this really what I had looked like back then? There were subtle differences in the shape of my lips and chin that gave me the sensation of looking at a stranger, and I felt a tingling of electricity course through me as I realized that perhaps I wasn't me after all. I dismissed the thought quickly, as it made me uneasy.

I opened the front door and slipped out onto the porch, with the seamstress following a few steps behind. I pulled a cigarette and lighter from my garter. The cigarette appeared to be hand rolled, and the lighter wasn't a modern plastic one but an old-fashioned type made of metal that was heavy in my hand.

Though I'd never done it before, somehow, I sparked the flint like an expert. I placed the cigarette between my lips and took a long drag. The action seemed as natural on the one hand as it did completely foreign to me on the other, like I was two people inhabiting the same body, with all the memories and knowledge of both.

"Say, do you know of any places on the island where a girl can get a drink?" I asked.

My new friend took the cigarette from me and gave it a few puffs as she thought. "Depends. Do you like music?"

I nodded.

"What type?"

"Jazz, of course." I was quick to reply, even though I considered the stuff about as thrilling as elevator music.

"Now, that's the berries!" she replied. She flashed a conspiratorial smile. "You're in luck. My beau, Freddy, plays piano at a speakeasy down by the docks. If you can sneak out Saturday night, I'll take you there. It's run by Bertie Chase, the most infamous bootlegger in all of the northeast."

"A bootlegger?" I swallowed, uncertain how to feel about this revelation.

"Oh, yes. But don't be concerned. Everyone loves Bertie. He's ever so suave and debonair."

Before I could reply that I liked suave and debonaire, she pulled out a pin and stabbed it into my left breast.

My eyes popped open as a searing pain jabbed me like a needle had been inserted into my nipple. I couldn't breathe.

"Meow."

"Buster!" I shook the cat off of my chest. "You stabbed me in the boob."

He glared at me like I'd deserved it.

"Where am I?" My eyes started to focus. I was still in the living room, but now it looked like it'd been put back together the way I expected. Sunlight streamed in through the window, but I suspected this time it was because it was actually morning.

Yet I was still wearing the black silk dress, and a hint of rose hung in the room. Maybe I was dreaming.

Rubbing my eyes, I contemplated going back to sleep, but then I remembered the previous night. Had Alexander Tate come back, and I'd slept through it?

"I better check—"

Before I could finish, a scream from outside forced me off the couch and sent me racing for the door. My feet were bare, the black silk rustling around my legs as I ran.

At the edge of the lawn where the grass sloped into the cove, Celia and David stood together in the water, soaking wet. They were pulling a massive, hulking something from the sparkling water. Even once it was on the grass and I could see, it took several seconds for reality to hit me.

It was Alexander Tate, who no longer seemed to be of this world.

CHAPTER TEN

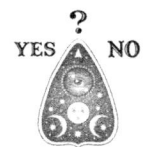

Nora knelt at the edge of the water, still wearing her dark suit from the night before, as she searched the man's body for vital signs that almost certainly didn't exist. I wasn't entirely sure how she'd gotten there. Had I called 911? I couldn't remember. It had only been a few minutes since I'd woken up in the living room to the stab of a claw in my boob and the sound of Celia's scream, but it felt like an eternity.

A cloying scent of roses still hung in the air.

"This can't be happening," I said to no one in particular. But no matter how much I insisted it was impossible, it wouldn't change reality.

"I'm afraid he's dead," Nora announced solemnly, removing her stethoscope and placing it in the backpack full of medical supplies she'd grabbed from her car when she'd arrived.

My vision blurred, and I staggered forward, gooey mud squeezing between my bare toes. Celia, dripping wet, let out a strangled cry, while David remained stoic but white as a sheet.

A hulking black SUV crunched its way along the long driveway, coming to a stop at an angle that displayed the gold sheriff's department logo to good effect. The engine shut off, and the sheriff got out, followed by a deputy. A second cruiser soon pulled in behind.

"Do not disturb the crime scene!" the sheriff barked as the deputy pulled out a large roll of yellow crime scene tape.

"Who said anything about a crime?" I asked before thinking, probably not the smartest thing I'd ever done. The look she gave me should have required registration as a lethal weapon.

"I'm the law on this island, Miss Shipton. If I say something's a crime, then it's a crime. You got that?" The sheriff turned her back to me, addressing the doctor instead.

Looking back at the house, I gulped as the deputy secured one end of the tape to a fence pole and began stretching it across the property in a way I was pretty sure would be visible from space.

"Nora, can you tell me—?" the sheriff stopped short, taking in Nora's clothes. "What exactly were you doing before the victim's body was discovered?"

Nora, who had opened her mouth in preparation to

respond, snapped it shut. That was obviously not the question she'd been expecting.

"Miss Shipton," she eyed my vintage gown, wrinkled from a night spent sleeping in an armchair, and my tousled hair. "What were you doing in the time leading up to the body's discovery?"

"I was sleeping."

"Is that right?" The sheriff's eyes narrowed. Whatever thoughts were going through the woman's mind, I didn't want to know. "You weren't up making breakfast? This is a bed-and-*breakfast*, is it not?"

"Well, yes. But I didn't get home until late, and—"

"How did you get home, exactly?"

"Now, hold on," I protested, reaching my limit of her bizarrely jealous behavior and frankly not wanting to risk admitting Nora had driven me home. If she didn't trust her own girlfriend, that was one thing. But she had no right to take it out on me. "I fail to see how this has anything to do with Alexander Tate's death. Aren't you going to investigate?"

"I already know who killed him." The sheriff pulled a pair of handcuffs from her belt. I held my breath, fearing she was coming for me, but she marched directly toward David, who was shaking his head vigorously and barking unintelligible sounds of protest. "David Spencer, you're under arrest."

The sheriff clapped her handcuffs around David's wrists, holding him until one of the deputies could put down the crime scene tape long enough to take the prisoner to the cruiser and haul him away. The previous night, she'd said people frowned upon arresting people without proof. Sure, David had threatened Alexander Tate, but was that enough to warrant an actual arrest before anything was ascertained? Not wanting to offer these thoughts out loud, my eyes questioned Nora who seemed as surprised as I was.

I'd nearly forgotten Celia's presence until she sank to her knees as if her legs had given out. Nora rushed to her, lending physical support while checking her pulse.

"Bonnie, I'd like to get Celia to the clinic, if that's okay with you," Nora said. "The EMTs are on their way and should be able to assist with transporting Mr. Tate's body to the dock. I'll arrange a spot on the next ferry and alert the morgue on the mainland."

Bonnie? Until that moment, it hadn't occurred to me that the sheriff had an actual name, aside from scary. A quick check of her badge revealed the last name of Gray. At least now I knew who I was dealing with.

"Yes, that's fine," Sheriff Gray said in a much softer tone than she'd used up until this point. But it didn't last long. The moment Nora and Celia were out of earshot, the sheriff rounded on me, and I let out a squeak. "Obviously, with a victim as high profile as Alexander Tate, we'll be launching a thorough investigation. My team will need to search the inn."

"Yes, of cour—wait." Belatedly, my brain emerged

from its fog to fully engage. "Why do you need to search the inn? Mr. Tate clearly died in the water."

"Don't you think it would be wise to leave the investigation up to the experts?" Something told me this was a rhetorical question, so I kept my trap shut while Sheriff Gray whipped out a notebook and pen. "Ms. Shipton, I'm going to need all your food service, personnel, and health and safety files."

"Uh—" My mother hadn't given me the location of any of these documents before leaving for the hospital.

"You do have a food preparation certificate, do you not?"

"Me, personally?" I shook my head. "I don't actually, you know, cook."

"I see." She snapped her notebook shut. "Effective immediately, the kitchen of this facility is closed, pending proper documentation and a complete inspection of the premises."

"What does this have to do with Mr. Tate drowning?"

"Who said he drowned?" the sheriff demanded. "Are you saying you know the cause of death before a trained professional like Dr. Kenworthy does? You're in enough trouble without me issuing a citation for practicing medicine without a license."

That settled it. Sheriff Bonnie Gray was out of her freaking mind. She's clearly looking for ways to add fraudulent charges to scare me, and it was working because the woman had a badge. And as normal—

even, to my surprise, nice—as Nora Kenworthy appeared to be, there was clearly a screw or two loose in her head if this woman was her girlfriend. I would do best to steer clear of them both.

Sheriff Gray went to the trunk of her car, pulling out half a dozen large, red signs that read *Closed by Order of the Goode Harbor Sheriff*. The fact she drove around the island with a stack of these told me a lot about how she operated.

"If you could post those on all the entrances to the crime scene, I'd appreciate it."

I bit my lower lip in consternation. "The entrances. You mean, like, the beach?"

"The property, Miss Shipton." She said this in a tone that implied I was the insane one. "Front door, back door, fences, driveway—"

"Driveway? You want me to put this on the road?" As if this wasn't already going to be grist for the island rumor mill, the sheriff seemed intent on making the inn into a complete spectacle. "People will see it."

"That's the whole point."

Yeah, I'll bet it was. For whatever reason, Sheriff Gray was out to make me a laughing stock.

I was growing delirious from frustration and lack of caffeine, and by the time I was finally allowed to go back inside, all I could think of was how desperate I was for a cup of coffee. The sheriff's deputies, however, had been busy. Yellow tape was woven like a plastic tapestry to seal the kitchen completely. This in addition to one of those big red signs, declaring the space closed, in case all that crime scene tape wasn't a big enough of a clue.

Stifling a groan, I peeled back a loose edge of tape and peered into the room beyond. My heart sank. Every drawer had been emptied and every cabinet opened. A twenty-five-pound bag of flour had been overturned in the pantry and spread across the floor like freshly fallen snow. What were they even looking for? My guess was nothing. The sheriff simply had them do this because she could.

Slapping the tape back into place, I made my way to the dining room, sank into a chair, and buried my head in my arms.

If this were a regular Sunday at the inn, there would have been eggs and thick slices of bacon in silver chafing dishes on the sideboard, towers of fresh fruit, and the aroma of cinnamon and vanilla hanging heavily in the air from homemade waffles and muffins. My stomach grumbled, but with the thorough job the deputies had done, I couldn't even get to the cupboard for a bowl of cereal without committing a crime.

I swiveled my head as a light tapping came from the back door on the far side of the kitchen. I could just make out the edge of Nora's face in the window, and as we made eye contact, she held up a large paper sack. I recognized the logo of the island's best donut shop and grinned.

"Is that what I think it is?" I called out as loudly as possible, hoping she could hear me through the glass.

"A dozen donuts," she confirmed. "And hot coffee."

"I'll be right there!"

The obedient citizen in me told me I needed to go out the front door and walk all the way around to the back. The rebel in me gave the crime scene barrier a long, hard look. The deputies had outdone themselves, but plastic tape wasn't exactly as sophisticated a deterrent as laser beams. With a little flexibility and some blatant disregard for the law, I shimmied my way through a gap near the bottom and dashed across the room with the speed and care of a thief in the middle of a museum heist.

"Bonnie mentioned something about all this," Nora remarked as she took in the tape. "But it has to be seen to be believed."

"Do you think she's serious about keeping it closed?" I nearly accused the sheriff of being a maniac on a power trip, but then I remembered who I was talking to. The maniac's better half. And she had donuts and coffee with her. Best not to burn bridges.

"Serious enough that I wouldn't test her on it this morning. I can give a call over there for you later and urge one of the deputies to give the all clear."

"You're a lifesaver." I took the bag from her, my eyes growing wide at the huge cardboard container she still held, a plastic spout sticking out from its side. "Now this is what I call a coffee."

"The Gallon of Joe is one of Holey Moley's specialties. It even comes with paper cups and all the fixings."

"Which is useful when getting some half-and-half out of your own fridge is a federal offense." I led Nora into the dining room, lifting up the police barrier for her to pass under and then smoothing it back into place to erase all signs of our trespassing. "We speak of this to no one."

"My lips are sealed."

Hers lips twitched with humor, and as she came up close beside me to set the bag on the table, my pulse quickened. The sheriff's warnings echoed in my head. She'd wrecked my kitchen and shut down the inn already. What additional torment would she come up with if she happened to walk in right now and witnessed *this* scene?

I took a slow breath and put some distance between us under the pretext of grabbing some dishes from the built-in china hutch in the far corner. Better safe than sorry.

THE HOUSE WAS EERILY QUIET THAT EVENING. As soon as news of our guest's demise reached her,

Mira had offered to keep the girls another night. I accepted at once. The last thing I wanted so soon after living through the drama of an FBI raid in Cleveland was for my daughters to discover their new home had been declared a crime scene. With no one in the house except Celia, who'd gone directly to her bedroom with a strong sedative the minute she'd returned from the clinic, I wasn't sure what to do with myself.

I tried to read a book in the living room, but all I could think of was the strange dream I'd had the night before. My stomach rumbled, reminding me I hadn't eaten since the donuts and coffee that morning. Given the disastrous state of my kitchen, that was what I planned to eat for dinner, too.

The clock on the mantel chimed eight times. I glanced up the stairs to the darkness of the second-floor landing, catching a thin light beneath the crack of Celia's door. My guest was up. The least I could do was offer her some donuts and room temperature coffee. No one could accuse me of being a bad host.

I arranged the meager offerings on a tray, balancing it in one hand as I tapped on the bedroom door. My stomach tightened at the sound of movement on the other side. Would the woman be hysterical in her grief? I stiffened as the doorknob turned, bracing myself for an onslaught of rage at the worst, or uncontrollable sobbing at best, but when the door opened, I was puzzled to be met with a face that radiated calm.

"Yes?" she said, her tone quiet, almost soothing.

I pressed my lips together and swallowed. "I brought you something to eat. It's not much."

"I appreciate it." She took the tray from my outstretched hands and set it on the bed.

I hovered in the doorway, uncertain what to do or say. As the silence dragged on, I finally opted for the timeworn, "I'm so sorry for your loss."

"Thank you," she replied, her eyes remaining dry.

"If there's… uh… anything you need," I stumbled, confused by her lack of emotion. She might as well have been thanking me for bringing her an extra towel or telling her the time of day. Was she in shock?

She nodded. "If you'll excuse me, I have a lot of work to do."

She turned her back and walked to the plain metal desk in the adjoining office, the one where Alexander Tate had spent so many hours those past couple of weeks, typing away. Before the door closed all the way, I could make out a haziness in the space. It was unidentifiable, no more solid than a wisp of smoke or a smudge on your glasses, yet it chilled me to my core. I tried to turn and leave, but my feet refused to move.

Seconds ticked by, and my body grew increasingly cold until I had to wrap my arms across my chest to soothe the gooseflesh that had erupted on my bare arms. At the same time, the space around me shifted slightly, almost imperceptibly, like the room had become trapped inside a bowl of clear Jell-O that someone had given a good shake. When the jiggling stopped, Celia was gone, and she wasn't the only thing. All the modern furniture was gone, too.

My eyes shifted from the gleaming wood of an antique bed, past the gold velvet draperies that hung in thick folds from the windows where moments before only sheers had been. They settled on a sturdy yet feminine desk and upholstered chaise lounge that had taken the place of the metal desk. I was certain I'd never seen any of it before.

Buster was curled in a ball in the middle of a delicately patterned, oval rug that had definitely not been in the room moments before. It wasn't the only change, either. As the room came more into focus, I noticed the phone was missing from the nightstand.

Before I could get a good sense of it, the room wobbled around me again, bringing that same Jell-O sensation I'd experienced, and with it an unsteadiness in my legs so unexpected and pronounced that my arm shot out toward the nightstand so I could steady myself. My fingers stung as they made contact with the phone that had gone missing, which apparently had chosen that moment to make its return.

"What was that?" I asked out loud, bringing my fingers gingerly to my lips as if to kiss away the pain.

"Excuse me?" Celia, who was standing exactly where I'd left her, turned to me with a frown. The bare pine floorboards under her feet shone brightly, lacking both the floral-print rug and the napping cat that I had been looking at a second ago. "I'm very tired. Did you need something from me before I go to bed?"

"No… no, nothing," I muttered, easing myself into the hallway and shutting the door.

What the hell was going on around here?

CHAPTER ELEVEN

I woke the next morning in my cozy bed in the attic room, and for a blissful second, I thought about rolling over and going back to sleep. After the terrible events of the day before, not to mention a near constant lack of sleep, I was mentally and physically fried. But before I could act on this impulse, the phone rang. It was one of the sheriff's deputies, calling to give me the all clear to tidy up the kitchen. The premises would have to remain closed until further notice, but at least Mom and Aunt Izzy wouldn't return to a flour-encrusted cyclone.

Heaving a sigh, I tossed the covers off me and forced myself upright. To say I was an unhappy camper was an understatement. I was supposed to be keeping a low profile. Considering my past, I would do best to stay off the radar of both traditional law enforcement and the Shadow Council, but instead I'd gotten caught right in the middle of a major investigation of a celebrity death. I should have felt terrified, but in truth, I was mostly numb. This was all way too much to deal with so early in the morning. The only thing that made being awake tolerable was the recollection of the single leftover donut waiting for me on the sideboard.

"What the—" My hands flew to my hips, and I stopped in my tracks as I caught the furry feline red-handed, his tongue scraping the last of the cream cheese icing off *my* donut. "Buster!"

The cat hurled himself from the sideboard to the floor and skittered out of sight. His work of ruining my morning was done. I briefly considered eating what remained of the donut, but I couldn't stomach it. Maybe that was a good thing. No matter how bad my life had gotten, I hadn't hit rock bottom.

It just felt like it sometimes.

Peeling away some of the police tape, I entered the kitchen and stared, overwhelmed, at the disaster zone that had once been my mom and Aunt Izzy's pride and joy. I grabbed a slice of bread from the breadbox and nibbled on the crust, trying to convince myself it was "raw toast."

Have I mentioned how much I dislike cats?

"Hey there." Dana appeared at the back door, wearing a pair of denim overalls and a red bandanna tied around her hair. The smile on her face faded when she surveyed the damage. "Wow, this is…"

"Yeah." I nodded in agreement with her unspoken sentiment.

"Now would be a good time for your aunt's famous cleaning spell."

"It truly would be, if only I'd managed to learn it." I plucked at some remaining yellow tape, gingerly at first and then more vigorously, until it tore away from the doorway in strips and chunks. I kicked at an overturned basket on the floor with my toe, leaving a trail in the powdery white flour that coated every tile. I went to the sink and turned on the faucet, letting the water run until steam rose up from deep within the basin. "I guess I'll have to do this the old-fashioned way."

"You mean *we* will," she said. "I'm afraid I don't know any good cleaning spells, either, but I know my way around a broom."

"Is that a witch joke?" I teased. "How did you know I would be doing this, anyway?"

"You just said it. I'm a witch, remember?" Dana laughed as she put her fingers on the sides of her head, implying she'd read my mind. "I'm kidding. Mira told me she'd kept your girls another night and that the sheriff's guys had left you with a terrible mess. This is worse than I expected."

"I get the feeling Sheriff Gray doesn't like me much. It's almost like she did this on purpose."

"It was definitely on purpose." Dana grabbed the aforementioned broom and got to work taming the floury floor. I wanted to know more about why she thought the sheriff hated me, but I was afraid to ask.

We both got to work, putting stray items back in place and scrubbing surfaces until slowly the room once more bore some resemblance to its usual self. Though I wasn't pleased with the sheriff's office in the least for the mess they'd made, there was something oddly therapeutic about doing such a simple task. As much as I appreciated the convenience of Aunt Izzy's cleaning spells, it occurred to me that using a little bit of elbow grease from time to time wasn't such a bad thing. It cleared my head and helped me think.

"Excuse me?"

I'd been on my knees, deeply engrossed in thought while cleaning grout between the floor tiles, but this unexpected voice startled me out of my head and back to the present moment.

Looking up, I saw Celia standing in the doorway to the kitchen. I'd almost forgotten she was still in the house. Her face was pale and drawn, and her tone had an almost robotic quality, devoid of emotion. "I'm having trouble with the Wi-Fi. Is it down?"

"Not that I know of." I patted my pockets but couldn't locate my phone, so I turned to Dana, who was busy wiping flour dust off the jars and cans in the pantry. "Dana, can you see if you've got a Wi-Fi signal on your phone?"

Dana pulled her phone from the top pocket of her

overalls and squinted at the screen. "Looks fine to me. Would you like to borrow it?"

Dana held the phone out toward Celia, who shook her head. I was relieved to see some of the color had returned to her cheeks, and when she spoke, it was with a much more natural tone. "No. Thank you, though. It's really sweet of you to offer. I'm in the middle of doing some research, and I really need to be able to access it on my laptop."

I frowned, wondering once again how, with her fiancé so freshly departed from this mortal realm, her first thought could possibly be about work. She'd said nearly the same thing the night before.

"You might try the library." Dana fumbled with the phone in an uncharacteristically clumsy way, missing her pocket twice before finally stowing it safely inside. "As it happens, I'm the head librarian, so I'd be happy to show you around and get you settled in. We've got computers there, and if you promise not to tell anyone, I'll let you print whatever you need for free."

The woman's face melted into a grateful smile. "I would really appreciate that. I've got a terrible deadline looming, and I absolutely can't afford to miss it."

Was she for real? Sure, people grieved in their own way, but this couldn't be normal.

"Right, I'll finish up here," I muttered as the two women left the kitchen together without so much as a backward glance, "and then go check on the upstairs router." There was no reply, and I could hear them chatting as the front door shut. Looked like I was on my own, although at least with Dana keeping Celia entertained, I didn't have my guest to worry about for a while.

I put the cleaning supplies away, retrieved my phone from my bag, and headed upstairs. Though the router in the hall closet seemed fine, I reset it to be sure then poked my head into Celia's room with the intention of checking the signal strength on my phone.

My nerves jangled as I recalled the strange occurrence from the night before, how the room had shifted, morphing into something unrecognizable and strange. Everything was back in its usual place now, but the temperature was frigid, and there was this odd blue-green light shining from the corner of the room.

A laptop was open on the desk, with piles of notebooks all around, some of them open while others sat with their black and white speckled covers shut. I inched closer, noting the discolored pages and the way the sections written in pencil seemed to have smudged and faded with time. What was more, the desk, the laptop, and all the journals, were fully engulfed by a tissue-thin, luminous orb.

I still can't explain why I didn't run from the room, screaming, but I sensed the light source… needed something. But then I blinked, and it was gone. Feeling silly for the thoughts I'd had, I chalked up the whole experience to a trick of the morning light.

Absolutely nothing was glowing, and I would be a fool to insist otherwise.

I'D TAKEN A BREAK FROM CLEANING AND WAS enjoying the last of the no-longer fresh dregs of yesterday's Gallon of Joe when Tabitha and Sabrina rushed through the door, screaming, "We made a sign!" They held up a big piece of poster board that read, "Welcome Home, Grandma."

Mrs. Crenshaw stood behind the girls, grinning. "Mira's kids helped us make it yesterday while I was babysitting all of them. Go get changed into clean clothes, girls."

The kids shot up the stairs with their sign, eager to please Mrs. Crenshaw.

"Mrs. Crenshaw," I said, "I truly don't know what any of us would do without you."

"It's my pleasure. Now that I don't have foster kids anymore, I have so much time on my hands, and leftover art supplies, too. Speaking of, I've brought over some extras for the girls to enjoy. I used to buy all this kind of stuff in bulk, but now it's sitting around collecting dust." She set down a reusable grocery bag. I peeked inside and spotted dozens of water color trays, composition books, crayons, and more.

"I'm sure the girls will make good use of all this," I

said gratefully. Her thoughtfulness would save me a small fortune in back-to-school shopping.

"Knock, knock." Nora stood in the open door. "I'm here to check on my patient. I prescribed Celia a sedative yesterday, and I want to make sure she's doing okay."

A sedative? I'd forgotten that fact. Maybe that explained her strange behavior, like her flat tone and total lack of human emotion.

"She's actually gone out with Dana—"

"Mom?" Sabrina interrupted, bounding into the room, clueless as usual that I was talking with another adult and that it would be polite to wait. "Why is there yellow tape all over the porch?"

"Shoot," I whispered to Nora. "I hadn't gotten to cleaning out there yet. I don't want them to know."

"You mean that police tape?" Nora asked in a loud voice, coming to my rescue. "Have you ever seen a house getting toilet papered? Well, the sheriff likes to pull practical jokes sometimes and does the same thing with crime scene tape."

"Why?" the girls asked in unison, breathless with fascination.

"Because she's a little bit odd."

I couldn't help noticing when Nora said this, it was spoken with utter conviction. I held in a snort. I mean, who was I to argue? Nora was certainly in a position to know.

"Grammy's coming!" Tabitha ran to the front door, dragging her sister along. "We need to get the sign!"

"Welcome home!" the girls shouted when my mom walked through the door.

"Girls, use your inside voices," I scolded. "We don't want to send Grandma back to the hospital."

"Don't you yell at my grandbabies," my mom scolded right back, wrapping them in her arms. "They're happy to see me."

When the kids had wriggled from her arms and run off to get into whatever mischief they could manage, my mom turned and gave me a hug.

I sank into the embrace. "I'm so glad you're home."

"How are you feeling, Diana?" Nora asked.

"Never better, Dr. Kenworthy." My mom jutted out her chin as if challenging Nora to dispute her claim.

"I'm very glad to hear it." Nora shot me a look that said she wouldn't be taking my mother's word for it. "I'm sure the full results of your tests will be waiting for me when I get back to the clinic. Speaking of—"

Sabrina shot out of the kitchen, crime scene tape wrapped around her like a scarf. "Tabitha's making me a mummy!"

Tabitha was right on her sister's heels, several yards of tape clutched in each hand. They raced out the door and down the porch steps, tumbling onto the grass.

"What's going on with all this?" Aunt Izzy asked.

She lowered her voice to a whisper and added, "I thought they found the body in the cove."

"Maybe it would help if we got the little ears out of here for a bit," Nora said. "I was just heading to the clinic. Would you like me to take the girls to art camp at the library?"

"Art camp!" I slapped the heel of my palm against my forehead. "I forgot all about it."

"I'll take that as a yes."

"You're not planning on putting them both on the back of your motorcycle, are you?"

"Only if they ask nicely." Nora winked, and I bit back a laugh. "You know darn well I have a car, Tallie. Or do you not remember me giving you a ride home in it the other night after the awards?"

"Tabitha? Sabrina?" I called out, ignoring Nora's question. "Time for camp!"

"Where are they?" Nora pretended not to notice either of the girls as they came inside, now both mummified with crime scene tape.

"Right here," Tabitha squeaked.

"Where?" Nora placed a hand on top of Tabitha's head. "Are you in there?"

Tabitha giggled, and I shook my head at the silliness, but deep down, I was uplifted. It had been a tense several months since the girls' father skipped town and the life they'd known had fallen apart. I wanted nothing more than for things to get back to normal for all of us. But was moving to Crescent Cove, with its magical residents, vindictive sheriff, and now a dead body on top of it all, really the way to make that happen?

"Give it to us straight," my aunt said as soon as Nora had driven away with the girls (in the back seat of her sensible sedan and not in a sidecar on her motorcycle as I had imagined). "Why did the sheriff toss our place? What's really going on?"

"I promise you I don't know," I answered. "I suspect it's because Sheriff Gray doesn't like me. Dana agrees."

"Dana would probably know," my mom said, and Aunt Izzy nodded.

"Why is that?" I asked.

"No reason," my mom said, but I could've sworn they exchanged a guilty look.

"Do you think it's because the sheriff knows about Phil, and she thinks maybe I'm crooked?"

"Not being straight would definitely be at the top of her concerns," my mom said with a smirk.

"Diana!" Aunt Izzy wagged a finger at her, even as she grinned from ear to ear.

"Please. Like you weren't thinking it, too," my mom said in retort and then turned to me with a deceptively innocent smile. "How considerate of Dr. Kenworthy to drop by and take the girls to camp."

"And give you a ride home," my aunt added. "After taking you to the awards gala."

"Yes, it—no, hold on." I crossed my arms, belatedly

picking up on Aunt Izzy's insinuating tone. "First of all, she didn't take me to the awards gala. Dana did. Nora only brought me home because Dana had her hands full with two missing finalists. But are you honestly suggesting the sheriff setting her deputies loose in our kitchen like hungry dogs with a Thanksgiving turkey has something to do with Nora being nice to me?"

"Well, there's being nice," my mom said, "and then there's… being *nice*. Wouldn't you say so, Izzy?"

"Definitely," my aunt agreed. "Nora's been very *nice*."

"You two have it as wrong as the sheriff does," I insisted. "There's nothing going on. I mean, obviously. I can't even believe you two would think such a thing."

It was bad enough to accuse Nora of flirting with another woman under her girlfriend's nose, but to think I would encourage it. I wasn't perfect by any stretch of the imagination, but that was one of my hard and fast rules, and I couldn't understand my family encouraging such behavior.

The wrinkles in my mother's forehead deepened. "You know that if there were, that wouldn't make any difference to us, right?"

"I can't believe you would say that, Mother." I put my hands on my hips. "In fact, you've made your feelings on the subject perfectly clear."

Mom pressed a hand to her chest. "When have I ever? I'm a witch, darling. I've never subscribed to any of those silly ideas about sexuality that the non-magicals do. We've always understood that same-sex attraction is as much a part of nature as anything else."

"I wasn't talking about *that*," I corrected, thoroughly confused. "I meant how you feel about witches and non-magicals. You flipped out when I told you I was marrying Phil."

"And I was right," she insisted. "For the record, it had nothing to do with him being non-magical, and everything to do with, well, with him being *Phil*."

"I couldn't agree more," I said. "Which is why I told you right after he left that I was finished with romance."

"Actually, dear," Aunt Izzy cut in, "you said you were finished with men."

"It's true. You did," my mom said with a firm nod. "You screamed it, as I recall, and then threw a coffee mug at his photo on the wall."

"It was my favorite mug, too." I sighed, whether out of sadness for my shattered mug or for the mess my life had turned into, I wasn't sure. "Anyway, it's a moot point. I have too many other things to worry about right now."

"Such as?" my mom prompted, her voice gentle once more.

Where to begin? Ever since I'd returned to Crescent Cove, weird things had been happening. Unsettling dreams. The storms. Now, someone had died in the ocean.

Just like with Maya twenty-five years ago. I couldn't shake the feeling that coming back to Crescent Cove had been a huge mistake, that somehow, all of this was happening because of me.

But I couldn't say any of that, not if I didn't want to cause my mom a full-blown stroke so soon after her release from the hospital.

"There's dinner to worry about, for one thing," I said instead. "I was allowed to clean up in there, but until we haul every piece of documentation we have over to the station, Sheriff Gray might arrest us if we so much as light the stove."

"We'll order pizza," my aunt declared. "No matter how good a kitchen witch I may be, nobody can make a pizza better than Tony's."

"I'm sorry if my coming home has caused trouble," I said, my heart too heavy for even the prospect of a Tony's extra-large pepperoni to lift it from the pit of my stomach.

"Nonsense," Aunt Izzy said with added firmness. "This has nothing to do with you. Not Phil. Not the kitchen, and certainly not that poor man who drowned in the cove."

"I know we're not supposed to speak ill of the dead," my mom said, "but Alexander Tate was not an agreeable man. If it turns out he had some help sending him off into the great beyond, I'm sure it was because he pissed off the wrong person."

"Did the sheriff really arrest David Spencer?" Aunt

Izzy asked.

I nodded. "Took her all of two seconds to make up her mind what had happened and slap on the cuffs."

"The sheriff is making some questionable decisions," Aunt Izzy said, "and I'll be speaking to someone about it."

With that, she went upstairs, leaving me to wonder who the someone was. Knowing my aunt, anyone from an alderman to an oracle was fair game.

"Can I get you anything?" I asked my mom.

"I think I might lie down. The travel is catching up with me." She patted my cheek. "Nothing to worry about. Why don't you go to town and get an ice cream?"

I laughed because that was something she'd said when I was a kid.

"I just might." I grabbed my purse, but I had much more important things on my mind than choosing between mint chocolate chip or butter pecan. There was something urgent I needed to do.

I never thought the day would come, but here it was. I had too many questions and worries weighing on me to continue trying to face them alone. I couldn't talk to my mother or my aunt, but that didn't mean I was out of options. Not on Goode Harbor Island, home of one of the oldest magical communities on the eastern seaboard.

I headed to the library to find Dana. I needed her to call a meeting of her coven.

CHAPTER TWELVE

We gathered that night in the Scott house—the huge Victorian house near Main Street that Mira and her kids shared with her mother, Phoebe, and grandmother, Betsey. A three-story tower in the center of the house rose above matching gables on each side. A small room at the top of the tower had been set up as a room for magic.

It was everything their cheerful Victorian tearoom was not.

This space overflowed with an otherworldly vibe. The deep-green walls sucked in most of the faint light emanating from a single brass chandelier that hung from the embossed tin ceiling. Old wooden shelves bowed from the weight of books, crystals, and other magical objects.

"Welcome, Tallie," Mira said when I entered. She

MIDLIFE IS THE CAT'S MEOW

sat alone in the room, so it seemed I was the first to arrive. "How is your mom doing? And the girls?"

"Oh, they're all fine," I assured her, too busy taking in the surroundings to elaborate any further. "This is quite a room you've got."

My eyes fell to the large round table in the middle of the room, surrounded with chairs and draped with a velvet cloth of deep forest green that was heavily embroidered in gold thread with a pentacle in the middle. A scattering of mystical symbols all around represented the wheel of the year. A thick book, almost certainly the Scott family grimoire, sat on a carved wooden holder. Its heavily ornamented leather binding was covered in mysterious occult symbols, and its slightly yellowed pages were no doubt filled with spells. It was a far cry from the Shipton grimoire, which looked like a 1970s cookbook.

I'll admit it. I had a little bit of grimoire envy.

"My grandmother gets most of the credit," Mira said. "She used to bring clients up here for readings, but the stairs are too much for her knees now, poor thing. Do you not have a Craft room at the inn?"

"Not like this," I said with a snort. After twenty-five years in the suburbs, it was hard for me to think of a craft room as anything other than a place where you kept a sewing machine and a hot glue gun. "Of course, they're kitchen witches, so that's where most of their spells are worked."

I couldn't help noticing the odd look she gave me

when I described my family as kitchen witches without including myself, but she didn't comment on it. A moment later, footsteps on the stairs announced Dana's arrival.

"How's Celia?" Dana inquired after greetings and other pleasantries had been exchanged. She avoided making eye contact as she asked, and I could tell she wanted to know, but I felt she was trying to give the impression she didn't care either way.

"I haven't seen much of her, really," I admitted. "She's been holed up in her room. I can't imagine what she's going through, especially being on an island where she doesn't know anyone. It's not like she can leave in the middle of the investigation."

"Sorry I'm late," Brigit announced as she entered the tower room. "I was putting a new window display together at the shop and lost track of the time."

"It's okay," Mira said, waving her toward a chair. "We were chitchatting before getting started."

My nerves zinged. Part of it was because of the condensed power of so many other witches in a small place, but another part of it was because I remembered the real reason I was there. I needed answers only witches could provide. From the look of things, I'd come to the right place.

On the same table with the grimoire, candles had also been positioned to form four corners, and the four spaces in between contained a variety of magical objects. There was a heavy silver chalice filled with what appeared to be dark red wine beside a shallow dish containing bite-sized cakes. A stick of incense sat in a mahogany holder that had a design traced in a mother-of-pearl inlay, and a brass dish sat nearby, holding a bundle of sage. A cut crystal dish contained salt, while the matching one beside it held water.

All of these things were mysterious and exciting. I'd been so young when I'd left the island that I'd hardly experienced any of it up close. Sadness weighed me down at the realization that I could never fully take part in what should have been my heritage. But as I studied the magical implements in front of me, a silver-handled knife with a long, sharp blade struck fear in my heart.

Whatever that was for, these witches weren't messing around. I could only hope they would always be on my side.

"Tallie, do you want to tell everyone why you're here tonight?" Dana prompted, as the others took seats around the table. I'd given her only the bare bones earlier that day when I'd asked for her help. Now it occurred to me that if this was going to work, I would have to reveal every secret I'd been guarding all these years.

"I'm not sure I can do this." I wanted to run back down the stairs and right out the door, but my knees wobbled, and I sat down in one of the chairs instead.

Dana sat beside me. "You can do this."

"I don't know where to start." I gulped.

"Start wherever you'd like," Brigit encouraged, her softly accented voice as soothing to my nerves as classical music. I suspected as a glamor witch, this was one of her powers.

"I don't even know what kind of witch I am, or where I come from." All at once, I knew that was the only way this story could begin. "For generations, the Shiptons have been kitchen witches. Granted, my mother wasn't as gifted as Aunt Izzy, but that didn't explain why I could barely boil water. For the longest time, it didn't seem to matter. I lived without magic, after all."

"Because your ex didn't accept it?" Mira asked, repeating the convenient excuse I'd hid behind for so long.

Only this time, I shook my head. "Because of something I've never told anyone. Not even my mom or aunt."

"What is it?" Dana grasped my hand, squeezing it in encouragement.

"I stopped being a witch because after Maya died, the Shadow Council bound my magic." For a moment there was silence except for the ringing of my own voice in my ears. Had I really admitted that out loud? There was no going back now.

"They did what?" Dana said the words slowly, as if trying to digest them.

"They performed a spell to bind my powers," I said in a voice barely above a whisper. "It was right after I'd left for college. They came to my dorm room and made me agree to have my powers bound and to never return to Crescent Cove."

Dana's jaw dropped. "Why would they do that?"

I closed my eyes to hold back a rush of tears. "I suppose because they thought I was to blame for my sister's death."

"But there was no trial," Dana argued. "No conviction."

"No," I confirmed. "It was kept quiet. I don't know why, except there must not have been enough evidence for them to act in an official capacity."

"Because you didn't do anything wrong," Dana said with confidence.

I swallowed hard. "I wish I knew for certain that was true. But from the time I started to get my powers as a teen, they didn't behave the way I was told they should. I couldn't do the simplest kitchen spell. I made more than one pie explode."

"I've done the same," Brigit assured me, though looking at the elegant Parisian, it was hard to imagine she didn't grow up with a cook. "But what happened? Your family must have known."

"Maya covered for me," I explained. "She was such a gifted witch. She could do just about anything. Meanwhile, the abilities I had frightened me."

"Like what?" Dana leaned closer.

"Like controlling the weather," I said, shivering. "Only it was never in my control. More like at any moment, it would take over *me*. And you don't have to say it. I already know. That's not something a good witch can do."

"I wouldn't go that far," Mira said. "There are many types of witches in the world."

"That's true," Dana said, her tone taking on a teacher-like quality. "When Crescent Cove was first settled by those who escaped the witch hysteria that swept through New England in the seventeenth century, it was chosen because it's a place of great natural power. And while the community was mostly made up of healers, psychics, and mediums, that doesn't mean there weren't others with more unusual gifts."

"Plus, I don't know that any power on its own is truly bad or good," Brigit pointed out.

Considering the next secret I needed to reveal, Brigit might soon change her mind. Still, they'd taken everything surprisingly well so far. It was time to see if that streak would last.

"What about seeing ghosts?" My stomach tightened, and my heart pounded in my throat. "If I can do that, does it prove I'm bad?"

"Seeing with your eyes?" Dana asked by way of clarification. "Not communicating with them through a spell or a spirit board?"

I shook my head. "If I tell you something strange, will you promise not to think I've lost my mind?"

"Of course," Dana said, and the others murmured their agreement. "What is it?"

"I think the inn might be haunted. There was this one night." I closed my eyes, trying to conjure a clear vision in my head. "I heard music coming from the living room, and when I got there, the Victrola was playing by itself, and the room changed all around me, like going back in time. I know for certain it wasn't a dream, and it wasn't the only time, either. It happened again the other night, and immediately after, I swore I could see a glowing orb, right at the desk where he always sat. I think the inn is being haunted. Maybe it's Alexander Tate's ghost, and maybe another entity, too. I don't know."

"If nothing else," Mira said, a hint of caution in her tone, "this is strong evidence the binding spell the Shadow Council cast isn't working. When you say they exiled you from the island, what exactly did they say?"

I sat silently, letting my mind take me back to that moment. "There were two of them, a man and a woman. The man said I could never go back. Then the woman said I didn't want to know what would happen if I did, or something like that." I couldn't remember her words, but the recollection of her tone made me shudder.

"Like a threat?" Brigit asked with a frown.

"Basically." I shrugged, willing myself not to dwell on the dread that was building inside. No good would come of it. "That was how it sounded to me. It was like we don't even know what we'll do to you if you decide to disobey."

"Unless," Mira said, "what if she meant it more like we really don't know what will happen if you return?"

"I mean... I guess?" I clasped my hands together, twisting them as I tried to square this new interpretation with what I could recall from that day. As I flipped the message upside down in this way, my head went with it, making me as dizzy as a loop on a roller coaster. "Yes, she could've meant it like that, I suppose. But they're the Shadow Council. Don't they know everything?"

"Not as much as they want us to believe, I'm sure." Mira gave a low, throaty laugh, thick with sarcasm. From the way they were exchanging looks and nodding, I could tell Brigit and Dana agreed with this assessment.

"Now that makes a lot more sense," Dana weighed in. "Binding spells are tricky, and as I said before, this island is a place of tremendous power. Maybe they knew if you came back for any length of time, what they did would weaken or wear off completely."

"Then whatever powers I was meant to have would start to appear again." A lump formed in my throat, matching the one that was settling deep in my soul. "There's something else that happened, that I didn't mention before. The night Alexander Tate died, I was wearing that dress I found in the attic. I had a dream. It was like I was myself, but not exactly, and I was in the inn, only I'm pretty sure it was the inn from long ago."

"You slept in that beautiful dress?" Brigit put a hand to her mouth, horrified.

"I dozed off. It was an accident." I bit my lip, knowing I wasn't explaining it right. "Honestly, since coming back to the island, I've felt off. I keep flashing to things that I didn't experience or using words I don't know, only I do know them somehow. Crazy, right?"

Instead of bursting into a fit of laughter, Dana traced a finger along her chin, deep in thought. "Like a past life? Maybe that's where these unusual powers are coming from."

"Or maybe it's someone in my past. In my real family." I scuffed my foot along the rug and looked away as Dana's eyes drilled into me, demanding to know more. I hadn't meant to mention that part, but there was no way out of it now. "The trunk I found in the attic belonged to my grandmother Abigail. Aunt Izzy told me. She said it had been her sister's, that she'd brought it with her when she came to live in Crescent Cove. When she was adopted."

"Your grandmother was adopted?" Dana breathed.

"She was never really a Shipton at all." I choked on a cry that rose up from deep within. "Which means neither am I. I should have realized ages ago from the red hair. We all had it, but Aunt Izzy didn't, and neither did her mother. I assumed it was a recessive Shipton gene, but I guess I was wrong."

"Honey, there's no way you could have guessed," Dana said soothingly.

The more I thought about the repercussions of this secret, the more desperate I grew. "I don't know who I am, or what I'm capable of. And I'm afraid of what it means for myself and for my girls."

"Right," Mira said, rising from her seat. I feared for a moment that she was going to force me to leave, but instead of dragging me from the table by my ear, she went to one of the dusty shelves and began searching its contents. "I think we've heard enough of Tallie's story to conclude there's only one thing to do."

"There is?" I had no idea what this one thing could be, but both Dana and Brigit didn't seem perplexed at all. Instead, they were already working together to clear the items off the table, even the velvet cloth, until it was down to bare wood. "What's going on? What are we going to do now?"

"We need to attempt to make contact with the spirit world." Mira said this like it was as simple as shooting off a text.

"Have you ever used a spirit board, Tallie?" Dana asked as Mira came to the table with a smooth wooden board printed with the alphabet.

"You mean a Ouija board?" I asked, recognizing the item that was placed in the center, along with a wooden pointer.

"That's another name for it," Dana said. "We generally prefer the term spirit board. People think of Ouija boards as a slumber party game."

Brigit brought a thick white pillar candle to the table. It was unlit, but suddenly a sulfurous smell tickled my nose and caught me up short, tying my stomach into a knot. The wick had burst into flame, but there was no sign of a match.

This was getting real.

Brigit placed the candle in a brass holder beside the board. Then she, Dana, and Mira joined hands. Dana reached out to take hold of mine, too, but I shook my head.

"I can just watch. I'm not supposed to be practicing magic. Besides, how will we put our fingers on the planchette if we're holding hands?" I'd seen enough people use Ouija—I mean spirit—boards to know how things were supposed to go down.

"Whether you like it or not," Dana said in a soft tone, "your magic is back. It's flowing through you already, no matter what you do. You might as well use it."

"As for the planchette," Mira said, "we don't touch it."

"You'll understand in a minute," Brigit added, answering my unasked question.

Giving in, I held out my hands, taking Dana's in one and Mira's in the other. The moment our fingers touched and the circle was closed, a current of electricity moved through my arms. I jumped and tried to pull my hands away, but the other witches tightened their grips.

As the four of us stared at the board, I thought all was lost as the seconds ticked by. Right when I was about to declare the mission dead, my skepticism waned, replaced by a mounting apprehension. What would I do if a spirit did come to us? What if it revealed truths I didn't want to know?

I forced myself not to pull away. Whatever was out there, I had to face it. Even if it meant finding out I was an evil witch. Even if it meant I had caused my sister's death. I had to know, if not for myself, than for Tabitha and Sabrina. There was still time to protect them if I had to.

After a few moments, the sharp tingling I'd initially felt settled into a more manageable hum, and my muscles relaxed, though my pulse continued to throb as if I'd run up a flight of stairs.

"We must center ourselves," Mira spoke in a serious tone. "Take deep breaths and clear our minds of any distractions."

Despite my grave misgivings and having failed miserably at both yoga and meditation in the past, I respected the present company enough to give it a shot. I didn't have high hopes, but shockingly, I could almost feel the stillness entering my body as I drew my first breath.

"I think it's working," I said with much surprise,

followed by a long inhale and exhale. "Now, what do we do?"

"I think we need to start by finding out if Alexander Tate's death was accidental or foul play," Dana suggested. "It's best to stick with yes or no questions. Asking it to spell out too many long messages can take all day."

"Tallie, I think you should be the one to ask," Mira said.

"Me?" All at once, I was on the verge of gasping for breath. I hadn't expected to be put on the spot like that. No wonder everyone was so obsessed with deep breathing. I should have taken that part a lot more seriously.

"Yes, I agree," Brigit said, either not noticing or choosing not to comment on my sudden panting.

"Come on, Tallie," Dana urged. "You can do it."

It may have been silly, but the confidence the others showed in me was contagious. Of course, I could do this. It was just words, right? At least I could try. They all believed in me. Maybe I needed to believe in myself a little, too.

"Spirits, was Alexander Tate's death an accident?" I asked loudly, feeling about as ridiculous as one might expect when addressing an inanimate object. I knew magic was real, but I'd never had much belief in spirits, at least until now. Even after seeing what I believed to be a ghost, I had more than a few doubts. What if there was a simpler answer? Like I was losing my mind? I stared at the board, but nothing was happening.

"You're doing great," Dana assured me, squeezing my hand. "We just need to be patient. The spirits will come when they're ready."

I was so relaxed from all the breathing that my body could have been made of limp spaghetti. I kept my mouth shut and stared intently at the wooden planchette, breathing to the point I feared I might hyperventilate.

The first time the heart-shaped scrap of wood moved on its own, I thought I had imagined it. My head was dizzy from the breathing, and the movement was so slight that it could easily have been attributed to my eyes playing a trick on me. I blinked a few times and had decided that the movement had been in my mind when it moved again, and not just a little. Without a single one of us touching it, the planchette slid shakily across the board all on its own, coming to rest on the word no.

For several seconds, I was no longer breathing at all.

"Did you see that?" I whispered.

Dana nodded. "Spirits, how did he die?"

"That's not yes or no," I said, biting my lip, uncertain what to expect. Would the spirits respond?

After a few tense seconds, the planchette jerked and chugged across the board until it landed on the letter A, followed by the letter L.

I gasped, accidentally dropping Dana and Mira's hands in the process.

The candle's flame flickered and went out.

"What comes next?" I reached for their hands, desperate to reconnect and get some real answers once and for all.

But Dana shook her head, looking both sad and drained. "I don't think we're going to get anything else tonight."

The heavy weight of exhaustion pushed my shoulders to a slump, and I knew she was right. It didn't make it any easier to accept. I had so many questions, but the answers remained beyond my grasp.

CHAPTER THIRTEEN

I yawned, stretching my arms overhead, as I started down the back staircase the morning after the coven meeting. For once, I'd slept solidly, and without any of the strange dreams that had plagued me since my return to Crescent Cove. Even so, I was dragging. I felt like every ounce of energy had been drained from my body. Was this what it felt like being a middle-aged witch?

I entered the kitchen, eager to be greeted by a tower of waffles. Instead, the kitchen was empty. I let out a groan as I recalled that the island's jealous excuse for a sheriff still hadn't lifted our cooking ban. We could walk through the space, but heaven forbid we kick on a gas burner. I was desperate enough for coffee and a hot meal that it was almost worth risking it, but knowing how badly the woman had it out for me, I half expected she was rigged to blow if her orders were disobeyed.

With a sigh, I swiped a banana from the counter, hoping it didn't contain a hidden detonator, and headed to the dining room. My mother sat with a can of diet cola in front of her, the local newspaper spread out on the table. I couldn't remember the last time I'd seen the news printed on actual paper. It was possible our house was the very last subscriber to this edition.

"Where are the girls?" I asked. "I'd like them to come in here and witness this. I'm not sure they've ever seen a real newspaper before."

"They've already left for camp," Mom replied, ignoring my dig.

"What time is it?" I patted my ratty T-shirt and sleeping shorts but realized I'd left my phone upstairs.

"A little after ten. You know if you wore the nightgown I got you, it has a pocket." Mom slanted her head, her brow creased with worry. "You look exhausted."

"I'm fine," I lied. "How could I still be tired when I slept past ten? I could use some caffeine, though. Do you think we can risk using the coffee pot?"

"Why do you think I'm drinking this?" Mom held up her can. "It was the last one, though. Maybe you should head downtown for a cup of coffee."

"Downtown?" I raised my eyebrows mockingly. "I love how everyone here calls it that."

"Don't put on airs just because you've lived in the

big city. You grew up here. No disrespecting where you're from." She lightly tapped me with a hand.

"Child abuse," I joked, exactly like I used to when Maya and I were kids. It seemed to strike us both at the same moment, the memory cutting as a silence fell between us. "I miss her."

I regretted saying it the moment the words left my mouth. No matter how great my pain was, it didn't compare to my mother's grief, and I feared any mention of my sister would bring the carefully crafted normalcy she'd managed to build over the years crashing down.

Instead, my mother smiled fondly, only a hint of sorrow in her eyes. "She's here with us. I feel her all the time."

My eyes welled up, and I swallowed a sob. "I think I might head to town for a cup of joe, after all."

"Okay, sweetheart." That was her way of saying she knew I needed time to pull myself together.

Even after all of this time, talking about Maya without a lump forming in my throat and the threat of tears was nearly impossible. Not to mention being racked to my core with guilt.

It was a beautiful mid-July day on the island, the kind tourists paid good money to enjoy. I opted to ride my bike, each spin of the wheel taking me closer to Main Street while easing the sadness in my soul.

The summer air tickled my skin. The strong scent of flowers and the saltiness of the ocean waves hung heavily around me. The sky was a soft blue, which hopefully meant the temperatures would stay in the upper seventies and not go any hotter.

By the time I locked my bike outside the coffee shop, my stomach was rumbling, and the skin around my eyes started to contract. Meaning I needed caffeine stat to stave off a killer headache.

I opened the door and was met with ten pairs of staring eyes, coupled with deathly silence, aside from soft music streaming through the shop's sound system. For a fleeting moment, I thought I must be glowing like the ghost haunting the inn, but it only took a second for my flaming red hair to give away my identity. Once they'd figured out who I was, it was business as usual, and the normal hubbub you'd hear in a crowded place hit my ears.

"Tallie, over here!" The voice was intoxicating, and before I figured out who it belonged to, I got this sensation of someone wrapping a towel fresh from the dryer around my shoulders. Soft, warm, and reassuring.

My eyes adjusted to the indoor lighting, and through the crowd, I spied Nora sitting across from Dana at a small table.

Had it been the doctor's voice that made me feel like that? Strange. Nothing like that had ever happened to me before. I wondered if it had something to do with the return of my powers. I would have to keep an eye on it and see if anything similar happened elsewhere.

Nora stood to pull over a chair. "Plenty of room."

I made my way to their table, weaving through the people. Some were prepping for a day at the beach, a few kids already in swimsuits and barefoot, despite the sign that read: *No shirt, No shoes, No service.*

Ah, to be a kid again, when everyone let you do what you wanted.

"How's your mom?" Dana asked.

"Struggling under the circumstances but doing the best she can."

"Is she feeling okay?" Nora asked with sudden concern. "Her test results came back better than I'd expected, but I told her to call if she had any symptoms."

"Physically, she's fine," I said. "I was referring to the fact that she and my aunt aren't allowed to cook anything. That's much more likely to kill her than a stroke."

"Your kitchen can't possibly still be closed." Nora's eyes narrowed, and her jaw clenched. "Please tell me it isn't that ridiculous police order."

"I'm afraid it is. We managed to get permission to walk through it, but—"

Nora let out a pained sigh. "I'll talk to Bonnie. This is getting out of hand."

I had a sudden desire to demand to know how she could stand being with a woman like that if she thought it was so unreasonable, but I managed to keep the thought to myself. It was none of my business. But the reminder of the good doctor's better half cast a shadow over the conversation, at least from where I was sitting.

"Anyway, sorry to interrupt your coffee break," I said, getting up from the chair. "I only popped in for a cup of coffee, but my stomach is reminding me that I need food."

"It's always a pleasure," Nora said, and it might have been odd, but I actually thought she was being sincere. "I suggest getting a cinnamon roll. We're both waiting on a fresh batch to come out of the oven."

Dana rose from the table as well. "As soon as they do, I need to get back to work. My fifteen-minute break was supposed to be over five minutes ago."

"Good thing you're the boss," Nora joked.

"Can I get my order to go?" I asked, keeping an eye on Nora, who didn't appear to be going anywhere.

"You can, but if you want some company, I'm planning to have mine here." Nora supplied the information casually, but I got the sense that she hoped it'd change my mind about leaving.

"Good to know." The more I thought about it, the less I relished the thought of drinking my coffee while cycling home. "Maybe I will."

I followed up this totally banal statement by giving a toss of my head like I thought I was still in high school, and the head cheerleader to boot. I felt my face and neck go up in flames. What on earth was I thinking? Dana stifled a laugh behind her hand as Nora grinned foolishly.

I finally understood why my kids always acted so embarrassed around me. I was one step away from telling everyone in the coffee place that I'd never met myself before, just like Tabitha and Sabrina would've done.

I watched as a gray-haired woman with saggy jowls came around the counter, handing Dana a paper sack with her order. My confidence was buoyed a bit. I was no head cheerleader anymore, but at least I was still relatively young compared to many. That was a blessing, right? The old woman looked vaguely familiar. As I tried to recall which of my high school friend's moms she might've been from way back when, she spotted me.

"Tallie Shipton, is that you?" She smiled broadly, showing off teeth stained yellow from years of smoking. "It's Jennifer Bates."

Jennifer Bates... The name did sound familiar, but I wasn't quite placing which kid could've been hers. Who had I known back then with that last name?

"They called me Jenny-Jen back then."

Jenny-Jen? The nickname squeezed the air out of my lungs. Surely not...

She smiled broader. Oh God, there was a gap where one of the teeth was completely gone. "We had chemistry together junior year, remember?"

I waved dumbly, wishing I could sink into the floor. Here I'd been imagining myself to still be cute and young compared to this poor old thing, and we were the same damn age. Actually, there was a chance I was older.

Oh shit.

But the thing about growing older that no one warns you about is you don't ever feel old. Okay, my bones might ache at the end of the day, my joints creak when I bend too fast, and I'm always tired. But in my mind, I still feel like I did my senior year. And every time I look in the mirror, that's the face I expect to see looking back at me.

I'd transitioned from maiden to mother willingly enough back in the day, but I wasn't ready for crone.

"It's great to see you, Jenny." I couldn't do it. I couldn't add that last Jen. It sounded absurd. I hopped off my chair to give the woman a hug.

"How are you doing? I've been hearing all about that bad business at the cove and with your mom."

"Oh, I'm hanging in." Other than being suddenly confronted with my rapidly approaching mortality, that is.

Only no. It wasn't getting older that bothered me. It was the years I'd wasted on someone who didn't deserve me. Phil had ignored me for years and taken me for granted. And while I wasn't looking for another man—or a woman, as my mom and aunt had hinted at the other day—I did want to feel like it was possible. I wanted to be cute and flirty, damn it.

"What can I get you?"

A way to turn back the clock ten years, I thought, but said, "I won't turn down a coffee and cinnamon roll."

"Coming right up."

"One meal taken care of today." I turned to Dana. "My girls are going to a birthday party tonight, and my mom and aunt have plans, too. Would you like to grab some dinner with me?"

"Oh, I would, but I kind of have plans already."

"Dana Wardwell, do you have a date?" I couldn't help teasing, noting how she answered without meeting my eyes.

"Oh, goodness. Look at the time. It was lovely to see both of you." Dana fled the joint like it was on fire.

"Guess that means I'm on my own for dinner." I laughed, feeling like the biggest idiot on the planet. My best friend was going on a date, and I didn't even know she was interested in anyone. I ran through all the single men I'd encountered since coming home, wondering which one it was. The most likely candidate, David Spencer, was still behind bars. That left me stumped.

"You know," Nora said, "we still haven't had a chance to go over your mom's test results."

"You're right." I pulled out my phone. "Do you want to schedule something now, or should I make an appointment at the clinic?"

"Actually, since you don't have other plans, I thought maybe we could discuss them over dinner."

"Over dinner?" I swallowed, contemplating that my attempts at being cute and flirty may have been more successful than I'd believed. But flirting with the one woman on the island whose girlfriend's jealousy could make my family's life a living hell was not what I'd intended.

"We both have to eat, right?"

Jenny buzzed by with our coffees and cinnamon rolls, causing us to giggle like kids.

"We do, and dinner sounds nice." It did. In a strictly professional way.

I took a sip of my coffee, warm and soothing.

Nora eyed her cinnamon roll like if she took a bite, she'd combust.

"I can take it home to my mom if you don't want it."

"You're a life saver." Nora sighed. "I should get to the clinic."

"Patients aren't so patient?"

She laughed like this was the funniest joke she'd ever heard. "Pick you up at seven?"

I swallowed and nodded, the lump in my stomach dissipating once I'd sealed the deal. Which was silly. It wasn't like I was going on a date or something. Nora was just being nice, trying to reassure the daughter of a patient. I needed to face reality and stop reading into things to flatter my own ego.

Still, it was nice to spend time with someone who listened when I talked and laughed at my jokes. When was the last time Phil had laughed at one of my jokes? I couldn't remember, that was how long ago. Probably way back when poor Jenny-Jen still had all her teeth.

I RETURNED TO THE HOUSE AROUND NOON, and the first thing I heard was the tapping of a keyboard. It had become such a familiar sound over the past few weeks that for a moment, I almost forgot Alexander Tate was dead. But he most certainly was, and that left two possibilities I could think of. Either that glowing orb I'd been convinced was his spirit had taken on corporeal form and was upstairs writing his book, or his fiancée was.

Given what little I knew about ghosts, my money was on Celia. But knowing the sound had a living human source didn't mean it made any more sense to me than the alternative. Ever since Celia had returned to the inn after Alex's body had been taken away, she'd seemed strangely concerned with work and deadlines. While he'd been alive, I'd gotten the impression she was not only engaged to him, but also served as an unofficial assistant of sorts. But now that he was gone, it was like she didn't know how to relinquish the role.

No, it was more than that. The woman was acting

like these deadlines were hers. In a way, it was like she was turning into Alex Tate. I was truly concerned for her sanity. Grief impacted everyone differently, but working oneself to death after losing a loved one seemed extreme.

With the goal of checking on her welfare, I knocked on her bedroom door. "Celia? Are you in there?"

I had no idea what I planned to say when—if—she opened the door. It wasn't like I could tell her what I truly thought, that the man had been a real ass to her, and that while I would never wish anyone dead, she'd kind of dodged a bullet with this one. You know what they say. What do you call one busload of ex-husbands at the bottom of the sea? A good start. I think that joke was originally about lawyers, but I liked it better this way.

And to think some people had tried to tell me my divorce from Phil was making me bitter.

The typing continued on the other side of the door without slowing. I was about to turn to leave when it stopped abruptly. A few seconds later, the door cracked open.

"Yes?" she croaked, her face wan. "Sorry. I didn't hear you before."

My breath caught at how terrible she looked. "It's a lovely day outside. Have you thought about getting some fresh air?"

Celia blinked as if not understanding a word I'd said. "Fresh air?" She sounded out the words as if that would help her make sense of my meaning. She edged out of the room, squeezing through the crack as if she didn't want me to see inside. "I do have a headache."

"I imagine you do," I said.

"It's the strangest feeling. I'm almost woozy, like when you've been painting a room all day and have been breathing in fumes."

"Do you smell something in the room?" I asked quickly, wondering if I needed to call in a repair person. Could there be a gas leak? Maybe it was a good thing the kitchen had been shut down, after all. Had the jealous sheriff done us a solid?

"No, it's nothing like that." Halfway down the staircase, her cheeks were already starting to pink. "I was feeling odd. That's all. I feel better now."

"I still think a walk would be good for you."

She nodded, her eyes seeming to adjust to the sunlight in the entryway. "I think you're right. I'll give it a try."

After she'd gone out the front door and it closed behind her, I thought once more about her comment about fumes. Perhaps she hadn't smelled anything unusual, but that didn't mean nothing was there. Carbon monoxide, for instance. I climbed back up the stairs and stood outside the closed door.

I should go in, I thought. Just long enough to check the batteries in the carbon monoxide detector. We were running a business, and it would look terrible if we lost a guest to carbon monoxide poisoning two days after having one drown in the cove. People would think the inn was cursed.

The minute I stepped inside the room, I knew carbon monoxide wasn't to blame.

What had been a faintly glowing orb the day before had morphed into a much more recognizably human form. I'm not saying I could look at it and identify him as Alexander Tate like it was some kind of police lineup. But there was no way this was a trick of the light. This room most definitely was housing a ghost.

Energy radiated from him in waves, like ripples moving across an unseen pond in all directions, forming a sort of bubble that extended several yards beyond the core of his being. I approached with extreme caution. With each step, my head grew lighter, taking on a dizzy quality. Celia was right. The effect was similar to the slight buzz of inhaling paint fumes. I doubted she had seen the ghost, but if she'd been sitting at the desk, working on the laptop, there would've been no escaping it. That whole area was engulfed.

"Alex?" I asked, turning back to quietly shut the door behind me. I'd yet to mention his presence to anyone in the house, and the last thing I needed was to be caught talking to someone who wasn't supposed to be there. "Is that you? Tell me how I can help you. What do you need to move on?"

I'll be honest. I had no idea what to expect when asking these questions. I didn't know anything about ghosts or how to help them move on. It was something I'd heard about in television shows, same as anyone else. It wasn't like this type of thing had ever happened to me in Cleveland. I'd never seen a ghost before, let alone tried to rationalize with one.

"Look, Alex," I said, taking a step closer. The rippling vibrations seemed to change their frequency, which I took as a sign he heard me. "I don't know what you're doing here, but I want to help."

As I drew closer, the ghost's appearance continued to change. He was nearly in a solid state, glowing so brightly I needed to shield my eyes. I could make out his form and features much more clearly than before. The best way to describe it might be to say he was like a plastic or glass sculpture of Alexander Tate, through which a blue-green light shone.

The desk and the laptop were fully engulfed in this light, and it didn't take an expert in ectoplasm to peg that as the source of Celia's earlier Wi-Fi interference.

"Alex, you've gotta tone down whatever you've got going on with these energy waves, okay? It's interfering with the internet connection."

Really? I asked myself. You're talking to a dead man whose spirit is trapped in the earthly realm, and you think he's gonna care about your freakin' Wi-Fi?

On impulse, I prodded the periphery of the energy field with a finger. Not my index finger, mind you, but the pinky on my left hand. It wasn't a digit I used all that often, so if it got zapped or whatever, I figured I could still live a long life.

Nothing catastrophic happened, but the temperature of my finger turned to ice. A faint chill traveled up my arm as I allowed the rest of my hand to follow, although whether it was because of the supernatural vibrations or my imagination, I wasn't certain.

Again, I asked, "Alex, what can I do to help?"

The air shifted around me, overwhelming me with a sense of helplessness and despair. I wanted to curl up on the floor in a ball, and it took all my strength to drag myself away.

"I'm going to try to figure this out. We can't have you trapped here for eternity. You gotta trust me."

Why he would was beyond me because I was pretty convinced at this point that I'd lost my frigging mind. Or maybe it was a sudden midlife crisis setting in. Was that a thing, hitting your forties and suddenly thinking you could become a ghostbuster?

CHAPTER FOURTEEN

"Hot date tonight?" My octogenarian aunt waggled her bushy white brows in a way I never knew she could. Frankly, I could have lived my entire life without that image seared into my brain.

"I'm going to dinner if that's what you mean." I adjusted one of the straps of my sundress while looking in the hall mirror. I'd chosen it to look nice while not too fancy, as I was pretty sure the place we were going was a burger joint down by the docks. "But it's not a date. Nora wanted to talk to me about Mom's test results."

"You know, they're my results, but when she talked to me about them the other day, I didn't even get a snack," Mom said wryly. "Sounds like a ruse to me."

My aunt nodded in sage agreement. "She's coming here to pick you up, right?"

"My car is out of gas," I argued as I fluffed my red

curls on one side where they looked a little flat. "I don't know why you two insist on continuing to tease me about this when I've already said there's exactly zero percent chance of romance between Nora and me."

"Oh, but why?" my aunt persisted.

Because I didn't have a death wish, I wanted to scream. Had they both forgotten Nora was dating a woman who carried a gun for a living? I always knew my family's view on sexuality was more openminded than most, but I'd never realized how unconventional they were if a person being in a committed relationship didn't give them a moment's pause. There was no use arguing about it, so I simply rolled my eyes and changed the subject.

"You know who is going on a date tonight? Dana. I don't know who with, and she insists it's not a date, but you should have seen how red her cheeks got when she mentioned it."

"Do you think one of us should mention how red *her* cheeks get?" my aunt said as an aside to my mom. They both snickered while I glared.

"How come your friend can say she's not on a date and you don't believe her and tease her about it, but when we do that to you, you don't like it?" Mom regarded me with a knowing smirk, the proverbial straw that broke the camel's back.

"Argh!" I crossed my arms and huffed. As I smoothed my dress after my outburst of temper, I began second guessing myself. "Am I overdressed? I was going for casual beach chic, but I think I overshot. Maybe I should change."

"Where are you going?" Mom asked.

"I wasn't paying much attention. I think it was Michael something. She said it's by the bridge." I shrugged. "Given her love of biscuits and gravy, I assume it's some sort of greasy spoon diner."

"Are you talking about the Whale's Tail?" Mom's eyes widened. "It's not by a bridge, dear. The chef's name is Michael Bridge."

"We're going to a restaurant that has a chef?" I still had the urge to change, but not into a T-shirt and shorts. Now, I was afraid I was completely underdressed for the evening. "Why would Nora want to go to a fancy restaurant to talk about Mom's tests?"

"Because it's a date," my mother and my aunt said in unison. At this point it was obvious they'd lost their grip on reality and were trying to get my goat.

Before I could protest, the doorbell rang. My stomach flip-flopped as Aunt Izzy took my face into her wrinkled hands, pulling my forehead to her lips. "Have fun on your date."

I wished they'd stop saying date. For all I knew, the sheriff had the place bugged. She was that type of crazy. Before I could caution my aunt to be careful with her words, she opened the front door and pushed me out onto the porch, shutting the door behind me so I couldn't do anything about it.

"Hi," Nora said, her eyes flicking from my carefully fluffed hair and sweeping quickly down my sundress before making sustained contact with mine. "You look beautiful. Are you ready to go?"

"I'm, uh..." Did she say beautiful? Once again, a simple compliment had my cheeks engulfed in flames. I took in her black trousers and shiny shoes, the exact opposite of casual beach chic. "Am I dressed okay? My mom and aunt seemed to think we were going someplace fancy."

"What's your definition of fancy?" Nora opened the passenger side door for me, waiting while I took my seat.

"Linen napkins," was the only thing I could think to say.

"Then yes." She closed the door before I could protest.

"Should I change?" I asked when she got behind the steering wheel.

"Never."

I sank my front tooth into my lower lip. What the hell was that supposed to mean? I was still trying to puzzle it out when the scratchy sound of a jazz band rang out from the car speakers. It took only a couple of bars to recognize it as the same song that had been playing on the Victrola that strange night a few weeks before.

My heart pounded in my throat. "Can you hear that?"

"What?" Nora cast a confused glance my way as she pulled out of the driveway.

"That music?" I reached for the armrest on the door, grasping it tightly. "Where is it coming from?"

"My iPhone," Nora replied with a laugh. "It's this invention we have here called Bluetooth. I've got my playlist set to a random shuffle."

I let out a breath, feeling foolish. But not too foolish. Thinking there was ghostly music in the car that only I could hear was admittedly over-the-top, but what were the odds that Nora, a twenty-first century doctor, would not only be listening to hundred-year-old jazz, but to the exact song that had been playing on my haunted gramophone? Go ahead, I dare you to try to calculate that.

Ignoring her teasing, I closed my eyes and focused on the song. Except for that night in the living room, I was certain I'd never heard it before. I'd almost convinced myself I'd imagined it.

"I'll see you in my dreams," Nora said.

"What?" My heart did a weird skipping thing in my chest. Was there some hidden meaning in her words? Sweat beaded on my brow as I tried to figure out how she could've known about my strange dreams.

"That's the name of the song. It's called 'I'll See You in my Dreams.'"

"Oh." Now I had even more questions than before.

Sure enough, Nora breezed right past the burger

place I'd thought we were going to and pulled into the parking lot for the Whale's Tail. This was definitely the restaurant my mom had been talking about, although I was still adamant this wasn't a date. I maintained this stance as Nora hopped out of the car and zipped around to open my door before I had a chance to do it myself.

"Let me help you out." Nora held out her hand for me, and honestly, what was I going to do? It would've been rude not to accept it as the friendly gesture it was surely meant to be. I was raised to have manners, after all.

I took her hand and steadied myself as I got out of the car. "Thank you."

"I've been wanting to try this place since it opened," Nora said as she led the way from the parking lot to the front door.

"How long has it been here?" I asked.

"Only since the start of the season. Michael, the chef, trained in Paris and runs several restaurants in New York, but he married a Goode Harbor Island woman, and they decided to open this place for the summers."

"Is it not open year-round?"

"Only May to October. It's a little pricey for the locals, I guess, but the food is locally sourced, and they serve every type of seafood, caught fresh from the bay. I should have asked before. You're not allergic to shellfish, are you?"

"You can't live on an island if you are," I said with a laugh. "It's a law, I think."

"Funny you should say that because a certain island sheriff I know can't even touch lobster without breaking out in hives."

"Is that right?" Inside, I was breathing about a hundred sighs of relief. Now it all made sense, why Nora was taking me here instead of Bonnie. I was convenient company, that's all. Though I was no big fan of the sheriff, hearing Nora mention her girlfriend had the result of putting me more at ease. There was nothing sneaky going on here, and clearly my family's theories about Nora's intentions were as off-base as I'd thought. I could relax and have a good time.

Threading my arm through hers in a chummy and not at all romantic way, I took in the restaurant's deep navy-blue storefront. It overlooked a particularly scenic part of Main Street, which offered views of both Penobscot Bay and Turner's Pond from a lovely outside deck where drinks were served while patrons waited for tables.

After letting the hostess know we'd arrived, Nora and I went to the deck, where I stayed while she fetched me a drink from the bar inside. The sun dipped low in the sky as I made my way through the well-dressed patrons on the deck and tried to pretend I didn't notice the raised eyebrows my flimsy dress and sandals were generating compared to their much nicer evening attire. I was pretty sure Nora was right. There wasn't a local in the bunch. The place reeked of New York money.

As I took a step toward the deck rail, I spotted the back of a head sporting a familiar dark brown librarian bun. Dana? I stood corrected. There was exactly one other local in the house tonight. The start of a giggle tickled my insides as I tried to figure out who her date would turn out to be. No doubt a summer resident who wanted to impress her with how rich and sophisticated he was. I was dying to find out.

I craned my head, but there was no one seated on the other side of her. I assumed that he, like Nora, had gone inside for drinks.

It would be awkward if I didn't go over and say hi, right?

There were dozens of people on the deck, so it took me longer to get to my friend than I'd expected. By the time I worked my way close enough to say hello, Dana was conversing with another familiar face. Celia, the sole guest of the Shipton Inn. Now that was an odd coincidence.

"What are you doing here?" Coming up from behind, I placed a hand on Dana's shoulder.

Dana jumped at the sound of my voice, sending the drink in her hand sloshing dangerously close to the rim. "Oh, you scared me."

"We keep running into each other today," I said with a laugh. I turned my attention to Celia, noting that though she was dressed nicely and had put on a touch of makeup, the woman's complexion still had an unhealthiness to it. "It's good to see you're taking a break. Are you meeting up with some friends from the city?"

"Actually," Dana said, her voice a bit shaky, "she's having dinner with me."

"But you're supposed to be on a date." The words were still in the process of leaving my lips when the warning bells went off in my head. The way Dana had fumbled her phone when offering it to Celia the other day. The way she blushed deepest crimson whenever the woman was around or her name was mentioned. No way... "Dana, is she your date?

Celia answered, "Yes," at exactly the same time Dana said, "This isn't a date."

"It's not?" Celia demanded, right as Dana said, "Is it?"

"I was kind of hoping it was," Celia admitted, her eyes downcast.

I gasped. Her fiancé's body was barely cold and she was already on the market again? "Oh my God, how could you?"

Something dark flashed over Dana's features, and instantly, I knew I'd gotten something wrong. I wondered how far I'd stepped in it. But did she not see how suspicious Celia's actions were?

"Tallie, may I have a word with you." Dana stood, grabbing my arm with urgency and pulling me aside. "What are you doing?"

"Me?" My heart was racing. "I'm not the one on a date with a woman—"

"I had really hoped you wouldn't be homophobic about this," Dana cut in, hurt evident in her eyes. "Aren't you here with Nora Kenworthy?"

"Okay, that's not the same thing. And besides, you didn't let me finish," I protested. "I was going to say a woman whose fiancé has been dead for less than a week. Think about it, Dana. She's barely shed a tear. All she's done is locked herself away in her room, working night and day."

Halfway through me talking, Nora had joined us, and now she looked from me to Dana to Celia with an expression of utter confusion. "What's going on?"

"I think maybe I should explain," Celia said. "And I can, I promise. Why don't we see if we can get a table for four? I think you all deserve to know what's really going on."

THE HOSTESS LED US INTO A ROOM WITH RICH wood paneling that reminded me of an old ship. The ceiling was covered with heavily embossed tin tiles, from which hung pendant lights that looked like lanterns. One full wall was covered with dozens of small apothecary drawers from some previous incarnation of the space, of exactly the type I'd expected to see at Mira's tearoom. I almost pointed this out to Dana, but I got the sense from the way she refused to look at me and kept her back turned that she wasn't in the mood for chitchat right now.

Some uncomfortable silence passed while we perused our menus, after which the server came by to take our orders. Once those formalities were out of the way, Celia cleared her throat.

"I think I should start by saying while I was engaged to marry Alex, it wasn't because I loved him. It was a business arrangement."

"You're a hooker?" I asked in a hoarse whisper. Dana instantly shot me a death stare, and I sucked my lips into my mouth so hard I'm surprised they didn't shoot out the back of my head.

To my surprise, Celia offered the ghost of a smile at my remark. "No, a lesbian. Although, I don't think this is coming out the way I intended. There is something about Alex's masterpiece, *Oceans of Glass*, that to my knowledge only three people ever knew, and two of them are dead."

I shifted uneasily. "Are you saying someone murdered Alex and that you might be next?"

"Not exactly, no," Celia rushed to assure me. "I'm not in any danger. You don't need to worry about your loved ones or the inn, if that was your concern."

I relaxed into the cushioned booth behind me and urged Celia to continue.

"One thing you have to understand about

Alexander Tate is that ever since he was born, his father thought he was destined to be the next Hemingway. And he had reason to know, having actually met and worked with Hemingway as a young man. You see, Alex's dad was a big deal in the literary world."

"Are you telling us that *Oceans of Glass* was published because Alex Tate was a nepo baby?" Dana let out a hollow laugh. "I mean, even if that's true, there's no denying it's a brilliant book."

Celia shook her head. "The funny thing is, even with all his dad's help getting his foot in the door, Alex could never get anyone to publish his work. And God knows he tried. Wanting to be a great writer and actually being one are not the same thing."

"He was bad at writing?" Nora asked.

"He was terrible at writing, but he had an excellent imagination, ever since he was a kid. That's the whole reason his father had such high hopes. But the most his dad's name ever did for him was help him land a job teaching creative writing at a community college in rural Maine. He was in his forties by then. That's where we met."

"You were his student?" Nora guessed.

"Fellow faculty member," Celia corrected. "Well, faculty's a pretty fancy sounding word for the job I did. I was barely out of college myself, but this was basically the type of place where students enrolled because someone told them they had to. They didn't care who was teaching them, and it paid the bills and gave me time to write."

"You're a writer, too?" I guessed. "Like Alex?"

"Actually, almost the opposite of Alex, which is important. He could dream up amazing stories, but the words failed him. As for me, words are my thing. Nonfiction's my jam. Stories, not so much." She said all this in a humble way, none of it coming across as bragging. "The funny thing is, Alex really enjoyed teaching. That was his true calling."

Despite what a jerk the guy had been, I found myself able to relate to many aspects of his past. No one had known how bad I was at basic witchcraft growing up, but at least my family hadn't put such unrealistic pressure on me to be the best. I felt sorry for him, and I got the sense Celia did, too. I wondered what my true calling was, not able to come up with a thing.

The server arrived with four orders of lobster bisque, and I couldn't resist sampling mine. It was rich and creamy on the tongue, so sweet and succulent I almost forgot what I'd been about to say. I took a second bite, and then a third, before turning my attention back to Celia. "How does Alex being a teacher relate to everything now?"

"About fifteen years ago, a bit before my time, Alex had this student. He was a little older, more like twenty-two or twenty-three, rather than the typical eighteen- and nineteen-year-olds who came through the program. To his dying day, Alex regretted how he treated the kid." Celia stopped for a drink of wine, leaving me on the edge of my seat.

"What did Alex do?" I breathed, noting how both Dana and Nora were equally engrossed.

"This kid looked up to him," Celia said, putting down her wine glass. "One day toward the end of the semester, he came to Alex's office after class with this stack of composition books. It was a manuscript, handwritten. He wanted Alex's opinion on it. Alex kind of brushed him off—gruff as he was, you know. And like a week later, the kid's dead."

"Suicide?" Dana whispered.

"No, a car crash. It was the fall semester, and there was an early storm that turned the roads to ice. Complete accident. But, Alex felt so guilty, and he still had all those journals, so he sat down the very next day and read every single one. They were brilliant. Best damn story he'd ever read, and the way the kid had told it brought Alex to tears. That kid had been the complete package."

"Oh my God," Dana said, clapping a hand to her chest. *"Oceans of Glass."*

"You win the prize, Miss Wardwell." Celia winked at Dana, her cheeks flushing as she took another fortifying sip of wine. "I don't want you to get the wrong idea. Alex didn't set out to steal the story. For years, he kept the manuscripts. He tried to find next of kin, maybe help them make contact with a publisher, but there was nobody. The kid was an orphan, a ward of the state until he aged out at eighteen. It's why he was so much older, working his way to pay for every class."

"That's terrible," I said softly. "But how did Alex's name end up on the book?"

"Like I said, he sat on that manuscript for years, unsure what to do. Then he found out his dad was dying, and I think he lost all sense of perspective. All he could think was how his dad would go to his grave believing his son to be a total failure." Celia drained the last of the wine from her glass. "So he submitted the manuscript as his own."

I sucked in a breath, even though I suspected the story was heading down this path. "I know the author was dead, but it's still stealing. It's wrong."

"I don't disagree," Celia said with a nod. "I don't think Alex thought it through, and he definitely never believed the book would become such a hit. I know that for a fact because he signed a contract that stated if it sold more than a million copies, he would have to write a second book."

I had no idea how many copies the book had sold, but the way Dana snorted at the mention of a million made me think it had gone way over that.

"Was there a second book?" Dana asked cautiously. "Had the student written another one?"

"He had not," Celia said, confirming what I'd suspected. "Which is where I come into this story."

"I'm not sure I understand," Nora said, echoing my own thoughts.

"Like I said, I do the words. You give me a story, I'll write it exactly how you want it." Celia paused, adding. "I'm a ghostwriter."

The veins in my neck bulged as I struggled not to burst into laughter at this revelation. What were the chances a ghost writer was being haunted by a real ghost. Dana gave me a warning glance, and I had no doubt by her expression that Nora thought I'd lost my mind.

Pretending to cough, I reached for my water and took a long swig. "I'm sorry. Please, go on."

"By this time, I'd left the college, as had Alex, but he tracked me down. He said he remembered how I had a knack for masking my own voice and taking on the style of other writers, which is a must for a ghostwriter, of course. And then, after making me sign about a million non-disclosure agreements, he offered me a job, along with a proposal."

"When you say proposal, do you mean marriage proposal?" I asked.

"I do." At this, Celia giggled, making me feel a little better about my near slip-up with the ghostwriter situation. "Alex was paranoid people would find out about his fraud. Who can blame him, right? He decided the safest way to keep me quiet was if we got married. He knew I was a lesbian. There was never any thought of a real relationship between us, but he felt that was the best way to ensure no one could make me testify against him if it came to that. There would be strong legal protections for me, as well."

Our meals arrived, and we ate for some time without talking. All the while, so many questions swirled through my mind that I could barely enjoy the butter-and-garlic-covered scallops I'd ordered.

"I have to ask you something," I began slowly, after the chewing around the table had lessened. "Given what you've told us, how do you think Alex died?"

"I think he killed himself. The guilt of what he'd done was eating him from the inside, and I think in the end, he gave into it." Celia didn't hesitate a second in offering this assessment, and to me, it made sense. It certainly tracked with the blackness of despair I'd sensed for his ghost's aura. "There's another thing. Alex never told me anything about the identity of the man who actually wrote *Oceans of Glass,* but I couldn't help noticing how his personality changed after his publisher told him about being nominated for the Chesterton Prize."

"You mean he wasn't always—" I bit off the rest of my sentence, realizing that even if Celia wasn't actually the man's true fiancée, there was no polite way to call someone an ill-tempered asshole, especially a dead guy.

Celia laughed, clearly knowing what I'd been about to say. "He was always...quick tempered. I mean, the man popped blood pressure pills like Tic Tacs. But the way he started to act when we got to this island, and how he would spend hours walking through the cemetery, looking at each headstone—well, it led me to wonder if the author he'd stolen the manuscript from was originally from Goode Harbor."

We all sat in silence after this, digesting what Celia had told us along with our food. Was that why Alex Tate's spirit was still trapped in this world? I'd assumed he wanted justice for his killer, but perhaps what he wanted was redemption for his sins.

But was I the one who could give it to him?

CHAPTER FIFTEEN

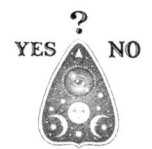

I felt like a criminal as I slid Mrs. Crenshaw's credit card into the slot at the gas pump on Friday morning, but I had no choice. My car's gas tank was nearing empty and my own credit card's balance was approaching its max. It wasn't like she hadn't given me the card for this exact purpose. Her own car was in the shop, and she needed something with plenty of trunk space to help her get the products from her garden to the Goode Harbor farmers' market.

Suburban mom vehicle to the rescue!

Though she'd insisted on giving me her card, saying it was payment for my time even if I secretly suspected she didn't want me to feel embarrassed about my situation, I refused to put in more than five gallons. It was a small island, after all. That would last until I got my money situation figured out. Once I was done at the pump, I drove in the direction of her cottage, which was on the far side of town.

In a seaside resort like Goode Harbor, it wasn't unheard of for rich people to build multi-million-dollar mansions and quaintly refer to them as cottages, as if doing so instantly made a twelve-bedroom house less ostentatious. But the house Mrs. Crenshaw lived in truly lived up to the spirit of its name. Behind a row of tall hedges that nearly blocked the whole thing from view was a charming Cape Cod style house with weathered gray shingles, surrounded by the most beautiful garden I had ever seen.

I parked my car in her drive and got out to admire the profusion of blooms that seemed to cover every surface at once in a way that was chaotic and delightful in equal measure.

"Right on time." Mrs. Crenshaw, wearing a loose cotton dress and garden gloves, came from around the back of the home. "I do so hate being late to the market. I like to claim my tent space before the garden club gets there. I enjoy seeing the look of consternation on Doris Greene's face."

"We wouldn't want to miss that." I opened the back of my wagon, exposing the empty space, which I had been sure to clear of all the random toys and junk before heading over. "Tell me what I should grab."

"There are some boxes of honey and jams in the entryway," she said. "Beeswax soaps, too. I'll go get the buckets with the flower bouquets."

I started hauling boxes to the car. When she came to the trunk with the second bunch of flowers, I couldn't help but say, "These bouquets belong on a magazine cover. The whole garden does, really."

"Well, thank you, dear, but that might raise some eyebrows."

"Why's that?"

"Have you heard of hardiness zones? That's what tells you the types of plants that can thrive in your region, based on how cold it gets," she explained, no doubt sensing my total ignorance without me saying a word. "Now, here on this island, we're a 5b, or maybe a 6a, depending how close you are to the water. That means we need plants that can survive down to negative twenty. See those gardenias right there?"

"They're beautiful," I said, inhaling their rich, fragrant scent.

"That particular variety is a zone eleven. That means around the time a true Mainer is thinking about putting on a sweater, that gardenia bush will have frozen to death. And yet," she added with a sly grin, "I've had it right there in my yard for ten years."

"Magic?" I guessed.

"Oh, yes," she chuckled like a child who was excited to have a secret. "I grow a lot of special flowers and fruit trees here to keep my bees happy, but anyone who knows anything about plants might get suspicious if they look too closely."

I nodded with understanding. "That's why you have those thick hedges along the road."

"That, and it worked better than a fence to keep the children in the yard, back when I had all the little ones running around." There was a wistful look in her eyes, and I could tell the old witch missed those happy times a great deal.

"Mom told me you took in quite a few," I said gently, not sure if she would like to talk about it or if it would make her sad.

"Dozens and dozens. I've got their photos hanging up on every wall inside." She sighed, but it was a happy sound, like the memories of all those children brought her joy. "I loved each and every one like they were my own. I always said, the best thing you can do for any child, or any person for that matter, is love them for who they are, no matter what."

"Even the naughty ones?" I joked, although my conscience was pricked by her words, and I couldn't help but remember how Dana had accused me of being homophobic at dinner the night before.

"Especially the naughty ones," Mrs. Crenshaw answered with a laugh. "The trick with them is they're usually not naughty. They're bored because they're too smart for their age, and everybody underestimates what they can handle."

"Is that right?" I immediately thought of my younger daughter, all sass and snarky temperament. "Do you think that's Sabrina's trouble?"

"She's a smart cookie, for sure," Mrs. Crenshaw assured me. "Reminds me of one boy I had here, used to get into so much trouble, until I finally figured out what he needed."

"What was that?" I asked, hoping whatever it was might work for Sabrina, too.

"To express himself. That's usually the way to unlock their potential. The trick is figuring out the right key, 'cause each kid comes factory equipped with a different lock. Sometimes it's through art, sometimes stories, or athletics. You have to find what works." Mrs. Crenshaw put a hand on my arm, warm and comforting. "Don't you worry about Sabrina. Kids are much more resilient than we give them credit for."

"I appreciate you saying that, only now something else has me concerned." I thought again to what Dana had said. "I'm afraid I got carried away and wasn't careful with my words. I think I may have upset a friend and made her feel like I didn't accept her for who she was, when that's anything but true."

"It's so easy to let passion get the best of us sometimes." Mrs. Crenshaw let out a long, low sigh. "Tell you what. Would you like to bring some flowers to your friend? You can have one of my bouquets."

She reached for one of the bundles of flowers from a bucket in the car, but I stopped her right away. "I couldn't possibly take one you plan to sell."

"I'm giving it to you for helping me out today."

"But you've already done enough by filling my gas

tank." The woman had been a teacher. She didn't need to tell me she was on a fixed income for me to know it was true.

Mrs. Crenshaw screwed up her mouth like she planned to argue but then said, "How about a compromise? After we finish loading the last few boxes of honey into the car, I'll give you a pair of snips and you can cut some flowers fresh for her yourself."

"Dana would like that," I said, giving in as I pictured the smile it would bring to my friend's face.

"Dana? I've always like her. Straight as an arrow, that one."

"Only not so straight, as it turns out," I said before I could stop myself. "I shouldn't have said that."

"Why ever not?" Mrs. Crenshaw didn't appear to be the least bit shocked by what I'd said. "It's hardly a secret that Dana prefers female company."

"It isn't?" My features settled into a deep frown. "In that case, why didn't she tell me? I stumbled on the discovery last night. I've been replaying what I said to her, and it was no wonder she thought I was being homophobic. But I wasn't, I swear. The whole way I handled things makes me cringe."

Mrs. Crenshaw patted my shoulder. "Well, I have good news for you. It's hard to hate someone who gives you flowers." She reached into her pocket and pulled out a pair of small garden scissors. "Here. Why don't you get started while I run in for a few last items from the kitchen?"

"Do you happen to know which flowers say I'm sorry?"

"All flowers do." She chuckled. "But, I would avoid the *rhododendron simsii*. Those are the pink ones there, with the thick leaves."

"Do they mean something bad?"

"Not at all."

"Then they must be rare," I guessed. I didn't want to wipe her out of something that was worth a lot of money.

"Considering that specific variety only grows in the highest elevations in Nepal, and yet here it is growing happily at sea level in Maine, I suppose you could call it rare." Mrs. Crenshaw chuckled. "Unfortunately, it's also a bit toxic."

"It's poisonous?"

"Don't be too alarmed. Hundreds of plants are. Foxglove. Hemlock." Mrs. Crenshaw got a dreamy look in her eyes that would have been entirely at odds with the current topic if I didn't know she was a witch. "During my last trip to England, I visited the Alnwick Garden in Northumberland. There's a special section they keep behind black iron gates. A poison garden. Some of the most dangerous plants are in their own cages."

"Are the rhododendrons like that?" I asked, horrified that such beautiful plants might need to be locked behind bars.

"Oh, no. But they can bring on dizziness, sweating,

even the occasional hallucination if you're not careful. It's best not to mess around with plants you don't know."

"I think those wise words can be applied to just about anything you're not certain of," I said.

Including other people's sexual orientations. And sometimes maybe your own.

ALMOST EVERYTHING ABOUT MY LIFE HAD changed since the day the FBI had shown up at my door and I'd discovered what kind of man my husband really was. But there was one thing that remained even more constant than death and taxes: the chaos of dropping off and picking up my kids from extracurricular activities.

After leaving Mrs. Crenshaw at the farmers market, it was time to get the girls from art camp at the library. I'd tracked down Sabrina, but Tabitha was nowhere in sight.

"Where's your sister?" I asked, hoping she didn't sense desperation in my tone the way an apex predator senses fear.

"Probably with her boyfriend," she answered with a smirk.

Oh, yeah. She was aware of all my weaknesses and more than happy to exploit them.

I placed a hand on my hip, attempting to reestablish my dominance. "Tabitha is not old enough to have a boyfriend!"

"Tell them that." Sabrina pointed to where Tabitha and Marcus had emerged from a nearby bookcase, standing shoulder to shoulder.

Never had I felt more in tune with a nun at a Catholic school dance, waving around a ruler and screaming, "Leave room for the Holy Spirit, you two!"

"Tabitha," I said in a loud whisper. Which, although loud, *was* still a whisper, and therefore not really effective at instilling fear in my offspring.

Marcus yanked on Tabitha's braid and then ran off with Tabitha hot on his trail, soothing my nerves somewhat. Despite my grown-up fears, they were acting like kids. It was a relief, and I hoped they would stay this way for a good long while.

"Hi, Tallie!" Mira waved one hand as she held Ruby's hand with the other. "My kids want to go to the beach. Would yours like to come along? You, too, of course."

"Can we, Mom?" Sabrina pressed her hands together like she was the dramatic heroine in a play. It was possible that made me the villain with whom she was pleading to spare her life.

"Yes, okay." I told her, eliciting a cheer that was nowhere close to a whisper. "Do you mind going on ahead with them? I need to speak to Dana for a minute, first."

Mira gave a knowing nod, and my spirits sank. Damn. I had hoped none of the others in Dana's coven were aware of how I'd acted like an ass. But if Dana had told Mira about last night, it could only mean I wasn't blowing it out of proportion. I really did have some apologizing to do.

Approaching the circulation desk, I tried catching Dana's eye. She either was making a point by ignoring me, or she was frazzled by the transfer of all the kids to their rightful guardians. I was crossing my fingers for the latter, but I had my doubts.

"Those are pretty flowers," Ruby said.

"Thank you. They're for Dana. Would you girls like to give them to her for me?" That may have been a cowardly move, but I had an ulterior motive. I wanted a moment alone with Mira to talk without little ears listening.

Sabrina and Ruby skipped off with the flowers, shouting, "Miss Dana! Miss Dana!"

I was really going to have to talk with my youngest about library rules.

"What's your opinion about Dana and Celia?" I asked when they were out of earshot.

"I'm not really sure," Mira replied, "but whenever Dana talks about her, she has a glow."

I'd noticed that, too, but I was concerned about something else. "You don't think it's too soon?"

"For who? If you mean Dana, she's been single far too long, if you ask me. As for Celia, I thought her engagement was a sham." Mira's nose wrinkled a bit. "Okay, I'll admit that should probably be a red flag, but I don't know. Life's a mystery sometimes. If anyone can manage to find happiness in it, even for a little while, should we really try to stop them?"

I sighed, knowing Mira had a point. If Dana had found someone whose company she enjoyed, far be it from a nearly divorced woman and a widow to get in her way.

The girls came back from their mission, and Mira took Ruby by one hand and held out the other for Sabrina to take so they could head to the beach. I was about to inform my friend that Sabrina had stopped holding my hand in public three years ago, but my youngest accepted Mira's without a fuss. Marcus and Tabitha whizzed after them, playing a game of tag, looking so young but not as young as I'd like them to be.

"They're cute together, aren't they?" Dana said it to me, which meant she was on speaking terms with me, but a certain warmth I'd grown accustomed to was lacking.

"They are, but I'm not sure I'm ready for the teenage years." I squared my shoulders, not wanting to put off what I'd come here to say any longer. "I'm so sorry for being an ass last night about Celia. It's possible I was projecting a lot of my own issues with relationships onto a situation that is none of my business."

"Your failed marriage, you mean?" Dana clearly wasn't planning to pull her punches, which was fine. I was her friend, which meant she shouldn't have to.

"That, for sure. It's hard to trust anyone when you've had the wool pulled so thoroughly over your eyes by someone you thought you knew." I pressed my lips together, carefully formulating what I wanted to ask next so as not to step in it all over again. "Dana, why did you never tell me you liked girls? Not now—I mean when we were younger. I get that I've only been back a few weeks and you might not feel like you can trust me completely, but we used to be best friends."

"Because I didn't know. I was a typical late bloomer, I guess." Dana shrugged. "Do you remember me ever telling you a single person I had a crush on back then?"

I thought for a moment and shook my head. "Now that you mention it, no. You were the smart one. I guess I figured you had more important things to think of than boys."

"I kind of thought the same thing. I assumed I liked boys, you know, as a default setting or something."

"It *was* just assumed, wasn't it?" I agreed. "Especially back then. You're going to be a boy-crazy teen, and then you'll get married and have two kids. I certainly never questioned it."

"Exactly. Only when I eventually did get around to thinking those thoughts—you know, when I ran out of more important things, I guess—it turned out I wasn't thinking about boys after all."

It wasn't hard for me to empathize. I'd learned from my life with Phil how easily one could simply go with the flow... until the FBI put a stop to it, at least. As far as I knew, there were no SWAT teams for sexuality.

"You really didn't know before that?" If she hadn't wanted to tell me, I could understand. I'd proven to be less than reliable as a friend more times than I'd like to count.

"I really didn't, or I would've said something. But you were gone by the time it all clicked. And when you came back, I wasn't sure what to say." Dana picked up the bouquet the girls had given her, admiring the blooms with a faint smile. "The flowers are lovely. I should put them in a vase so everyone can enjoy them."

Dana disappeared through a door marked *staff only*, and I didn't try to follow. I figured she might need some space. Besides, I had hundreds of thoughts whirling through my head. Like, was it really possible not to know something as basic as your own sexuality? If so, once you did figure it out, was it set in stone? Or was it possible to change your mind if you met someone—say a flirty doctor, for instance? Minus the jealous girlfriend? If she happened to have this way of looking at you that could make your heart flutter like you were thirteen again, what did that mean?

Yeah, it was probably best that Dana had gone off for a moment. I apparently had some things of my own to sort out.

"You done for the day?" I asked when Dana returned, the flowers now displayed in a tall glass vase. "I thought you might want to walk with me to the beach to meet up with Mira and the kids."

"Yeah. That sounds nice." Dana smiled, and this time I could feel the warmth radiating toward me. "It's a lovely day. Spending time with all of you at the beach is just what my soul needs."

"Mine too." I fell into step next to Dana, not talking about much in particular until we reached a point where the stone church was just down the street in the opposite direction from the beach. "Hey, Dana? You wanna make a quick detour? I'd like to check out the cemetery."

"Okay, goth girl," Dana teased. "Why the cemetery?"

"I can't stop thinking about what Celia told us last night, how Alex was obsessed with taking walks through there and checking the headstones."

"You think we can find the guy who really wrote that manuscript?"

"It's worth a try. I put my accounting skills to work and did the math," I added. "I think the guy we're looking for was born in the late 1980s, maybe 1990, and probably died around 2012."

"So young." Dana's tone was full of melancholy,

and I couldn't blame her. Back when we were that age, we'd felt so grown-up, but from the perspective of another couple of decades, it felt very different.

I hadn't been past the cemetery since the night I'd arrived on the island, but in the daytime, it hardly looked like the same place. It was pleasant almost, with beautifully carved headstones and lots of shade-giving leafy trees. Not saying I'd want to spend the day there, but it was actually a really lovely place to take a stroll.

We made our way past the oldest tombstones, some of them barely legible, until we came to an area of newer graves.

"Here's one. Paul Granger, born 1989 and died in 2013." I pointed to the grave marker while Dana jotted the name down in a small notebook.

"Let's see if we can find any others," Dana said. "I'll research the names when I get to the library tomorrow, maybe see if my mom can check the historical archives for other candidates, too."

By the time we'd reached the far end of the cemetery, we'd found three possibilities, though one had a gender-neutral name that I wasn't sure about. It was harder than I'd thought, although I'm not sure what I was expecting. Maybe I'd figured that now that my powers seemed to be returning, the grave we were looking for would light up in flashing neon or something.

"I think that's the best we can do for today," Dana said, putting her notebook away.

My eyes drifted to an ornate structure in the center of the cemetery. It was marble and shaped like a church that had been made out of gingerbread. I recognized it as the building I'd seen surrounded by mist the night I'd arrived.

"What is that?" I asked, making my way toward it almost as if my legs had a mind of their own.

"That's the Chesterton mausoleum," Dana said, following me.

"Like Chesterton Manor?"

"Same family," Dana confirmed. "They couldn't take all their money with them when they died, so I guess they used as much of it as they could to build something special to be buried in."

"Sounds like something rich people would do." I peered through a leaded glass window, covered with grime, into the dim interior. I could just make out names carved in individual plaques along the wall. "Roland Chesterton. I remember that name."

"Yes, his father was one of the robber barons who turned Goode Harbor into a Gilded Age summer resort." Dana joined me in looking through the window. "Florence and Roberta. Those were his daughters."

"You would know that, you nerdy librarian," I teased. "So, who's that other one? It's so covered in moss I can barely read it."

"Let me see." Dana squinted so hard I was afraid she would strain herself. "Looks like it says Prudence Mayfield."

"Why is her name with the Chestertons?"

"I honestly don't know." Dana jotted the name in her notebook as she wandered away from the mausoleum. "I thought I knew just about everything when it came to island history and the Chestertons, but I've never heard of her."

I remained in place for a moment, contemplating the names on the wall of the old crypt. Out of nowhere, the air turned cold, and a blast of wind lashed my face.

Though Dana was only a few yards ahead of me, she seemed completely unaffected by the sudden shift in temperature, not a hair on her head out of place.

"Let's go." I wrapped my arms around myself, shivering uncontrollably. "It's kinda creepy here."

CHAPTER SIXTEEN

*D*ana spent the next several days scouring every record she could find at the library, but even so, we were left with several possible candidates for the real author of *Oceans of Glass,* and no clear way to narrow it down more. There was only one person on the island who might be able to shed some light on the matter, but asking him for help would open a whole new can of worms.

"Are you sure we should tell him?" I whispered to Dana as we stood on David Spencer's front stoop, waiting for him to answer the bell.

"Celia said it would be okay," Dana whispered back. "Anything to help solve the mystery of who actually wrote the book."

"I was more concerned with the effect it would have on David," I corrected. "His ego was big enough already. Discovering his rival was a fraud is going to make him insufferable."

"Maybe jail changed him for the better," Dana suggested.

I shrugged, not believing it. From what I could tell, the man was a self-appointed know-it-all who believed he was better than the rest of us. "If anything, you'd think finding a dead body might have changed him."

"Like reminding him life is short and to embrace everything?" The look on Dana's face as she said this suggested she wasn't buying what she was saying any more than I was. "Maybe he'll keep his gloating to a minimum, at least."

My finger hovered above the doorbell, poised to press it again, when the door opened a crack, revealing little more than an eyeball, bloodshot and crazed. "Oh, it's you. Quick, come in before they see you."

David—at least I assumed it was him, not because that one eyeball had looked familiar, but because I was pretty sure I recognized his voice—grabbed each of us by an arm and yanked us into the house, slamming the door and sliding the lock into place.

"Pests," he intoned with disgust. "They should be exterminated."

"Mice?" I asked, my head whipping to and fro as I scanned the floor.

"Should I get you a chair to stand on?" Dana cracked, earning her a salty glare.

"The paparazzi." David went to the window in his

front room, peeking out the curtain. "I caught one of them going through my trash. My trash!"

"You have paparazzi?" I asked, unable to wrap my head around it.

"David, that's terrible." Dana put a hand to her heart while shooting me a warning glance, as if to remind me not to insult the man when we needed his help.

"That lady sheriff has no idea the wrath my lawyer is about to bring down on her. She's messing with the wrong David Spencer." His phone rang, and he excused himself with a raised finger.

"I can't decide whether to react to his use of the term *lady sheriff*," I said in a whisper, "or to wonder how many other David Spencers there are, and whether he's the worst of the bunch."

"Shh," Dana warned. "Don't antagonize him."

"Come on, though. Lady sheriff? Sounds like she should have to wear a pink uniform," I muttered. "I'm amazed he found a lawyer so soon. Do you think it's a lady lawyer?"

"I highly doubt it," Dana said. "I have a feeling it's his copyright attorney. That's the only lawyer David knows."

"I'm not sure this is a smart move, getting him involved if the press is snooping around." I cast a wary eye toward the street. "I had no idea people cared about authors that much. I could walk by Stephen King, and I probably wouldn't know it, and I've actually read some of his books."

Still, if we were going to make any progress getting Alexander Tate's ghost to stop haunting the inn, we needed to know who had really written his book. If there had ever been another person on the island with the potential to be a rival, David Spencer was the type of guy who would know.

Finishing his phone call, David motioned for us to take a seat on the couch. He perched on the arm of a brown leather wingback chair. "What'd you want to see me about? But please don't say Alexander Tate. I never want to hear that man's name again."

"Uh…" I looked to Dana, who plastered on a smile.

"How are you doing, David?" Dana asked in that soothing way of hers. "I'm so glad the sheriff released you from jail. I couldn't believe the news when I heard you'd been arrested. Who could believe you capable of murder?"

"Exactly—wait." David frowned as if taking Dana's reassurance as an insult. "I could've, you know. I wanted to kill him. If given the chance, I would have."

At one point, I'd been surprised the sheriff had held David as long as she did, essentially waiting as long as the law would allow before letting him go. Hearing him now, I was amazed he'd gotten out at all. Did the man have no preservation skills? It was like he had to convince everyone he was the best, all the time. Even if it meant claiming he would make a good murderer.

"I have some news about your nemesis that might please you," Dana said in a tantalizing way that was sure to make him want to know more. I had to admire the way Dana honored David's request by not actually saying his name.

David leaned forward, wobbling on the arm of the chair. "I'm listening."

"What would you say if I told you a certain someone never actually wrote *Oceans of Glass*?"

"He was a fraud?" David's eyes widened, a smile tugging at his lips.

"It seems the real author was a student of Alex Tate's, once upon a time," Dana confirmed. "The young man died, reportedly without any kin, before his book could be published."

David jumped to his feet, nearly sending the armchair tipping onto the floor. "I knew it! You know what that means?"

"That someone else out there might have a motive to kill Alexander Tate?" I suggested.

"No!" David smacked his fist into his palm with such force it made me wince. "It means I win the Chesterton Prize! Oh, yeah. Come to Papa, baby. I've got a spot for you waiting right here on my mantel."

Was he for real? A man was dead, and we might have stumbled onto a motive for his murder, and all this dude could think about was some stupid trophy? Also, the pervy way he was talking to the imaginary trophy seriously made me fear for the poor thing's safety.

"I don't know the protocol for that," Dana hedged, looking as shocked over this turn in the conversation as I was, "but I'm here about something else. We have reason to believe the real author of the book lived on the island. We've narrowed it down to a handful of individuals. We thought, given your familiarity with the literary scene in Goode Harbor, one of them might stand out to you from the rest."

Reaching into the bag she'd brought with her, Dana, took out three yearbooks from Chesterton Academy, with the photos of the likely candidates marked by bright pink Post-it Notes.

David reached for a pair of reading glasses on the end table and inspected each of the books before shaking his head. "I can't say any of them look familiar, but based on the years of these books, it was a little after my time."

"Is there anything you noticed that might help?" Dana asked, a hint of pleading in her tone.

"I see they were all members of the school literary magazine. I helped found it, you know." David puffed out his chest, once again exercising his skill in bringing everything around to him.

Dana bit down on her bottom lip.

"Seems like a dead end," I said, immediately regretting my choice of words.

"Not necessarily," David said. "If he attended

Chesterton and was a good writer—which I'm not necessarily saying he was, since he *did* write *Oceans of Glass*—but chances are whether it's one of these guys or someone else, the author was a member of the lit mag. If you talk to some of the members from those years, someone may remember something."

I flipped through one of the yearbooks, locating the pages dedicated to the literary magazine. "There's gotta be two dozen people from each year, and we've only narrowed it down to about a three-year span. How are we going to find all of them to talk to?"

"I think I know." Dana grinned. "The 150th anniversary celebration for Chesterton Academy is this coming weekend. Everyone who ever attended the school was invited. If our guy did go to school there, there has to be somebody who remembers his writing style or maybe read a rough draft. I can't believe I didn't think of it before."

I translated her words to, "Why did I waste my time with David?"

"It's not your fault," David said consolingly. "You simply lack the natural imagination of an author."

I'm not saying I agree with people being locked up in jail without probable cause, but in David's case, maybe the sheriff had been onto something.

"Indeed," Dana managed to say. "Thank you for your time."

We both rose from the couch.

"You're not leaving, are you?" he asked in alarm. "We haven't discussed the most important thing."

Dana tilted her head. "Which is?"

"My award, of course. I'll get my lawyer to contact the Goode Harbor Literary Festival if I must," he added, wagging his finger. "It's my award, fair and square. I won't settle for less."

Once we made it back outside, I took a good look around. All was quiet. "I don't see any paparazzi, do you?"

"David does have the imagination of a writer," Dana said with a smirk.

"I don't know how more authors don't end up dead. I'll be happy if I never have to talk to another author for as long as I live."

"In that case," Dana said with noticeable caution in her tone, "I have some bad news for you. David's right about us needing to talk to former members of the literary magazine."

"Us?" I tensed against what I feared was coming. "What do you mean us?"

"Guess who's going as my date to the reunion?" Dana pasted on a cheery smile that left me seeing red.

I crossed my arms defiantly, or at least as defiantly as was possible when I was also left with little choice but to comply. Not if I wanted to rid the inn of Alexander Tate's ghost. "If you think I'm putting on another dress and heels, you've got another thing coming."

Squatting in front of my closet, trying not to grimace as my knees crackled like a toddler with a sheet of bubble wrap, I peered into the abyss to find my other flip-flop.

"Come on. I know you're in here." I was breathing as heavily as I used to on the treadmill at the gym. Except I wasn't at the gym. I was literally just bending. When had that happened? "Ah-ha!"

I grabbed the missing shoe from the back of the closet, and almost instantly, I wanted to commit murder of the feline variety. The foam platform had tooth marks on the edges, which I was certain were the work of a pesky black cat who had it in for me. If Buster and Sheriff Gray ever joined forces, I was a dead woman.

"Meow."

Speak of the devil, here came the furry little Satan now. And he had something shiny dangling from his mouth.

"What do you have there?" I shifted slowly, trying not to let on that I was about to grab whatever it was right out of his mouth. At least, that was the plan until something in my knee popped. Tears sprang to my eyes as I fell backward and landed on my butt. "Sonofabitch!"

Intrigued, Buster stopped in his tracks. He

regarded me with an expression entirely devoid of emotion—in other words, his typical cat face—before dropping the item in his mouth on the floor in front of me. I would have called it a peace offering, except considering the source, I figured he'd probably done it to torment me.

"Thanks, but what I could really use is some help standing up."

As expected, the cat continued on his way without sparing me another thought. Meanwhile, I was stuck on the floor with a throbbing knee and no idea how I was going to get back on my feet. I rolled to one side so I could use the edge of the dresser for leverage, but an immediate twinge in my knee stopped me. I rolled to the other, but without anything within reach to grab onto, there was little chance of success. Finally, I went flat on my back and then rolled onto my stomach, my forehead pressed to the floorboards.

"Mom? Are you all right?" It was Sabrina. Of my two daughters, did it have to be the one who would be most likely to mock my predicament?

"Fine, honey. Just doing some yoga," I lied. But then I panicked. What if she believed me and left me there to die? "Actually, sweetie, could you come over here and give Mommy a hand?"

"Uh, okay."

A few seconds later, I was back on my feet, my dignity in tatters. "Thanks, kid."

"Mom, what's this?" Sabrina scooped the shiny

thing Buster had dropped up from the floor, a good thing because if it had been left to me, it would've stayed there forever. I was never going to attempt to bend like that again.

I held out my hand, and Sabrina placed the object in it, oddly warm against my palm. It was round in shape, the gold dark and mellow from age. I could make out the shape of a woman sitting on a crescent moon. There was a clasp on the side, but try as I might, I couldn't get it to open.

"It looks like a locket. Old, too. But it seems to be good and stuck, and the chain has a broken link." I put it in my pocket. "I'll take it with me to Brigit's shop and see what she has to say."

I drove into town with the windows rolled down, the better to conserve my precious half tank of gas. The humidity made my denim shorts and tank top stick to my skin, and my hair puffed out like a bright red Brill-o pad. And don't get me started on my chewed shoes.

What are you doing with your life, Tallie?

I pulled into a parking spot, glancing toward the clinic building before crossing the street in the direction of Brigit's shop. Nora would be working there all day. She had a grown-up job and wore a smart white doctor's coat. I bet her shoes didn't have a single tooth mark on them. Meanwhile, I was on a mission to spend my last few dollars on a dress I didn't want, all because of a ghost.

Yeah, I sure was a catch. Had I really thought for even a second that Nora was flirting with me these past few weeks? I must've been out of my mind.

With its black and white striped awnings and perfectly formed potted topiaries on either side of the door, the front of Brigit's shop screamed sophistication. Or whispered it quietly, rather, in that way that hinted everything you'd ever wanted to be could be yours if you stepped inside.

The mannequins in the window had on better outfits than I wore. That was for sure. To be fair, with two kids to raise and a husband who had checked out emotionally a long time before he'd skipped town, I'd stopped caring about my looks. That much was painfully evident as I studied my bedraggled reflection in the shop window. But maybe, if I tried, I could someday be half the woman those plastic mannequins were.

Brigit, who wore a vintage 1950s dress with tiny martini glasses on it, was adjusting dresses on a rack as I entered. She smiled brightly when she spotted me, showing off her perfectly white teeth. I hadn't even realized teeth came in that color except in magazines.

"Tallie, just the person I was hoping to see. I received a dress in my latest shipment that has your name all over it."

"Really?" I wondered if she meant that literally, half expecting her to bring out a dress with Tallulah stitched across the front. It seemed about as plausible as anyone looking at a dress of any kind and thinking of me, the queen of cut-off jeans.

"Dana gave me the heads-up about the anniversary celebration and told me I had to find the right thing for you to wear."

"I guess my lack of fashion sense is legendary."

"Don't think of it that way. If everyone was like me, I wouldn't have a job." Brigit came out from behind the counter, beckoning me with a finger to one of the dressing rooms. "It's a fabulous day dress from the 1920s."

"Day dress?" My head was already spinning from trying to figure out what made that different from any other kind of dress.

"My understanding is this party you're going to isn't a formal affair. Is that right?"

Brigit stepped away for a second, coming back with a dress on a hanger that she held out for my inspection. It was black chiffon with a white sailor collar and a white sash that seemed to be several inches below where my waist would be. The short sleeves were delicate and fluttered with the slightest movement.

"Geez. That's still fancier than pretty much anything I've ever owned."

"I'm certain you'll look smashing in it." Hearing Brigit say this in her French accent made me believe her words. "Go on. Give it a whirl."

I stepped inside the dressing room, drawing the curtain closed. As I began to undress, the locket I'd shoved into my pocket tumbled out and landed on the floor, skittering to the other side of the doorway. "I almost forgot about that."

Through the space between the curtain and the floor, I saw Brigit swoop down to retrieve the jewelry. I listened in vain for labored breathing or crunching noises coming from her knees, but apparently, I was the only one who was so easily exerted.

"This is exquisite," she said. "Where did you get it?"

"I found it back at the inn. It's lovely, but the latch sticks, and one of the links on the chain is broken."

"I can fix this right up while you try on that dress."

"Really?"

"I never lie where fashion is concerned."

As her heels clicked against the floor, I nearly asked what things she did lie about, but she was already out of earshot. Probably a good thing.

Standing in only my bra and underwear, the shop's air-conditioning turned my bare skin to gooseflesh. The chilliness intensified as I slipped the smooth, silky chiffon over my head. Although there were some hooks I couldn't reach, I could tell it fit as though it had been made for me. I wondered if Brigit had cast a spell. The coldness surrounding me intensified.

"How are you doing in there?" Brigit inquired.

"Okay… I think."

"Come on out. Let me give you my professional opinion."

Feeling self-conscious, I edged out from behind the red curtain, my arms hugging my stomach.

Brigit pulled my arms apart with clinical precision, her eyes sweeping from head to toe. "Magnificent."

As I stood in front of the full-length mirror, she closed the fasteners I had missed. She handed me a pair of black shoes with sturdy, low heels, and I put them on, completing the look. "It fits perfectly."

"I know."

I spun one way and then another as I watched myself in the mirror.

Rubbing her hands together, Brigit ran them over my head, smoothing my hair better than a stylist at a salon.

"I should have known you used magic."

"Only on the hair. It's as if the dress was made for you, with no help from me. Here, let me get the locket. It's just the thing to make it all sing."

"Did you get it fixed already?" I was surprised, but when she held it up, the locket, though still clearly an antique, shone like brand new.

"A pair of pliers and a silver cloth was all it needed. A simple fix. Turn around." Brigit affixed the necklace in place.

As soon as the silver touched my skin, a blast of air-conditioning hit me directly in the face, forcing me to close my eyes.

When I opened them, Brigit and the shop were nowhere in sight.

CHAPTER SEVENTEEN

I snapped my eyelids shut again, hoping to reboot my brain like a computer. It didn't work. I was not in the shop where I was supposed to be, but that wasn't my fault. The shop had completely disappeared.

Instead, I was standing in the middle of a restaurant, with crisp, white linen on the tables. Men and women were seated all around, dressed in fashions that felt impossibly antiquated. However, with the outfit I had on, I fit right in.

Out the window, I spied Model-T Fords alongside horse-drawn carts. I couldn't explain what had happened, but it all felt absolutely real. Every detail was perfect, including the honk of a horn outside that sounded like it was saying, "ahooga."

Patrons clinked their silverware against plates. A waiter breezed past me with a tray, and the pungent smell of onions tickled my nose. The next moment, it was replaced by the cloying scent of rose perfume.

"There you are. Come on."

My heart nearly stopped as I recognized the seamstress from my dream, the one I'd shared a cigarette with. She took my hand, leading me out the back of the restaurant into an alleyway. I really hoped she didn't want to smoke again. That was an experience I preferred not to repeat.

"Where are we going—Agnes?" I held my breath to see if my guess at her name was right. It struck me that my voice sounded slightly different, and I felt younger and nimbler, too. I was pretty sure if I tried to squat down now, nothing would crackle or pop.

"I told you earlier. Freddy's playing piano tonight."

It was like I had reentered my dream shortly after where I'd left off. The seamstress—whom I was now more convinced than ever was my great-grandmother, Agnes, since she hadn't so much as blinked when I'd called her that—was whisking me off to a speakeasy.

What in the Hecate was going on?

We stopped at a wooden door that looked like it might be used for deliveries. Agnes tapped her fist against it in a distinct pattern, two slow raps followed by three short ones, like a secret code. A tiny slot slid open in the door, about eyeball height, revealing nothing beyond it but shadow. A moment later, a pair of eyes emerged from the blackness and blinked. There was the scraping of metal as a latch on the other side was undone. Then the door swung open, allowing strains of jazz music to escape into the alleyway along with the odor of cigar smoke and perfume.

I'd be lying if I said I wasn't curious what I was about to experience. Also, freaked out. But more than intrigued. Who wouldn't want to witness the Roaring Twenties firsthand? With my great-grandmother as my personal tour guide, the prospect seemed less scary than if I'd found myself in this situation all alone.

Naturally, having seen my fair share of old movies, I expected the eyes behind the door would belong to some cartoonish brute of a bouncer. Instead, I was mystified when I got a good look at the sandy-haired young man who stood guard at the door.

"That's Tony," she said.

It's not that I didn't know staring was rude, but I couldn't help it. I stared at poor Tony so hard my eyeballs started to get dry, because while his name was in keeping with my expectations, Tony was shorter than I was, even while standing on a stack of wooden crates. The man could've had a promising career as a racing jockey or gone to Hollywood to play the role of a hobbit. In fact, as I took in his tousled hair and rumpled clothing, I found myself wondering if the scuffed shoes he wore covered hairy hobbit feet.

Except if this was really the 1920s, Hollywood was in its infancy, and Tolkien's Middle-earth wasn't even a gleam in the author's eye.

Fortunately, when I opened my mouth, I didn't let

any of what I was thinking spill out and simply said, "Nice to meet you." He didn't respond or make eye contact, and it occurred to me to wonder whether he could see me or if perhaps I was simply a soul in this experience, not corporeal.

How could my great-grandmother see me, then?

The door shut quickly behind us as I followed my guide down a narrow, dark hallway which had to be navigated more by feel than by sight. By the time we reached the main room, the dimly glowing lamps and a dozen or so votive candles scattered on tabletops provided ample illumination and a welcome relief from utter darkness.

I'd watched enough movies to have a pretty good idea of what a speakeasy should look like. I pictured a room full of gangsters carrying Tommy guns and women wearing short fringed dresses with feathers in their hair, all doing the Charleston while bathtub gin flowed freely from barrels marked XXX in black stencils. I could not have been more wrong.

The room itself was not very large, maybe the size of a private banquet room in a restaurant or hotel. There was no bar in sight. Instead, along the back wall was a bookcase that gave the place the appearance of a library.

On the other end of the room, a jazz quartet played on a raised platform. In between were numerous small tables, maybe fifteen or twenty in all, with groupings of two or four people at each. The patrons who occupied them were well dressed, with men in three-piece suits and women in silk gowns, the expensive embroidery and beadwork sparkling in the candlelight. I wished Brigit had given me an evening dress so I would fit in better, but no one seemed to mind.

Everyone drank from fine china teacups balanced primly on saucers, while several waiters in crisp uniforms circled the room holding teapots and doling out refills. If it hadn't been for the secrecy involved in gaining admission, I would have sworn we'd wandered in on a church tea party.

"This place is wonderful, like Alice's tea party, but for grown-ups." I whispered.

"You can say that." She looked at me as if bewildered I was so gobsmacked. "Welcome to Bertie's place. Have you really never been here?"

"No, never," I said, my brain churning. "Isn't Bertie that bootlegger fella you told me about? The one who's suave and debonair?"

"The very same." Her laugh tinkled like a wind chime in a light breeze. "I'm sure he'll want to meet you if he's here."

"I don't know," I said, my insides knotting. "Bootleggers are dangerous gangsters, aren't they?"

"Not Bertie. He's a thoroughly modern man with an entrepreneurial spirit and an adventurous streak." Even in the dim lighting, there was no mistaking the sudden flush of color in her cheeks or the dreamy quality to her tone.

"Sounds to me like you have a little crush on this Bertie person," I teased.

"Oh, he's a real sheik all right, and an egg to boot. If it weren't for Freddie—" Whatever she'd been about to say was swallowed as she pointed to a man in a sleek black tuxedo who was speaking in a hushed tone to the man playing piano. "There he is, right over there."

"Freddie?"

"No. Bertie Chase."

I followed her eyes to the man as he shifted just right so the stage lights splashed on his face, making my breath hitch. He was taller than I was by a few inches—not overly tall for a man—but his strong jaw and aquiline nose combined with his confident bearing gave the bootlegger the appearance of strength. His dark hair was slicked back impeccably. He wore a black tailcoat, his vest and bow tie stark white against a crisp white shirt.

Bertie Chase was a real sheik, all right.

Whatever that meant.

Now he'd made eye contact and was making his way right to me.

"I told you he'd notice you," Agnes said with a laugh.

"What should I do?" I whispered frantically. The last thing I wanted was to become acquainted with an outlaw, although if that was true, why was my pulse racing?

"Good evening, ladies." Bertie gave us each a nod, an almost regal gesture. He reached for my hand, taking it in his, while pins and needles pricked my skin. "I don't believe I've met this lovely lady before. Would you do me the honor of a dance?"

"I'm not much of a dancer." I couldn't take my eyes off the man, nor could I shake the sense that Bertie reminded me of someone, but I couldn't put my finger on whom. My nerves were firing like flare guns.

"Can you do the Duck Waddle?" he asked. "How about the Grizzly Bear, the Horse Trot, or the Kangaroo Hop?"

I looked at him askance. "Are we dancing or going to a zoo?"

"A simple foxtrot, then. Come. I'll lead." He led me to an open space that served as a dance floor. The reflection of candles on the tables that surrounded us twinkled in his dark eyes like stars. "All you have to do is follow. Do what I do. And look pretty, of course. But you're a natural at that."

Too overwhelmed by his flattery to argue, I allowed myself to be taken into his arms, my body moving to the beat of the music. Up close, his bone structure was finer than it had at first appeared, his fingers long and almost delicate, with skin as soft as kid leather. It didn't square with a rugged lawbreaker at all.

Still, he looked so very familiar. But why?

Before my brain could kick into a high enough gear to figure out who the man reminded me of, the band abruptly shifted tempo from sensual blues to a ragtime tune that was jarringly upbeat.

As if acting on cue, Bertie abandoned his dance stance and left the floor, but not before giving my hand a farewell kiss.

Agnes came running up to me, breathless. "It's a raid. Let's blouse."

"Let's what?"

"We gotta get outta here!"

All at once, spurred by the band's musical signal, waitstaff scurried toward the bookcases as patrons guzzled the contents of their teacups and set them clattering onto saucers. My friend darted toward the back wall, but my feet were glued to the floor. I watched, astounded, as one of the servers yanked at the books on a top shelf, which instead of tumbling to the floor, swung open to reveal a hidden cabinet jammed full of liquor bottles. He stowed his cocktail filled teapot inside and shut the compartment, while other servers repeated the process all along the library wall.

One bookcase had slid away from the wall entirely. It was toward this opening that a crush of people now swarmed, disappearing into the blackness like rats fleeing a ship. The shrillness of a police whistle pierced the air, and I heard someone call out, "Get moving!"

There was a pale face in the secret passageway, and the urgency reflected on it spurred me to action. I raced across the now empty club, zigzagging around chairs that had been strewn haphazardly. As I reached the entrance to what I could see was a narrow tunnel, my foot caught on a chair leg, and I stumbled forward.

Heat surged from my wrist through my arm as someone reached for me, and in the dim light, the locket around my neck glowed like a red-hot coal. Though thankfully not as hot as that, it did sting some.

I winced, navigating the first several yards of the escape route with my eyes squeezed tightly shut. When I opened them, I could see nothing but unrelenting blackness. My ears strained for the sound of footsteps or whispers, but I heard nothing.

I progressed as best I could, crouching as I ran my fingers along the rough walls of the corridor. There was a downward slope to the passage, which was filled with a salty, fishy smell that grew stronger the more I walked.

Finally, a faint light shone not too far in the distance. Soon I stepped out of the tunnel and found myself in a rocky outcropping near the shore. Lobster traps were piled high in front of the mouth of the tunnel, but other than that, the area was deserted. I blinked, looking frantically around me for any sign of my great-grandmother or the others from the speakeasy, but it was clear I'd been left behind, alone.

I hiked up a steep bank to the road. It, too, was deserted. I looked back to find stacks of lobster traps obscured the entrance to the tunnel entirely. No one

MIDLIFE IS THE CAT'S MEOW

would ever know it was there. At least the view from higher up told me I was not far from Main Street, while the sudden blaring of rock music from an approaching car radio let me know I was no longer in the 1920s. But how was it possible, when I'd been running from a police raid moments before?

"She's over here!" Dana shouted.

My head began to spin, and I shut my eyes, feeling consciousness draining from me. The last thing I was aware of was arms propping me up as I stumbled on my feet and the feel of a car's cloth seat against my legs. Then it all went black.

When I was able to open my eyes again, I was sitting in the back seat of a car. I could see the striped awning of Brigit's shop beyond my window. Dana sat beside me, holding my hand, while Brigit and Mira stared at me from the front seats with their mouths agape.

"What happened?" I asked, my entire body shaking.

"You tell us," Brigit replied. "One minute you were standing in the shop, and the next, you were gone."

"Gone?" If I'd felt cold before, it was nothing compared to the chill that overtook my bones as I repeated what she'd said. "How could I be gone?"

"I don't know." Brigit's voice trembled like she was barely holding it together.

"Tallie, did you teleport?" Dana asked, caution in her voice.

"No." The denial was automatic because teleportation wasn't real. Except, what else would you call what had happened? "I mean, I don't think so. I didn't mean to."

"What happened then?" Mira pressed.

"It felt like I accidentally slipped through a hole in time." Because that was so much better than teleportation, right?

"What does that—wait." Brigit's eyes widened. "Are you saying you traveled in time?"

"Don't be ridiculous. That can't happen." I ran a hand over my head. "Can it? It only felt that way. It had to have been a dream."

"That doesn't explain how you went *poof*, and we had to use a finding spell to locate you," Dana argued, making a reasonable point as she generally did.

"Did this place used to be a restaurant?" I asked, looking at Brigit.

It was Dana, historian extraordinaire, who answered. "Years ago. Why?"

"I think—I must have known that for some reason. Maybe I heard it somewhere. It had to be an illusion. Like before." I wanted to believe it. I truly did, despite the fact I could still detect a hint of roses in the air. All of a sudden, I had the distinct feeling that the dress was tightening around my body, suffocating me, and I clawed at the fabric to get it away from my skin. "Get me out of this thing."

"Stop," Brigit scolded. "That's no way to treat a vintage dress. Let's go inside."

My clothes were where I'd left them on the floor. I stared at the familiar pile as Brigit's expert fingers quickly undid the fastenings. I darted into the changing room as soon as I felt the last hook open. Only the prospect of Brigit's extreme disapproval kept me from leaving the gown in a heap on the floor. I pinched the fabric between two fingers, holding it away from me while touching as little of it as possible. "Here. I don't think I want it anymore. Maybe we should try something a little more... modern."

CHAPTER EIGHTEEN

I woke as the sun was coming up on Saturday morning with a sweet melody lingering in my head and the sensation of my body swaying on a long-ago dance floor fresh in my mind. When I was fully conscious, I had no doubt my rational brain would kick in and go through all the ways this memory was impossible, even for a witch more powerful than I could ever hope to be. Time travel simply couldn't happen. It went against every natural and supernatural law. Magic was real, but this was a fantasy, not unlike the ones my imagination had been spinning throughout the night with a certain dashing bootlegger in the starring role.

No matter how it had felt, it simply could not have been real. The speakeasy, the dance floor, and even Bertie Chase—no, *especially* him, with his dark, brooding good looks and effortlessly flirtatious ways—

were figments of my imagination. In reality, no man could be so charming, turning my knees to jelly with a quick press of his lips to the top of my hand. It was the stuff of dreams. That didn't stop me from closing my eyes again to revisit the moment while gently humming a ragtime tune.

Seconds later, a furry lead weight landed in the middle of my stomach.

"Oof," I grunted. "Am I going to have to put you on a diet, Buster?"

I opened my eyes, and the cat stared into them as if to communicate he knew I was full of hot air. For one thing, I wasn't responsible for feeding the little brute, so I couldn't put him on a diet if I wanted to. He shouldn't have been able to figure this out, and frankly, I was getting a little tired of his know-it-all attitude. I had two daughters on the verge of teen years. I had my fill of sass without adding a demanding cat to the mix.

"Meow."

"Not now. It's my day off." I had yet to think of a way to weasel out of the Chesterton Academy celebration that night, but since it was a weekend, I had the whole day ahead of me with little to do. I knew I needed to enjoy it while I could. These lazy days would be coming to an end soon. I'd gotten accustomed to having Celia as our only guest, but she'd be checking out on Sunday, and as of early the next week, the

Shipton Inn would once more host a full house of guests.

"Meow."

I groaned. It was no use. The obnoxious fuzz ball wasn't about to let me have my way. "What is it, huh? Did a mouse get the better of you?"

He hopped onto the floor, springboarding himself off my belly with all the enthusiasm, but none of the grace, of an Olympic diver. When he landed, he looked back at me through the fluff of his oversized tail. "Meow."

"You're a persistent little devil. If I get up to see, do you promise to leave me alone for the rest of the day?" I must have lost my mind if I was seriously bargaining with a cat.

I followed him into the hall, past the closed door of the bedroom where my children, free from the obligation of summer camp, would likely sleep until noon, and down the stairs to the second floor. The sound of typing came with the rapid-fire of a machine gun from the other side of Celia's bedroom door. It was awfully early to be up on a Saturday, but I guess I couldn't blame her. Buster strutted across the floor, stretched himself to full height, and began to bat her doorknob.

"Don't do that!" I hissed. "Leave our guest alone."

He didn't heed my words. Instead, the feline terror doubled his efforts, clearly to show me who was in charge. After something approaching seventeen-thousand attempts, he succeeded in turning the knob enough to send the door crashing inward.

"Meow." He disappeared into the room, and the typing ceased.

"I'm so sorry, Celia," I called out, but instead of a response, the door simply closed, and the typing resumed.

Befuddled, I headed downstairs.

"Did Celia come down for breakfast this morning?" I asked Aunt Izzy as I stacked fresh waffles and sausage on a plate, drowning everything in sight with luscious maple syrup.

"No. Poor thing must be heartbroken."

Since I hadn't yet filled in my mom or aunt about Celia's true situation, I simply said, "That must be it."

The clicking of the keyboard continued uninterrupted throughout the day. I could hear it as I slipped out of my lounge clothes and into the simple 1960s cocktail dress Brigit had chosen for me to wear to the Chesterton anniversary soiree. I continued to hear it as I tamed my frizzy curls with a flat iron and applied my lipstick. When the doorbell rang in the early evening to signal Dana's arrival—she'd insisted on picking me up, likely believing I wouldn't go if left to my own devices—there wasn't so much as a pause in Celia's typing.

Dana frowned as she stepped into the entryway, immediately aware of the click-clack coming from upstairs. "She's still at it?"

"All day," I confirmed, casting an anxious glance toward the darkened second floor landing. "I don't think she's come downstairs once, and Aunt Izzy even made bacon at lunch."

"That's hard to resist."

"If it weren't for the constant typing, I would've checked to make sure she was still alive." The instant I said it, a cold dread settled into the pit of my stomach. When you recently had one guest die, it wasn't the best idea to make light of the subject. "Do you think we should go check on her?"

"Maybe a quick hello," Dana said, already heading for the stairs.

It was so cold in the hallway outside her door I almost expected to see frost when I breathed. "Do you feel that?"

"I'm sensing something off," Dana replied, though she didn't seem impacted by the cold in the same way I was.

I tapped on the door. "Celia? It's Tallie. And Dana," I added, hoping that would encourage her to take a break.

The typing stopped, and I let out a breath—which did not freeze in front of my face, so that was good news, right? Only there was no answer from inside the room, not even when I tapped a second time.

"Celia?" The concern in Dana's tone was unmistakable.

"I'm opening the door," I called out, reaching for

the doorknob. But when I tried to turn it, the knob wouldn't budge, and it was like putting my bare hand on a block of ice. I pulled back in shock. "It's frozen!"

"Let me try." Dana grasped the knob and yanked it hard. The door swung open. Celia sat behind the chair, slumped over, and surrounded by a thick blue haze.

"Do you see that?" I asked as Dana charged into the room. "Is it fumes?"

"I don't see anything. But we need to get her out of this room. Now." Dana hunched down to wrap an arm around Celia's waist. "Help me get her up."

I did, but it wasn't easy. I'd have to work out more if lifting bewitched bodies was going to become a regular part of my routine.

We got her out of the room, and by the time we reached the stairs, Celia was capable of moving her legs.

"What are you doing?" She sounded groggy but didn't fight us off as we led her down the stairs and into the kitchen.

"I'll make some tea." It was really the only thing I could think of to help.

"No honey," Celia said.

"I remember," I assured her as I dug through the cabinet to find a box of the English Breakfast I knew she liked.

"Celia." Dana squatted in front of the woman. "Can you tell me what happened up there? I need you to explain what's going on."

"I should be writing." She started to get up. "My room."

"You can't go back there."

"I have to," she said as if in a trance. "Not much time left."

"Celia, listen." Dana took a firm hold of both the woman's shoulders. "I don't know how to tell you this, but I think your room is… I think there might be, well, a ghost."

I nearly dropped the teakettle on my foot. Not in a million years did I think Dana would let something like that slip out to a person who wasn't a witch. It was a reckless thing to do. Either Celia would think we were crazy, or the shock might be enough to kill her.

Instead of either of these expected reactions, Celia simply blinked. "Tell me something I don't know."

This time, I did drop the kettle. Luckily, not on my foot.

"What are you saying?" Dana asked, brushing hair off Celia's cheek. "Have you seen something?"

Like a thick blue, glowing haze? I wanted to ask but busied myself with finding a towel to sop up the spilled water from the floor.

"I haven't seen anything," Celia answered slowly, "but I know it's him."

"Who?" Dana prompted.

"It's Alex. I need him."

"I thought you said you two had a business

arrangement." Dana's hurt was plain to see beneath the accusation in her tone.

"I need him to finish the book."

"I don't understand," I said, not certain I'd heard her right. "Are you talking about the sequel to *Oceans of Glass*?"

Celia nodded. "Alex lied to his publisher, or else I'd really be in hot water. He told them the manuscript was finished, and after his death, I said we'd left it back in New York and that I'd send it as soon as I returned."

"But the book wasn't finished," I said.

"No. And if I don't finish it before I head back home tomorrow so I can deliver it to the publisher on Monday, I'm facing financial ruin." She was on the verge of crying, and I was pretty certain it was the first time I'd seen her this way since Alex Tate's death. "I don't have any savings. Alex took care of all my bills while I was in his employ, and I have a contract guaranteeing me a stake in this book. But if it doesn't get published, I'm out everything. An entire year wasted. How will I survive?"

"Are you saying Alex is somehow helping you write the rest of this book?" The prospect was so horrifying, I trembled as I asked. "How does that even work?"

"When I'm upstairs, it's almost like I can hear him. Not actually, but there's a strange sensation that comes over me, and I know what to write." Celia buried her face in her hands. "His story, my words."

"You can't keep letting it happen, though." Dana comforted Celia.

"What do you know about this, anyway?"

"Uh, I don't know how to tell you this other than to say it out right. I'm a witch."

Celia nodded, the word washing over her, given the way her eyes glassed over. "You're not talking about being Wiccan, are you?"

"It's a bit more involved," Dana admitted.

"You can do spells?"

"Yes."

"I wish we never came to this island," Celia muttered under her breath.

Hurt spread in Dana's eyes, but she kept it tucked in. It was hard to blame Celia for such a statement. Before she'd arrived, she probably thought witches and ghosts only existed in fiction.

"Do you know about ghosts?" Celia asked.

"Not a lot," Dana said. "But enough to know that communicating with him is draining you. It isn't safe."

"It's a risk I'm willing to take." Celia got to her feet. "I don't have a choice. I'm so close to being done."

"Celia, wait," I called out, but it was too late. She was already heading upstairs, and I knew there was nothing either Dana or I could say to make her change her mind.

"Do you think she'll be okay?" Dana asked, looking

half ready to bolt up the stairs after Celia but possessing enough self-control to stop herself.

"I hope so." I pressed my lips together, trying not to dwell on the terrifying cold I'd experienced upstairs or the way Alex Tate's spirit had surrounded Celia's workspace like a poisonous gas. "I really hope so."

CHAPTER NINETEEN

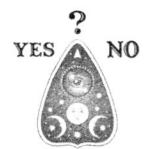

The evening was in full swing as Dana and I made our way into the gymnasium of Chesterton Academy. The sounds of laughter, clinking glasses, and music over a terrible sound system made me regret not hiding under the bed. After twenty-five years, the place still smelled the same, a mix of sweaty sneakers and raging hormones, despite the current occupants of the space mostly being decades past the prime of their youth.

"Do I look like I'm trying too hard?" I plucked at my dress, doubting my choices. Not just the overly fancy dress and another pair of high heels that made my ankles scream in protest, but all of them. Every single life choice that had led me to this moment was suspect.

"You look great. Now excuse me while I go track

down David. We have a mystery author to unmask, remember?" Dana left me before I could stop her.

Abandoned, I gravitated to the wall in the same way I probably had during my first school dance. There were hundreds of people filling the space—way more than I'd imagined—ranging from recent graduates to a few I wouldn't have been surprised to learn were part of the first graduating class. But it wasn't the crowded room in itself that caused every muscle in my body to seize.

Standing not five feet from me was Chad Kenworthy, the bully who'd made my high school years a living hell.

Chad sported the preppy good looks that were usually confined to the glossy pages of a Vineyard Vines catalog. He wore immaculately pressed khaki trousers and a button-down shirt that was definitely pink, but for some reason, people insisted on calling it Nantucket red.

"Hey there!" He flashed a distractingly white smile, oozing charm, but I wasn't fooled. "If it isn't Polly Parrot!"

He said it loudly enough that several heads swiveled to look in our direction. A couple hands went up to wave, and I could've sworn I heard someone from across the room yell, "Polly wanna cracker?" If I'd been worried the islanders had forgotten that incident, I could rest assured they had not.

"It's Tallie," I corrected through gritted teeth.

"You'll always be Polly to me." Chad gave a hearty laugh, the type that he probably thought made him irresistible to women but, in fact, made me want to punch him in the solar plexus. "Have you heard the good news?"

Your cholesterol is off the charts, and it's only a matter of time? I crossed my fingers, hoping this would be it.

Naturally, he didn't wait for an actual reply. He was more interested in hearing his own voice than anyone else's. "You're looking at the new owner of Chesterton Manor. I mean, technically my uncle, I guess, but it was mostly thanks to me. I'm in real estate, you know. It took some real finagling, which is utterly ridiculous, considering we're related to the old coot."

"Is that right? You're related to Roland Chesterton?" Personally, I'd put money on Chad being a direct descendant of a cockroach.

"Oh, yeah. You're looking at island royalty, right here. I mean, we haven't found that smoking gun in the DNA yet, but it's only a matter of time. Uncle Greg's sure of it. Anyway, we've had a whole slew of contractors working 24/7 on fixing up the place, and they're almost done. It's costing more than a 1939 Alfa Romeo Spider. I can tell you that."

"I assume that's… a lot?" I couldn't tell if everyone in Chad's social circle automatically knew how much this type of car—at least, I assumed it was a car—was worth, or if he was really that much of an insecure tool that he had to name-drop sports cars like they were A-list celebrities. I bet he didn't even own one.

"Is that a lot? That's funny!" Chad slapped a hand to his leg as he guffawed at the joke I hadn't been trying to make. "Polly, Polly, Polly. Man, you're funnier than I remember. Sexier, too. You know, we're planning an end-of-summer bash in August. You should come."

Me? Attend a party at Chad Kenworthy's house? I'd rather spend the evening giving Buster a bath. And had he called me sexy? Now I was the one in need of a bath. "I'm not sure—"

"It's going to be epic. I'm thinking a big Gatsby thing but with strippers serving the appetizers." He beamed with pride, and I could tell he thought this was a really classy take on the theme that was sure to impress me.

It was at this point I really wished I had stuck with those karate classes I'd taken when I was ten. I was picturing doing one of those Karate Kid moves, connecting my high-heeled shoe right in the middle of Chad's family jewels. The image made me giggle. Uncontrollably.

He seemed to think this was my way of flirting and took it as permission to let his eyes roam my body. "We really should catch up now that you're back, Pol."

"I'm pretty busy these days," I said, doing my best not to throw up on his boat shoes, which he wore without socks, naturally.

"So, you and me, drinks on the balcony later on? It's a full moon."

"No, it isn't. It's a waxing crescent." It was one thing to use a tired old line like that on non-magicals. In fact, I assumed he would be trying it on any female in the room under the age of seventy-five as the evening wore on. But don't ever challenge a witch when it comes to moon phases. Even a lapsed witch.

"There you are!" Appearing as if from nowhere, Nora came up beside me and slid an arm through mine. "You promised me a dance."

"I… what?" I nearly choked.

"If it isn't my cousin, Leslie." Chad's lip curled into a sneer. "I guess she's one of yours, then? That explains it."

"Her name's Nora, you idiot," I corrected. "Don't you know your own cousin?"

I may have started the evening feeling intimidated in the presence of my former tormentor, but the more I saw of the man, the more I realized I no longer cared what he thought, or what any of these people thought. He was a buffoon, and he would never be able to scare me again.

"That's my dear cousin's little nickname for me." Looking off in the distance, Nora lifted her hand and waved. "Hey, Chad. It looks like Linda's trying to find you. You remember Linda, your wife? Say hi to her for me."

Nora and I laughed as Chad stormed off toward a

blonde woman in an excessively tight red dress on the far side of the room.

"I see he hasn't changed one bit," I said.

"Not a chance. The man is in his forties and still thinks it's funny to call me Leslie because it sounds kind of like lesbian." Nora shook her head in obvious disgust. "Now that Uncle Greg's bought the Chesterton place, Chad's become doubly insufferable. I'm sure he's picturing himself as lord of the manor."

"What's this about your family being related to the Chestertons, anyway?" I asked. "I thought that whole line had died out decades ago."

"One of my uncle's crazier theories." Nora gave a chuckle that said she considered her uncle to be the family lunatic. "Roland had two daughters, Roberta and Florence. Neither married or had kids, but one of them—I can't remember which, and I only know the names because he can't stop talking about them at every family holiday—went on a nine-month trip very suddenly to visit a sick auntie somewhere back in 1929."

I raised an eyebrow, catching on. "Nine months, huh?"

"There were rumors back in the day, obviously," Nora said with a shrug, "though how he gets from there to we're the rightful heirs to the Chesterton legacy is the stuff of fever dreams and hallucinations."

An involuntary shudder passed over me at this comparison, making me think of Celia. Had I done the right thing leaving her at the inn without telling my mother or aunt what was going on? I feared I hadn't, but somehow, I hadn't been able to bring myself to explain what was happening. Not when my mother was in delicate health, and especially if it meant explaining the fact that I could suddenly see ghosts.

"What's wrong? Someone walking over your grave?" Nora's brow creased as I shivered again. Talk about an unfortunate choice of words. She didn't wait for an answer but grabbed hold of my hand. "Come on. I came over to get you to dance, remember?"

"I appreciate you running interference with your cousin," I said, digging my heels into the ground, "but you really don't want to dance with me. Not unless you want these spiky heels to accidentally end up in your feet."

"I'm willing to take my chances." She gave a slight tug, and my feet unstuck themselves from the ground without consulting the rest of me.

"Seriously, Nora," I argued, powerless to resist any more than that. "I'm not much of a dancer."

Where had I said that before? Before I could place it, I was on the dance floor, and Nora was wrapping her arms around me, pulling me into position with a gentle but sure confidence. The music, which was an eclectic mix from all the decades the school had been open, shifted to something jazzy.

"All you have to do is follow. Do what I do," Nora

said. "And look pretty, of course. But you're a natural at that."

"What did you say?" My breath caught as Nora whirled me in a circle, my mind racing as the memory clicked. Bertie Chase had said those exact words to me. He'd had the same dark hair, too, and the strong jaw and aquiline nose. The same hands, as surprisingly soft for a doctor as they had been for a gangster.

A woman's hands. I hadn't realized it then, but now it was crystal clear. Bertie Chase, the notorious bootlegger of Goode Harbor Island, was a woman disguised as a man.

The spinning came to an abrupt stop, and anger flashed in Nora's eyes as she let go of my hand and waist. "Geez, Tallie. It was... I don't understand you. Every time I think we're on the same page, I discover you're reading a completely different book."

"No, Nora, I..." I wanted to explain what was actually happening, but how could I? Instead, all I could do was gape as Nora left me alone in the middle of the dance floor.

"There you are!" Dana pulled me to the side as my brain struggled to process what had happened.

With my heart in my throat, I watched Nora leave the gymnasium, her head down. "I need to—"

"You need to come with me, is what you need to do. Have you forgotten we came here with a purpose?" Not noticing my state, Dana barreled on. "David's located Mr. Kimball, the teacher who headed up the lit mag until he retired a few years ago. You ready for some good-old fashioned sleuthing?"

Honestly? I was not. All I wanted was to chase after Nora and try to explain, but it was impossible. There was no explanation. We were us, not some people who only looked like us almost a hundred years ago.

Suddenly, solving a murder mystery and exorcising a ghost from my family home seemed easier by comparison.

"Okay, let's do this," I said, trying to muster as much energy and enthusiasm as I could. "Since the student we're trying to identify graduated around twenty years ago, this teacher, hopefully, will remember him."

We walked along the edge of the gym to where David stood with a man of maybe seventy-years-old, wisps of gray hair framing a balding head and thick glasses perched on his nose. I vaguely recollected Mr. Kimball as middle-aged, though he seemed impossibly old now. To be honest, so did almost everyone in the gym tonight, with the exception of a handful of recent graduates, who looked like children. Had any of us ever been as young as they were?

"Dana and Tallie," David said, "this is Ron Kimball, the founder of the Chesterton Academy literary magazine, and my mentor."

It was good to see that David had recovered from his brief incarceration and was back to his annoying self. I wondered how long it would be until he started pestering his former teacher to tell him what a great student he'd been.

"Mr. Kimball," Dana said, sticking out her hand to accept the one the man had offered. "Thank you so much for talking with us."

"Of course, Dana, but you must call me Ron." After shaking Dana's hand, he offered his to me. "And Tallie, wasn't it? I believe I had both of you in my English class your senior year."

"Yes, Mr. Kimball, you're right." I had no idea how he remembered that because I hadn't until he said it. Regardless, it was a good sign that his memory was still very much intact. We were counting on it.

"It's Ron, remember?"

"I just can't do it," I said with a laugh. "You know we have my teacher's aide from kindergarten working for us at the inn, and I still can't call her Alice? She'll always be Mrs. Crenshaw to me."

"The reason my friends wanted to talk to you, Ron," David emphasized the man's first name, more than happy to claim equal footing with his one-time mentor, "is that they're looking for a former student who may have passed through one of your classes or the lit mag around twenty years ago."

"And he's not here this evening?" the teacher asked, stroking his chin.

"Unfortunately, I'm afraid he's deceased," Dana said.

Mr. Kimball's face fell. "Oh, dear. Of course, if

you're a teacher as long as I was, it's not unheard of to lose a student, but what a tragedy. What was his name?"

"That's the thing. We don't exactly know," I admitted. I couldn't imagine what he thought of that, but judging by the look on his face, the teacher was beyond puzzled.

"We're trying to identify the author of… a piece of writing in the library archives," Dana said, her confidence rallying after a moment of hesitation midway through.

"Do you have it here? If I read it, I'm sure it might spark something." Mr. Kimball waited expectantly, and of course, it would have made sense for us to have the writing with us, if only that hadn't been a last-minute improvisation.

"I'm afraid I didn't bring it with me," Dana said, and I could almost hear the gears in her mind turning to get ahead of her earlier lie. "His writing style was very distinctive, though. Lyrical, wouldn't you say, David?"

"Er, I, uh, don't know if I'd say lyrical, exactly." It was amazing to watch David trip over his own jealousy like this. Even with both Alex Tate and the true author dead, he was turning positively green with it. "It had dragons in it."

No doubt he'd meant this as a criticism, but the instant he said the word dragon, Mr. Kimball's eyes sparked.

"Dragons, you say? You know, I am getting a memory." The teacher stroked his chin again, more vigorously this time, as if doing so would help the details fall into place. "He wasn't from any of the island families. I'm not certain of the situation, but he moved here from the mainland and was here less than a year. His stories were fantastic, though. I remember that. I always thought he'd end up in Hollywood."

"What was his name?" Dana's face glowed with possibility, although I couldn't help but notice that ever since his mentor had started to wax rhapsodic over some other student, David looked like he was ready to spit nails.

"It's..." Mr. Kimball tapped the side of his head in frustration, like he was trying to knock something loose. "I can see him so clearly, but I can't remember his name."

"Could you describe him?" I asked, trying not to lose hope quite yet.

"I might be able to do one better," Mr. Kimball said. "Follow me."

He led us to the hallway outside the gym where glass trophy cases lined the walls. Instead of my eyes being met with shiny awards, the cases were covered in thousands of photographs that seemed to be of students from every era of the school's long history.

"Here we are," Mr. Kimball announced. "They're not quite in chronological order, but from what I saw earlier, the decorating committee did a good job of grouping them by decade. How long ago was it, again?"

"About twenty years," I offered.

"Twenty years." The man shook his head slowly as he contemplated my answer. "Time really does fly. You're young now, but someday, you'll see what it's like to get old."

I nearly argued that I was far from young, but it struck me that youth is relative. To a man in his seventies, forty-three was the prime of life. As I followed Mr. Kimball down the hallway, I knew it would do me good to take this lesson to heart if I could.

"Here we go." Mr. Kimball stopped in front of a section of photographs, scanning them quickly with a finger raised in the air. All at once he jabbed it at one picture in particular. "Ah-ha! You were right. The young man you're looking for was part of the lit mag while he was at Chesterton. Here he is with some of the other members as they were putting together an issue to go to press."

"I'm sure we checked the official club photos in the yearbook," I said, squinting to make out the young man's face, which wasn't very memorable except for a crooked nose, like it had been broken and not set properly at one point. "I don't remember seeing him."

"I don't either," Dana agreed. "But now that we know who we're looking for, we can give it another try. Maybe there's a photo in the yearbook, or even the local paper from back then, that would have his name listed with it."

"Joel Franklin," Mr. Kimball announced with a satisfied grin. "Now that I see his face, the name came to me. I remember telling myself, Ron, you need to remember that name. Joel Franklin. Out of all your students, he's going to go on to do great things."

Standing behind his former mentor, a vein bulged in David's neck with such ferocity I feared it might burst. I almost felt sorry for him, finding out after all these years he wasn't his teacher's favorite after all.

After thanking Mr. Kimball for his help, Dana and I ducked out of the party as quickly as we could.

"That night Alexander was sleepwalking, or whatever that was," I said as we were walking toward Dana's car, "I thought he was talking to someone. It sounded like Joe or George to me, but it wasn't. It was Joel."

"Joel Franklin," Dana said as she turned the key in the ignition. "Do you know what this means?"

I nodded. "It means we can finally help Alexander Tate's spirit atone for his crime and cross into the light."

CHAPTER TWENTY

"Has anyone seen Celia?" Aunt Izzy asked as she set a fresh batch of waffles on the sideboard.

Though we only had one guest, it was the final day of her stay, so my mom and aunt had gone out of their way to make a full Sunday brunch in her honor. She'd still been working when I got home the night before, but the typing had finally stopped a little after one in the morning. I was certain of this fact because I'd still been wide awake, tossing and turning in my bed over the falling out I'd had with Nora at the anniversary celebration.

"Tallie, have you seen Celia?" This time it was my mom doing the asking, so I knew what that meant.

"Translation: you want me to go upstairs and check on our guest." With a sigh, I got up from my chair before I was able to have my first syrupy bite.

"What a lovely idea. Thanks so much for offering." Aunt Izzy and Mom exchanged cunning smiles.

I paused between my daughters, putting a hand on the top of each of their chairs. "Just so you know, I'm learning from the best. When I get old, you better watch out."

"We're not scared of you." Sabrina swiped a piece of bacon from my plate as if wanting to prove her point.

Tabitha circled her arms around her own plate to form a protective shield. "Mine."

"You're going to be the death of me, child." I grabbed a retaliatory bacon slice from Sabrina's plate to remind her two could play at that game.

Sabrina shrugged. "I hope you have your affairs in order."

Sometimes, my younger daughter's dark sense of humor scares the crap out of me, but that was something to deal with another day. Right now, I had a guest to check on. I lumbered up the stairs, flashing back to how I used to take them two at a time full tilt, without so much as a twinge in any joint. I wished I could say the stairs had gotten steeper in my absence, but I was pretty sure the house wasn't to blame.

"Celia." I rapped on her door. "It's time for breakfast. Do you need some help getting your luggage downstairs?"

There was no reply, not so much as a grunt or a cough. Surely, she was up by now. It was nearly eleven.

Checkout was at noon. If she was still asleep, she was likely to miss her ferry.

I knocked again, much louder, but still nothing.

"I'm coming in," I called out at the top of my lungs, turning the knob slowly to give her time to put on a robe if need be. "I hope you're decent in there."

The drapes were closed, and the room was nearly dark despite the bright sun outside. I blinked, letting my eyes adjust. There wasn't a peep from our guest. At this point, my muscles tensed as if preparing either to fight or flee. When I could finally see clearly enough to make out more than the bare outlines of the room, my heart clenched.

Celia was not in bed as I had assumed. She was at the desk, slumped, with her head on the hard wood.

"Celia?" I dashed across the room, taking hold of her shoulder and giving it a shake.

I don't quite remember what I did next, but I'm pretty sure I screamed my head off like the cool cucumber I am, because the next thing I knew, Aunt Izzy had joined me in the room while Mom stood in the hallway, blocking the kids from entering the room.

"Is she dead?" asked Sabrina, the ghoul, craning her neck to see as much as she could.

"She can't be dead. I'm tired of dead bodies," I sobbed, further establishing myself as one of the trustworthy adults in the house.

My aunt, on the other hand, took the sensible approach of checking the woman's pulse before losing her damn mind. "She's not dead, but her pulse is weak. And there's something..." Aunt Izzy breathed in deeply, like a bloodhound tracking a scent. She gave me a pointed look. "Is there any reason to think there's something other than exhaustion and too much work that could be causing this?"

"I'm not sure what you mean." My eyes darted to my daughters, who were still on the other side of the door and hanging on every word. I knew exactly what Aunt Izzy meant, but this wasn't a discussion I wanted to have right here.

"Let's try this another way. Do you think we will have more success reviving her by calling Dr. Kenworthy, or going downstairs and making a pot of tea?" The sternness in my aunt's tone made me tremble with a mix of fear and guilt.

"Tea," I replied in a small voice, knowing that was code for one of my aunt's magical healing brews. "You should make her some tea."

"As soon as we get her lying down," my aunt replied, leaping into action with the skill of a trained nurse. "Diana, come help me move Celia to the bed."

"I can help with that," I argued, but before I could act or even start to argue they'd both throw their backs out or worse, the task was done. I constantly forgot I lived with two witches who, unlike me, had total control of their magic and could use it at will.

"Tabitha and Sabrina, stay here and help Grammy,"

Aunt Izzy ordered like an officer addressing the troops. "Tallie, you come with me."

Suddenly, my aunt seemed less like an officer and more like an executioner. I'd been keeping information from her, and I was going to pay for it soon enough.

Tabitha did as she was told, but as I trudged across the room, Sabrina demanded, "Is she dead? Can I see the corpse?"

"For the last time, she's not dead." I winced at how snappish I sounded. I hadn't meant it to be, but something about that daughter of mine brought out the worst in me.

Corpse? Really?

In the kitchen, I let out an anguished sigh. "Should I be concerned?"

"About Celia? No. A little of my picker-upper brew will bring some life back to her cheeks, no matter what trouble she's gotten herself into."

"I was talking about Sabrina. She has this macabre side that worries me." I couldn't recall her acting this way when her dad was around, but I didn't want to say that part. It made me feel like I'd failed.

"My guess is that's why she does it."

"To worry me?"

"I know she's younger than Tabitha, but she's rapidly approaching the terrible teen years. And unlike her older sister, I think she plans to give you a real run for your money. You'll probably have white hair before Yule." My aunt chuckled, much more tickled by this prospect than I was. "We can be twins!"

My hand flew to my head. "Don't say that. I can't afford to go to a salon and have it dyed until I get a job."

"You have a job. You work here." My aunt fixed me with a stare so sharp it could cut glass. "Now, what's really going on with that poor woman upstairs?"

"It's her fiancé, Alex. Except he wasn't really her fiancé." As my aunt gathered the herbs she needed to make Celia's tea, I filled her in on the parts of the story she hadn't heard, explaining how Celia needed to finish the book before her stay was over or risk losing her livelihood. "But that's not the only reason it was a race against time. She had to finish before she left because she needs help. From Alex Tate's ghost."

"Are you telling me the inn's haunted by the ghost of that dead author?" Considering the shocking nature of this revelation, my aunt was taking it surprisingly well. That's one of the benefits of living in a household of witches. In fact, I think she would've been more upset to discover we had an infestation of mice in the pantry. At least Buster was good for something.

"His spirit has been able to communicate with her. Telepathically, it seems." I chose my words with caution, not wanting to reveal my own ability to see our ghost. Sensing a presence was one thing, but it was a rare witch who could see spirits, especially as clearly as I could. Most members of the magical community considered this ability to be one step away from Black Magic.

"No wonder she's so drained." After considering the contents of the pantry for a moment, she reached for a jar of honey. "A bit of this should do the trick."

"Celia doesn't like anything sweet in her tea."

"This isn't about what she likes. It's about what she needs." Aunt Izzy unscrewed the lid to the honey jar, and her nose scrunched. "I think this batch has gone bad."

"Hand me that." I grabbed the nearly empty jar, sniffed, and then tossed it into the trash. "I'll add it to the shopping list. Do you have anything else that will work?"

"Bee pollen should do in a pinch." My aunt took a small jar from the cupboard and added a sprinkling of the contents to the rest of the ingredients in the pot. "Now for the hot water."

When the tea had finished steeping, I brought it up to the room, and Mom helped me prop up Celia.

"Do you think you can handle it from here?" she asked.

I nodded. "I've had enough practice force-feeding Sabrina when she was a toddler."

"I had to do that with you."

Just what I needed, a reminder that my youngest and I shared the same stubborn streak.

Mom went downstairs along with my daughters, leaving me to sit alone in a chair beside the bed.

"Celia? I have tea that'll return some of your strength. You need to drink up."

There was a murmur, but Celia's mouth remained stubbornly closed.

"Come on, now." I placed my left hand on Celia's forehead to brush the hair off her forehead. The skin was clammy to the touch. Something needed to change, and soon, if we didn't want her shedding her mortal coil and joining Alexander Tate in the spirit world.

The second after I thought this, the ring on my left hand, the one I'd found in the attic and almost forgotten I was wearing because I was so in the habit, began to glow a burning red. I gasped. This was no trick of sunlight bouncing off the metal. The light was nearly blinding me, but I couldn't pull my hand away from Celia. I felt as if it'd been superglued in place.

I wanted to scream, but I couldn't. All the energy in my body flowed out of me, into Celia, whose cheeks began to pink with life. When her eyes popped open, the flash from the ring went out. My head and back were drenched, and my left hand trembled so badly I had to hold it with my right to keep it steady. What the hell had happened?

"Hi." Celia blinked, seeming a bit confused, but her voice sounded more chipper than a chipmunk drinking a triple espresso. As for me, I hadn't felt this exhausted since Sabrina was a newborn, and I was averaging forty-five minutes of sleep between feedings.

"Are you okay?" A quick scan of her forehead didn't turn up any signs of scorch marks, despite the fact the ring had been the color of molten lava.

Celia smiled. "Never better."

I studied the color in her cheeks, the brightness of her eyes, and the subtle sheen of her hair. She'd certainly never looked better, at least not in the time she'd been on the island.

Was that because of me? Or was it something to do with the ring? I honestly didn't know, and I didn't want to think about it.

"You should have some of Aunt Izzy's tea," I urged instead. "She made it especially for you."

"I'd love some. Are there any waffles?" After guzzling most of a mug like she'd never had liquid before, she inhaled deeply, and her eyes lit up like stars. "Do I smell bacon?"

I couldn't help but laugh. "I'm pretty sure I can rustle some up."

"I should get packed." She practically sprang out of bed like a cat, but I eased her back down just as quickly.

"I think you should stay another night to be safe. I'd feel better about you traveling if Dr. Kenworthy could give you a clean bill of health tomorrow when the clinic opens."

"Do you really think that's necessary? I haven't felt this good in years." There was so much enthusiasm in Celia's tone she was a step away from bursting into song. "The book's done, and I feel like this weight has been lifted."

I shook my head. "I insist. I'll give Dana a call and tell her you won't need that ride to the ferry until tomorrow."

At the mention of Dana's name, Celia's determination disappeared. She had a soft smile, one that had nothing to do with me. "Okay."

I'd expected a battle, but the woman gazing at me seemed almost childlike, ready to explore all the good things the world had to offer. She seemed completely reborn.

I twisted the ring around my finger with a growing sense of uneasiness. If all that renewing energy had come from me, what would the consequences be? Was I going to look in the mirror and see an old crone? I wished I could turn to Mom or my aunt for an answer, but I feared this was yet another secret I would be taking with me to my grave.

"Bye, Mom!" Tabitha waved, and she and Sabrina climbed into Mira's car right after breakfast Monday morning. There was no camp at the library that day, and Ruby and Marcus were already inside the vehicle waiting to go on the picnic Mrs. Crenshaw had planned for the four of them.

"Have fun, and behave yourselves!" I called out as I waved them off.

"You don't actually expect Sabrina to behave, do you?" Dana joked, though her smile didn't quite reach her eyes. I couldn't blame her. She'd gotten one extra day with Celia, but assuming Nora signed off on her health—which I saw no reason she wouldn't—the woman would be leaving the island in a few hours. It was no secret Dana had developed some intense feelings for our guest, and it had to hurt to see her go.

Which was why it was better not to bother with all that romance stuff to begin with.

"Did you tell Celia what we found out at the anniversary celebration?" I asked.

"Tell me what?" Celia joined us on the porch, looking like she'd caught up on a year's worth of missed sleep in one night. She almost glowed.

Dana took a fortifying breath. "Tallie and I think we figured out who the true author of *Oceans of Glass* was. His name was Joel Franklin. A retired teacher remembered him."

"He was a brilliant young author with a fantastical imagination," I added. "Apparently, he only lived on the island for a short time."

"I did some digging," Dana said, which didn't surprise me. There was nothing my librarian friend enjoyed more than research. "I found his obituary, and it was exactly as we thought. He had no family and had bounced around from home to home until he aged out of the system."

"What a sad legacy," I said.

"That's not his only legacy," Celia said. "He also wrote a bestselling book, don't forget."

"An award-winning book, too," Dana added. "Maybe I shouldn't say that, as the literary society hasn't announced it, but had we gotten that far, *Oceans of Glass* would have been named the winner of the Chesterton Prize."

Celia lifted her chin with determination. "When that award is finally given, I want everyone to know Joel Franklin is the one who earned it."

"But, what about *your* book?" Dana asked. "You said you'd finished it, but if the world finds out Alexander Tate wasn't the author of the original, no one will want the sequel. You need the money to live on, and the Chesterton Prize is another ten-thousand dollars on top of that."

Celia shook her head. "Use the money to create a scholarship in Joel's name. I won't need it."

"Are you sure?" I asked. "We wouldn't think badly of you if you decided to keep this a secret."

"No, but I would. Besides, with Alex's help, I've written a book that is sure to make me a fortune, or at least enough to live comfortably for quite some time. It's not a sequel," she added in response to the bewilderment on both our faces. "These past few days when I was writing nonstop, I didn't even know what I was doing. It was only when I was done that I realized it. Through whatever connection he'd established, Alex dictated a full confession before he moved on."

"You're certain he moved on?" I asked, though I had to admit I hadn't sensed Alex's presence since Celia had woken from her ordeal.

"I mean, it's not like he said goodbye, exactly, but he must have moved on when I was…" Celia's face scrunched as she sought the right word. "Indisposed. When I read back over what he'd inspired me to write, I could feel his relief at getting the truth out, but I couldn't actually feel him, anymore, if that makes sense. I will say, with my flair for words, it's a scintillating read."

"Right up to the author's mysterious death." I hesitated but couldn't help asking, "Did Alex tell you how he died?"

"He didn't," Celia said sadly. "But I could feel the anguish he felt, and given the nature of what he had me write, I do wonder if he might have jumped into the water on his own. In the end, the guilt was overwhelming to him."

"It would make sense, considering what the spirit board—" I stopped suddenly as I realized we'd never told Celia about that.

It was too late. Celia had trained a stare on Dana that was more powerful than a can opener and a crowbar combined. It only took a second for Dana to confess.

"We used a spirit board, or what you might call a Ouija board, to see if we could find out why Alex's ghost was haunting the inn."

"It said his death wasn't an accident," I added, unwilling for Dana to have to confess alone. "And it gave us the letters A and L before the connection was lost."

"It was spelling his name." A tear slid down Celia's cheek. "He wasn't an easy person to get along with, that was for sure, but he deserved better than that."

"What's going on? How are you feeling?" Nora, who had managed to ride her motorcycle all the way up the driveway without us noticing, climbed up the porch steps. She took Celia's wrist to check her pulse. "Dana told me how tired you've been. Any other symptoms of depression I should know about?"

"You mean the tears?" Celia laughed softly as she brushed her cheek with her free hand. "I'm doing well. I promise. I'm just sad Alex felt he had no option but to end his own life."

Nora's eyes widened in surprise. "Who told you that?"

"I... assumed, I guess," Celia stumbled, obviously realizing that telling a doctor you've been communicating with ghosts was not a great way to convince them you're in good health and fit to travel.

"In that case, I have some news, if you're strong enough to hear it." Nora waited for Celia to nod. "I got the preliminary autopsy report from the medical examiner on the mainland this morning. There was no water in his lungs, no evidence of drowning at all."

"Then, how did he die?" Celia choked.

"He was dead before he fell into the water. Most likely he suffered a heart attack while walking along the shore path by the cove, and his body tumbled over the edge into the water."

"He didn't kill himself?" Celia's voice was barely above a whisper.

"It doesn't seem so," Nora said gently, pausing to let the woman absorb the news before asking, "Had he been experiencing any symptoms of heart trouble leading up to his death? Like dizziness, vertigo, excessive sweating, or general weakness?"

"Yes." Celia's breath hitched. "Some stomach issues, too. I chalked it up to the stress he was under to meet his editing deadline. I should have done something."

"This isn't on you at all," Nora stated emphatically. "A lot of people ignore these symptoms because they are under stress and don't stop to think it might be something more serious."

"Will you share the final autopsy report?" Celia asked. "It doesn't have to be with me. I know Alex and I weren't married, so I'm not his next of kin, but his publisher will want all the details. Is it okay if I fill them in when I get back to New York?"

"Speaking of—" Dana reached for Celia's bag. "We better go, or you'll miss the ferry."

Celia turned to me. "I can't thank you and your family enough."

"Please. It was a pleasure having you, and we're so sorry... for everything."

Once Dana and Celia had gone, I was left standing next to Nora. With everything that had happened, it was only in the awkward silence that descended on us that I recalled how things had been left between us on the dance floor Saturday night. "Look, Nora, I—"

"I've gotta go, Tallie. We're short staffed at the clinic, and there's some big shot law enforcement type coming from the mainland to ask a bunch of questions about the local handling of all this Alex Tate stuff."

"Okay." I swallowed as Nora hopped on her bike and fired up the engine, my chest hollow, as if my heart had given up and moved on to greener pastures. Like Antarctica, probably.

I had no idea what I would've said if she'd let me have a chance to finish talking. What was there to say? I was just out of a bad marriage, not even legally divorced yet, not to mention a single mom with two kids and no career prospects aside from helping run a tiny inn. On top of all of that was the simple fact I'd never given even one thought all my life to having romantic feelings for a woman.

At least, not until I'd met Nora. Which, really, who could blame me? If there was going to be one woman on the planet who could give me second thoughts about sticking with my hetero lifestyle, why wouldn't it be a tall, dark-haired beauty who wore leather like a rock star, but also saved lives because she was a friggin' doctor. And charming, and funny, too. And the way she looked at me, like I was the most interesting person in the room, the only woman in the world…

Well, I mean, damn.

Only, of course it was all bullshit. I wasn't the only woman, because there was Bonnie. No matter how perfect I might want to think Nora was, she had a girlfriend. And if she was flirting with me while dating the sheriff—a woman who could lock me up and throw away the key with no questions asked, to top it all off—well, that meant good ol' Dr. Kenworthy wasn't such a *worthy* catch after all. Right?

I would keep telling myself all of this on an endless loop until I believed it.

With nothing better to do, and in need of the kind of distraction some honest manual labor could provide, I went inside and proceeded up the stairs to Celia's old room. A houseful of guests was expected the following afternoon, which meant there were sheets to change and trash cans to empty to make everything shipshape.

The door to the bedroom was open, and a window must've been, too, because as I stepped closer, a gust of cold air smacked me full in the face, slamming the door at the same time. I jumped, startled at the loud noise in the empty house. I may have yelped, too, but with the girls on their picnic and my mom and Aunt

Izzy on the mainland to stock up on food for the new arrivals, I was the only one who could hear how embarrassing I'd sounded. Except possibly Buster, but it wasn't like he had any respect for me to lose.

"Must be a storm coming," I muttered, detouring to grab an extra blanket from the linen closet at the end of the hall. Someone once claimed the coldest winter they'd seen was a summer in San Francisco, but the same could be said of coastal Maine. It was almost August, for heaven's sake.

Except, it wasn't a storm to blame for the cold and the wind. When I stepped into the bedroom, the culprit was staring me in the face. Literally. In the middle of the room, almost (but not quite) in the flesh, was Alexander Tate.

CHAPTER TWENTY-ONE

"Mira!" I barreled into the tearoom, waving frantically, before it occurred to me that the shop was open to the public, and a crazy red-headed witch swooping in for an attack probably wasn't the best look for business. Fortunately, mid-morning on a Monday wasn't exactly prime time for afternoon tea, and the place was empty.

Mira smoothed the last wrinkles from a floral cloth she'd been spreading over a table before my dramatic entrance momentarily derailed her efforts. "What's going on?"

"Alexander Tate is haunting the inn."

She tilted her head to one side, her oversized gold hoop earring coming to rest on her shoulder. "I thought we already established that a few weeks ago."

"No, but he's back. Or still there. I'm not sure which." I pressed my hands to my temples, hoping to slow my brain enough for my mouth to keep up. "Celia finished the book, and Nora said he didn't drown after all, and—"

"You thought he'd crossed over?" Mira guessed in an adorable attempt at understanding my meaning.

"Yes. That." I pulled in several deep breaths, suddenly gasping at the effort it had taken to get my point across. "There's something we're missing, only I'm not certain what. He's confessed his misdeeds in a tell-all book. We figured out the identity of the author he stole from. Celia's going to arrange for the young man to get all the credit he deserved. And according to the authorities, Tate died of natural causes."

"The autopsy results are in? I hadn't heard. What do they think happened?"

"Simple, really. He probably went for a walk along the water to cool his head, and he had a heart attack. He tumbled into the water, but he was no longer breathing when he went in." I tried to recall anything I'd left out. "Celia confirmed some symptoms leading up to his death that Nora said were consistent with early warning signs."

"What were the symptoms?" Mira asked. I rattled off the list, and she nodded at each one, nothing seeming to catch her by surprise. "What about that sleepwalking incident you told us about?"

"It was the weirdest thing." As I tried to think back to the first days of his visit, it felt like years had passed instead of weeks. "I remember he was freezing cold all the time, even though it was so hot outside. Then again, I was always cold in that room, too."

"Yeah, after it was haunted," Mira pointed out, straightening the silverware of the place setting nearest her as she spoke. "By him. He wouldn't have been experiencing that, unless you have another ghost hanging around the inn."

"Not that I'm aware of," I said, my laugh a little forced. That was the last thing I needed to worry about at a time like this. "That night with the sleepwalking, it was like he was hallucinating."

"Interesting." A shadow crossed Mira's face as a crease formed in her brow. "It's almost… but, no. I don't see how that would be possible."

My pulse revving, I leaned forward. "If you have a theory, I'm all ears," I prodded. "Nothing's crazier than having a dead guy living in your house."

"Well, the symptoms you described remind me of what can happen if you take too much of a certain folk remedy." Mira paused to fuss with the precise placement of a teacup, leaving me on pins and needles for more details for so long I thought I might pop. "It's not something you find around here, though. I'm sure it's a coincidence."

"The authorities are convinced he died of natural causes. Meanwhile, the spirit board said that wasn't the case, and it's cold enough to store ice cream in my guest room," I reminded her, impatience building, though not with her. All I wanted was to figure out what was going on and put things right. "I'm willing to consider the impossible."

"Fine. For the sake of argument, certain pollens contain a highly poisonous substance called grayanotoxin. In small doses, it's a traditional heart remedy and aphrodisiac. Larger quantities can lead to euphoria and psychedelic hallucinations, but too much can be dangerous and even fatal."

"Pollen?" Despite the serious subject matter, I couldn't help but laugh. "Are you suggesting Alex Tate went around licking flowers to get high?"

Mira laughed, too, shaking her head. "You don't lick flowers. You take it in the form of honey."

"Honey?" I was dead serious now, and a ball of dread was forming in my belly. The pistons in my mind were chugging like a locomotive, and I was pretty sure I didn't want to know where this train was headed.

"They call it mad honey, but it's very rare, and most of what you find online is fake. It takes a special kind of bee to make it, and a variety of flower that only grows in the highest elevations of Nepal."

Sweat beaded on the back of my neck. "Rhododendron."

Mira gave me an unsettled look, her head tilting. "That's right. *Rhododendron simsii*, specifically. But as I said, you can't grow it here." The uncertainty in her tone suggested otherwise and sent my spirits plummeting as that mental train of mine pulled into the station.

"Not unless you're a witch with a green thumb," I said, the ball of dread now doubled in size. It couldn't be. Except, it had to be. "Mrs. Crenshaw has it in her garden. She even warned me not to put the flowers in the bouquet I made for Dana. She brought a big jar of honey to the inn, and Alex had a lot of it. Aunt Izzy took one sniff of it yesterday and swore it had gone bad."

"Honey doesn't go bad. Do you still have it?"

"We threw it away." I pressed my fingers to my lips, my head spinning. "Poor Mrs. Crenshaw. She must not have realized. We have to tell her right away, before anyone else gets sick."

"That must be why Alex's ghost is still here," Mira agreed, already grabbing her purse and keys, pausing to turn the open sign in the front window to closed. "He wants to stop another accident. Come on. I'll drive."

When we arrived at the cottage by the sea, there was no sign of anyone in the garden. I frowned at the silence that engulfed the place. "Aren't the kids supposed to be here having a picnic?"

Mira wandered toward the back of the house. "Ruby? Marcus?"

"Mrs. Crenshaw?" I called out. "Girls?"

"Do you think they're inside?" Mira asked, worry pinching the corners of her eyes. When Mira knocked on the front door, it swung open. She put one foot gingerly inside the entryway, followed by the other, and I did the same.

"Hello?" I called out as I walked deeper into the house, willing my voice not to shake. Whatever was going on, surely everyone was fine. I just wished I knew where they all had gone.

"No one's here," Mira said. "I'm going to check Marcus's phone location."

"I'll look upstairs, just in case." I started up the staircase, which was lined floor to ceiling with dozens of framed photos containing Mrs. Crenshaw and what seemed like hundreds of different children. Despite my worry, I couldn't help smiling a little at the thought of all the lives she'd touched over the years.

"Found them." To my relief, Mira laughed. "They're at Prescott's Drug Store, no doubt getting ice cream at the soda fountain. Let's go meet up with them there."

I was halfway up the stairs when she said this, and as I turned to go back down, my eye was drawn to a familiar face in one of the photos on the wall. I had to grab the banister to keep myself from tumbling all the way down. "Oh my God. It's him."

"Tallie? Are you okay? You've gone completely white."

I couldn't speak, pointing to the photo, gasping for air.

"What? Use your words, Tallie." I would have laughed at this common phrase spouted by mothers everywhere had I not understood what, or who, I was staring at.

"It's Joel Franklin." In a snapshot on the wall, the young man Alexander Tate had stolen his masterpiece from stood beside a much younger Alice Crenshaw, proudly wearing his graduation cap and gown. The final piece fell into place. "A-L. The spirit board wasn't spelling Alex. It was spelling Alice. Alice Crenshaw was Joel Franklin's foster mother."

Mira's expression shifted to the same look of horror I was sure I must've worn. "It's not a coincidence, is it?"

"This is why his ghost hasn't moved on yet," I said as I slowly but steadily made my way down the stairs. "His killer is still on the loose. And she has our kids."

"Are your mom and aunt at home?" Mira demanded as her foot slammed on the gas pedal. "We're going to need every able-bodied witch we can find."

I shook my head, not sure whether to be more scared of the fact my daughters were being babysat by a coldblooded killer, or that the way Mira was taking the curves on the shore road, we were likely to end up in the sea before we reached downtown. "They went to the mainland today to restock all the household supplies."

"I've already called Dana and Brigit to meet us at Prescott's soda fountain. Alice will try to run if she knows we're onto her, but at least we'll have four of us so we can call the corners and cast a circle to contain her."

"She's a powerful witch," I agreed, remembering how the woman had carried luggage up a flight of stairs like it was a feather pillow. "Mira, I don't think I'm strong enough to do this. I'm out of practice, and my powers are untested. What if I let everyone down?"

"You won't. You're a mom. You can handle this." Mira didn't have time to continue her pep talk because an incoming call popped up on her dashboard display. For a moment, I marveled that not all that long ago, I too had been a proper suburban mom leasing a shiny SUV. Now, the front bumper on my used station wagon was attached with a bungee cord.

"Dana?" Mira answered the call with an urgency that bordered on frantic. "Have you found them?"

"The kids are at the soda fountain, but she's on the move. She's on foot now, headed toward the moped rental place next to the ferry terminal." With that, Dana hung up, and the dial tone echoed through the speakers.

"I think I should call Nora." I reached for my phone, unable to explain even to myself the desperate need I had to hear the doctor's voice telling me everything would work out. It was insanity, but this was hardly the time to think about it. "She said there's some high-ranking law enforcement type in town to investigate the way the sheriff's department handled the Alex Tate investigation. I think we need to get them involved."

We were in downtown now, the brightly colored flags at Rick's Mopeds and More coming into sight. Mira didn't so much as park her car as abandon it. Not having the time for a conversation, I sent the briefest text possible to Nora, asking for help.

"There's Dana," Mira said, pointing to the far end of a stretch of asphalt filled with mopeds and bicycles for rent. "And Brigit is right over there."

"I see Alice!" Now that I knew she was a murderer, I no longer felt the need to show deference by using her last name.

The old witch noticed me right away, and she must have seen in my expression I was on to her. I had never been the poker-face type. She made a break for it and tried to shimmy around the back of the rental office, but Brigit cut her off at the pass. Dana was on the other side. Without wasting time, Mira and I closed in to form a circle. As soon as we were in position, a surge of power hummed around us like a magical electric fence coming online.

"What a lovely surprise." Alice oozed calm, which I suspected was the result of more than a little magic of her own. She had to have felt what was happening, even if she wasn't ready to accept that she was trapped.

"We know what you did to Alex Tate with the honey," I said, seeing no reason for beating around the bush. "How could you?"

"I don't have the foggiest idea what you're talking about," the old witch bluffed. "If this is about the children, they're perfectly fine at the soda fountain. I was about to call you, in fact. My sister's in the emergency room on the mainland. I can't miss this ferry."

"You don't have a sister," Dana challenged. "My mother is the keeper of the archives. Do you think I don't know the personal histories of every witch on this island?"

Her bluff called, Alice tried to bust out of the circle, but she couldn't. After struggling for a moment, she closed her eyes, letting out a sigh. "I didn't mean for it to go so far. I only wanted him to suffer. It wasn't supposed to happen like this."

"What *was* supposed to happen?" Mira demanded. "You're a well-educated witch. You know the risks of mad honey as well as I do."

"I wanted him to think he was dying," Alice confessed. "But not actually die. I put a little enchantment on it to give it an extra kick. I wanted him to be wracked with guilt over what he did to my boy. Poor Joel!"

"How did you know what Alex did?" I asked, trying not to feel sympathy for the woman who was crying out for her lost son. As a mother, I could understand the depths of her anguish, but that didn't condone killing a man.

"It was happenstance, really," the old witch said. "The first time I cleaned his room, I noticed the journals on his desk. They reminded me of the ones I used to buy my foster kids in bulk each school year. You remember, Tallie. I brought some over for the girls."

"Please stick to the topic at hand, Mrs. Crenshaw," I pleaded, trying to remain strong. The exertion of painting the magic circle was draining my energy as well as my resolve, but I couldn't let her go.

"Very well. It wasn't until I moved one of the books to dust underneath that I spied Joel's name. It felt like someone knocked the air right out of my body."

"I'm sure it was a shock," I mumbled, even as I balled my fists, urging myself to remain strong.

"Joel wasn't with me long, but he was one of the sweetest kids I ever helped raise. Wicked talented, too. I helped get him into that writing program at the community college. The one where Alexander Tate stole his work.

"Even though he wasn't with me long, Joel would send me Mother's Day cards. That's the kind of boy he was. All he wanted was a family. When he died in that terrible car accident, I didn't think I'd get over it. It was like a part of my reason for being was snuffed out." She blotted her eyes with a tissue from her bag. "It killed me to know a man like Alexander Tate stole

Joel's words. But, I didn't want him to die for it. Fatalities are rare."

"That's true," Mira conceded, and I prayed she wasn't flagging, too. If we all lost our resolve, the circle would dissolve, and our captive would go free. "Even so, it's too dangerous to mess around with. I can't believe you would be making and selling mad honey in Goode Harbor."

"I would never!" Alice insisted. "I don't sell it. Most of my honey is completely benign. I only have one special hive of Apis laboriosa bees, which I keep right beside the rhododendrons. The honey is for medicinal purposes. I would never hurt anyone."

"You did, though," Brigit said accusingly. "You killed a man, and now his spirit is trapped on this plane, unable to move on."

"He wasn't supposed to die," Alice sobbed. "I gave him the mad honey to punish him, not to kill him. I only wanted justice for my son."

"I think I've heard enough." A man in a dark suit had come up to the edge of the circle, catching us all unaware when he spoke. He had a sharp crew cut and wore black shades with the unmistakable air of law enforcement. I shivered, recalling the FBI agents who had knocked down my door. Nora had joined us now, and I wanted nothing more than to fall against her with relief. Something about her calming presence had that effect on me.

"Tallie," she said, standing so close her shoulder

rubbed against mine. "We came as soon as I got your text."

"Yes, Ms. Shipton," the man said. "Thank you for alerting us to the situation."

"Of course," I said, not really convinced that what I'd said in my short message would have been enough to convince a high-ranking law enforcement official to drop everything and come running. Was that Nora's doing?

"Alice Crenshaw, you're under arrest for violation of SC code 722." The air crackled as the man stepped through the invisible circle, slicing it like a hot knife through butter. My body turned to stone. Now I knew why he'd been so quick to show up on the scene. This man was no ordinary cop, or even a special agent.

He was a warlock.

A chill passed through me as I realized that the "SC" code he'd referenced had nothing to do with any human laws. It stood for Shadow Council. I'd done everything I could to keep a low profile since returning to the island, but here I was, face-to-face with someone who could make my worst nightmares come true.

There was no question he must know who I was. Would he snap on some enchanted handcuffs and haul me away to whatever dungeon Alice was headed for?

If I'd had my wits about me, I'd have made a break for it, but everything inside me shut down. I'd spent decades learning to make do without magic. I'd become used to it, to the point I'd barely thought of myself as a witch. But in this moment, I would have given anything to have mastered some sort of incantation or spell to whisk myself to safety. Instead, I was a sitting duck.

The prisoner must've realized who this man was and what shadowy forces he represented at the same time I did. With the fear of a captured animal in her eyes, Alice looked from one of us to the next, too overcome to beg for help. Not that there was anything we could do.

"Mrs. Crenshaw, come with me." The man crooked a finger, and Alice obeyed. There was no need for handcuffs. Now that she was under the authority of the Shadow Council, this formerly powerful witch went like a docile lamb to the back of his unmarked sedan. A minute later, the car was pulling to the front of the line of cars waiting to board the ferry.

As my muscles unfroze, every inch of me trembled. Had I just witnessed my own future?

"Who was that?" I asked Nora, even though I knew. What I really wanted was an explanation of how on earth she'd ended up in the company of a Shadow Council member.

"That was the official from the mainland," Nora said. "He was in the clinic getting a statement from me when I got your text."

"Why was he getting a statement?"

"He's livid with the sheriff's department, but

Bonnie especially. The way she arrested David Spencer on the spot with zero evidence and encouraging her deputies to toss your inn for no valid reason. She's in a lot of trouble. But never mind all that. How are you?" Nora placed her hand on my shoulder, and I wanted to sink into the touch, but I knew it would be wrong.

The other three witches were a distance away, talking amongst themselves and leaving me with a small amount of privacy to speak to Nora. I decided to use the opportunity to address the elephant in the room—otherwise known as the relationship she conveniently liked to forget she was in whenever I was around.

I squared my shoulders, brushing her hand off me. "That must be hard for you."

"Why?" She seemed genuinely puzzled. "It has nothing to do with me or the clinic."

"I meant I know what it's like when your partner has done something wrong and has to face the consequences." I swallowed, forcing myself to continue. "When the FBI showed up looking for Phil, it was terrifying, and I couldn't help feeling guilty that I hadn't seen him for what he was earlier. But I'm sure this thing with Bonnie is nothing like that, and it will blow over in no time."

"I'm confused. What does your ex-husband have to do with the sheriff being investigated?"

I blinked, unsure why she wasn't getting it when

I'd been trying to be nice. "Because she's your girlfriend, and she's in trouble. I know what that's like."

"She's my what?" Nora staggered back a step before bursting into laughter. "Who told you we were dating?"

"Bonnie did." I bit my lip, trying to figure out what was so funny. "She told me at the awards. Actually, she said, 'Nora Kenworthy is mine. You understand? The doc belongs to me.'"

"Did she now?" The humor in her eyes faded.

I nodded. "Word for word. It was pretty much burned into my skull."

"That does explain a lot."

I wouldn't have thought a simple fact like that needed explaining. Then again, I hadn't been the one getting all flirty every time we were together. At least, I don't think I was. Maybe this was not a great thing to bring up in my defense.

"Tallie, you need to understand something." Nora put her hand back on my shoulder, and this time, she put the other one on the opposite side, holding me very still. "Bonnie and I are not a couple. Hell, we've never even gone on a date. I can remember having coffee with her once, but it was only because we were in the shop at the same time and there was one free table. Even on a small island with not a lot of lesbians, I don't think that qualifies."

"You're not Bonnie's girlfriend?" I had the overwhelming need to clarify this one more time to be certain.

"I am not. I never will be." Nora paused, her dark eyes holding mine with an intensity I could feel in my toes. "She's not my type at all."

I wanted to ask what her type was. I wanted to so badly, but I chickened out.

"I need to go check on Tabitha and Sabrina," I said instead. "It's not every day the babysitter gets arrested for murder."

"Thank goodness for that." Nora offered a faint smile, tinged with a touch of sadness. She squeezed my shoulders before letting go. "Check on your kids. We can talk more another time."

One thing about your kids accidentally being left with a babysitter who turned out to be a murderer, it made a foolproof excuse to leave uncomfortable conversations for another day. Not saying I was planning to make a habit of it, but I wasn't above using it to my advantage while I could.

CHAPTER TWENTY-TWO

"Why didn't you tell me Nora and Sheriff Gray weren't a couple?" I demanded before Dana had a chance to sit down at the dining room table with her coffee. She'd dropped in to check on us all in the aftermath of Alice's arrest. I was pretty sure by the look on her face, she was already regretting it.

"Why would you think for a single second that they were?" Dana shuddered visibly. "Can you even picture the two of them together?"

"No, but…" The more I thought about it, the more I wondered why that hadn't become clear to me on my own. "The question is, why would the sheriff literally tell me to keep my hands off Nora if they weren't?"

"No, sweetie. The real question is, do you want your hands to be on Nora?" The question was asked with a teasing twinkle in her eyes, but I could tell Dana wanted to know the answer.

I wished I knew what I wanted. "I find my thoughts confusing on that subject to be honest."

The teasing faded, replaced by understanding, as Dana put her hand on my arm. "What's got you confused, exactly?"

"I know I didn't have the best marriage at the end, but I married Phil for all the right reasons." I ran this assertion through my head, trying to decide if it was true. "We wanted the same things, at least before his love of money changed him. And I loved him. I was attracted to him is what I'm trying to say, and—"

"I think we can stop right there," Dana said, holding up a hand. "I don't need all the gory details of heterosexual wedded bliss. Are you saying you were never attracted to anyone else?"

I could tell by the way Dana said it that by anyone, she meant women. I gave her question some serious thought but came up blank.

"If people around me were attractive, I didn't notice, I guess," I said at last. "I was married. And a mom. I wasn't thinking in those terms anymore."

"That explains a lot about how you acted with Nora."

I frowned. "What do you mean? How did I act?"

"Oblivious. She's been hitting on you since the first day she saw you."

"Has she?" I drew in a breath, truly shocked by this revelation. "The whole time?"

"Yes." Dana laughed, but not in a mean-spirited way. More in the *I was such a dork* way.

"I assumed she was being nice. After all, consider her family," I argued. "That cousin of hers will hit on anyone with legs and tits. He tormented me all through childhood, and he still propositioned me at the anniversary celebration."

"Nora is nothing like Chad." Dana squeezed my hand. "She's a good person, but aloof. All this time I've known Nora, she's never reacted to anyone like she has with you. I thought you weren't interested and weren't sure how to handle it. That happens sometimes with you straight girls."

"What if I'm not?" I let the question tumble out before I could stop myself, and although part of me wanted to sink under the table, part of me was glad I had asked.

"What if you're not interested?" Dana asked cautiously.

I couldn't answer with words, only shaking my head. It wasn't that I wasn't interested. It was that I wasn't sure I was straight. Only I couldn't bring myself to say it, as if the words themselves held the power of a magic spell, one that had every chance of blowing up in my face if I dared try to cast it.

Thankfully, Dana seemed to catch my meaning. "Ah. Then I think you should talk to her about it."

I cringed. "Won't that be awkward?"

"Most heartfelt conversations about feelings are, but they're also vital if you want meaningful human relationships."

Fear had my stomach threatening to rebel. "But, I shouldn't. I can't. Even if I did feel like that, it'd be completely reckless of me to act on it."

"Why do you think that?" Dana squeezed my hand, and instantly, I felt more grounded and a little less terrified. "You deserve happiness."

I wished I could embrace her sentiment, but doubts swirled all around me. Happiness was for other people. I was far from convinced it was for me.

"Let's consider the facts. First, I'm not even legally divorced yet." I extended one finger in the air. "I've got the kids to think about."

"But what about you, Tallie?" Dana demanded. "Who is going to think about what's best for you?"

"I can't." I sniffled, trying not to cry and ashamed of how weak I felt.

"If you can't, it's going to have to be me. I'm going to tell you what I think, even if you don't want to hear it." Dana lowered her head to make eye contact with me. "You've been hiding for too long. Hiding your desires. Hiding your power. Hiding the truth. You're literally hiding on an island right now."

"I…" I wanted to say I wasn't, but it was a lie. My shoulders slumped. "I guess I am."

"Stop hiding, Tallie. There's too much at stake

here, including the possibility of something real." Dana added, her voice full of compassion. "I know your instinct is to run. From the Shadow Council. From your mom and aunt. From me. And from Nora. But—"

"But nothing," I said, the very mention of the Shadow Council reminding me what was at stake. "Dana, don't you see? Thanks to Alice's arrest, the Shadow Council definitely knows I'm back on the island now. Just because I didn't get arrested on the spot doesn't mean I'm off the hook forever. I might get whisked off to witch prison at any moment."

"What's this all about?"

My heart sank as I turned to see my mother standing in the doorway to the kitchen. My conversation with Dana had moved from whisper into barely audible when I got too wrapped up in my anxiety. "Mom, I—"

"What is this about the Shadow Council and prison?" Mom's panic level had kicked up a notch, and she was giving off the energy of a woman who was about to go ballistic unless she got some answers. "Why would you say something like that, Tallie?"

"I think I'd better go." Dana rose, grabbing her unfinished coffee. Dana always was the smart one.

"What's going on, Tallie?" Aunt Izzy stood beside my mother, and now I was good and outnumbered.

I had no choice but to come clean about everything. "I never told you what happened after Maya died."

"You went off to college and never came home; that's what happened," my mother said, all the pent-up hurt from the past twenty-five years rising to the surface, raw and exposed. "From that very first winter break when you made some weak excuse to stay with a friend instead of coming home for Yule, you abandoned us. You left your family when we needed you most. When I needed you most. You ran away from the life you were meant to live and married that pathetic, non-magical lump of a husband and settled in Cleveland."

Of all the injuries I had caused her, I believe Cleveland may have cut the deepest.

"Phil wasn't that bad," I said out of habit, the misplaced loyalty of nearly two decades hard to shake. When I realized what I'd said, I laughed. "Okay, he was that bad, but to be fair, I don't think any of us realized at the time how he would turn out. Not unless your crystal ball told you, and you decided not to tell me."

"You know I've never been very good at divination," Mom said sadly.

My aunt, who had gone to the kitchen a moment before, returned with three fresh mugs of coffee. She'd made them so quickly I was certain magic was involved.

As if having the same thought, Mom sighed and said, "I've never been that great as a kitchen witch, either, truth be told."

"What are you talking about? You're a great cook." I couldn't believe what my mom was saying. Was this the same woman who had hounded me about my magical studies since the day I had turned thirteen, to the point where my older sister had started working the spells on my behalf?

"I can cook, honey, but that's not the same thing as being a kitchen witch." There was a sadness in my mom's eyes I'd never seen before, a different sorrow than the loss of Maya had caused, less frantic and more defeated.

"Now, now, my dear." Aunt Izzy patted my mother's shoulder. "You know your mama did the best she could to teach you what little she knew."

"Are you saying you don't have powers?" I held my breath, waiting to see how far this little apple had fallen from the tree.

"Some, but not a lot, and not what you might expect," she said, confirming my suspicion.

"Like making the wind blow when you get frustrated?" I pointed to her coffee, which had ripples on the surface despite the fact she wasn't blowing on it.

Startled, she set the coffee on the table, some of the liquid sloshing over the rim. "Oh my! I haven't done that in ages. I'd completely forgotten. I thought that was gone."

"You've been able to do that all along, and you never told me?" I didn't know whether to be relieved or angry as this piece of crucial information snapped into place. I wanted to laugh and cry at the same time. "If I'd known, I might not have been so scared when I did it."

"Oh, Tallie. I never thought you'd—" My mother choked on her words, tears filling her eyes. "I watched so closely with you, but I never spotted a single clue. And Maya was so much more talented at magic than I'd ever dared hope. I really thought whatever hex our line of witches was under had lifted."

"Maya covered for me," I admitted. "She didn't like to see me get in trouble. But, are you saying that Grandma didn't have powers, either?"

"She did but not acceptable ones," Aunt Izzy corrected. "At least not for the time period. You know how things were back then. In schools, you couldn't even use your left hand to write. Imagine what they were like with a witch who could change the weather and was always talking to things that weren't there."

"What happened to her powers?" I asked my aunt, tensing for the reply.

"It was too cruel. No child should have their powers bound just because of superstitious adults."

I let out an audible gasp, which my mom must've mistaken for shock. Which it was, but not for the reasons she thought.

"They don't do that anymore, dear." Mom grabbed my hand. "Even if Tabitha or Sabrina show some tendencies in the future for less desirable magical traits, it never comes to *that*."

"But it does happen," I wailed, unable to control it. Even though I could feel the air around me stirring, moving the hairs along my neck, I couldn't keep it inside any longer. "It did. The Shadow Council thought I was somehow responsible for Maya's death, and they told me I wouldn't be punished if I agreed—" A sob choked me. "If... if.... If I let them bind my magic, and I agreed never to return to Crescent Cove again."

The energy in the room crackled, and for once, it wasn't coming from me. "They did what?" My mother thundered, and I shrank from the sensation of electricity filling the air before a storm.

"I'm sorry, Mom. I'm sorry," I babbled. "I don't know what happened. I was on the boat. And then I was on the shore. And the waves, and the rain..."

I squeezed my eyes shut against the memory of that white sail disappearing between the dual blackness of sea and sky.

"I'm not mad at you." My mom's arms were around me. The electricity was gone, and it felt safe and warm. "It's them I'm angry with. How could they do that to a child?"

"I was in college," I argued, though I wasn't sure why, since in principle, she was right. Being in college and being mature enough to make adult choices didn't necessarily go hand in hand. "They came to my dorm room in September."

"Need I remind you, you were still seventeen at that point?" Mom said, her cheeks flushing, and her eyes filling with rage. "Your birthday wasn't until November. That's below the age of magical consent. They had no right."

"They thought I was dangerous," I whispered. "They thought I had caused it somehow, that it was my fault." As I said it, I cowered, understanding how deeply I worried they were.

"Whatever they thought," my aunt said with steel in her tone, "they didn't know, and yet they scared you into agreeing to something you couldn't possibly understand."

"Tallie, sweetheart." There was pleading in my mother's tone, her hand pressing into mine. "Don't you see now how important it is for Tabitha and Sabrina to know as much as possible about who and what they are?"

The events that had occurred since I'd returned to the island cascaded into one another, a domino effect that forced me to confront a single truth: by trying to protect my girls, I might have put them in danger. Now, I was being given an opportunity to spare them the potential hurt and scars that could come from being sheltered. I swallowed hard before drawing a deep breath, rising, and going to the foot of the stairs. "Girls? Come down here for a minute," I shouted. "It's time for a family meeting."

"Family meetings are lame." Sabrina glared at me from the sofa in the family room, her legs curled up beneath her. It was not the first time she had lodged this complaint since finally making her way downstairs.

"Too bad," I snapped. "We're having one, and you don't get a say about it."

"Off to a good start." Tabitha smirked. She was usually the good kid, but ever since developing a crush on Marcus, she'd been pushing the limits a little more each day. "Score one for democracy."

I balled my hands into fists, counted to five, and relaxed them against my thighs. "I know you're both getting older, and in fact, that's the reason we need to have this talk. I—"

"Ugh, Mom. We already had the period talk. Why do adults keep harping on it? So gross." Sabrina dramatically tossed her head against the couch in yet another Oscar-winning performance.

"It's not about periods," I told them, focusing on a spot on the wall to keep myself from flying into a rage. When had my sweet babies turned into these sassy preteens? "It's even more important. I don't know how to say this aside from just saying it. That night when we arrived on the island—"

"When Grandma and Aunt Izzy were naked?" Sabrina cracked. "I bet you thought we'd forgotten about that, didn't you?"

"Actually, it does have something to do with that,

yes," I conceded, embarrassment welling up as it always did when sensitive topics where addressed. Did they think I'd enjoyed talking to them about menstrual periods, for heaven's sake?

"You aren't going to—" Tabitha slid her eyes toward the kitchen, where my aunt and mother were hiding out to give us some privacy but ready to spring into action in case they were needed. "You can't put them in a home. I know they act a little weird sometimes, but they're not crazy and senile."

"A home?" I burst into laughter. "No. Trust me. I know they're not crazy, at least not because of the naked dancing and the bonfire. That night, they were performing a ceremony. A sacred ritual for the solstice. It's one that witches do. Because they're witches, girls. And so am I. And so are you. We're all witches."

The girls stared in silence for at least five seconds before bursting into giggles.

"Good one, Mom." Tabitha slapped her thigh. "We thought you were going to say someone was dead."

"Do we have to all be witches?" Sabrina asked between gasps, unable to stop laughing. "I want to be a werewolf."

"No, you don't." My nose wrinkled as I recalled the single time many years ago when I'd come into contact with one of these elusive creatures. "So smelly. And if you think getting a period once a month is an inconvenience—"

"Okay, what about a vampire?" Sabrina pressed.

Tabitha held up her hand for a high five, and it was obvious neither one was taking me seriously.

"Girls!"

Both froze. Who needs magic when you've perfected your mom voice?

"Children, listen to your mother." Aunt Izzy came into the family room with a tray of snacks. Of course, she did. While I had no idea now what my mother and I were, or what my grandmother and sister had been, Aunt Izzy was a Shipton by blood and a kitchen witch through and through.

"Look at that lovely tray of food," I said. "Aren't you glad you aren't a vampire? You wouldn't be able to enjoy any of it."

"Who would want to be a vampire?" Aunt Izzy seemed genuinely puzzled. "Why live for eternity if you can't eat garlic?"

"It doesn't work that way, anyway," my mother said, joining us in the room. "You don't get to pick what you are out of a Halloween grab bag. You're a witch because you were born into a witch family."

Sabrina's expression grew serious, and I could see she was starting to consider the possibility that we weren't joking. "Is Dad a witch?"

"No, he is not," my mother couldn't help but say, her hands flying to her hips with indignation. "But I should've turned him into a toad when I had the chance."

"Mother," I warned, my eyes flashing a reminder

that we'd agreed not to speak poorly of Phil in front of the kids.

"Male witches are called warlocks," Aunt Izzy explained. "And people cannot actually be turned into toads, so don't listen to your grammy."

"Are you buying this?" Tabitha whispered to her sister.

After more time to think it over than I would've expected, Sabrina responded, "Nah! Come on. Let's go get our bikes. I can't wait to tell Ruby about this."

I gave my mom and aunt a *what can you do* shrug. This was going to be a long process to get them to accept the truth, but at least I'd finally had the courage to take the first step. We'd ease them into it slowly, let them see little examples of magic until they got over their suspicion that it was a trick and started to believe.

The girls were still laughing and joking with one another when they opened the front door. Instantly, they came to a dead stop in the entryway.

"Uh, Mom?" Tabitha said, her voice a little shaky. "There's someone here."

"Are we expecting anyone?" Mom asked Aunt Izzy, who shook her head.

"No check-ins until the afternoon," she answered.

I made my way to the door and froze. The man on the porch stared at me, his gaze almost as sharp as his buzz cut. There was no mistaking him. This was the man who'd arrested Alice Crenshaw.

"Go upstairs," I said quietly to the girls, wishing it hadn't sounded so much like a hiss. I wanted this to be done calmly so as not to spook them.

"You will not take my daughter!" My mom, not at all worried about spooking anyone—and in fact seeming to take pleasure in it—leaped into the entryway, blocking the man's access to me.

My daughters turned to me with panicked faces. "Mom?"

"I would like you to leave my home." Aunt Izzy strode to the door, somehow looking as if she was fifteen feet tall. "Otherwise, you can expect a formal investigation into why the Shadow Council entered into a magical agreement with an underage witch twenty-five years ago."

"There's been a misunderstanding. If you'll let me explain, I think we can put your mind at ease, Ms. Shipton." He spoke with sincerity, almost as if he hadn't arrived for the sole purpose of dragging me off to the witch slammer. "I don't know what happened back then as it was before my time, but I think it's safe to say things weren't handled exactly according to protocol."

"You're damn right it was handled wrong. No one spoke to either of us." My aunt motioned to my mother, indicating they were a package deal and a force to be reckoned with. "What kind of monsters are you? Tallie had just lost her sister, and you blamed her for it and then forced her to leave her family and give up her magic. I never thought the Council could be so cruel."

To his credit, the man didn't flinch at the barrage of anger being fired at him. "The details surrounding the binding decision go above my pay grade even now, but I can say one thing with confidence. She was never banned from the island," the warlock said. He turned to me, and the expression on his face was the same as someone might wear if begging you to call off the attack dogs at their throat. "Not in the way you seemed to have interpreted it, ma'am."

Oh, for the love of all that's holy, had this Shadow Council agent, who on closer inspection barely appeared old enough to shave, just ma'amed me? Like I was his mother or something?

"If I wasn't banned, can you explain why I was told never to return? Sir?" Damn. Said out loud, that didn't have the same snarky ring to it as ma'am did. One more reason to hate misogyny.

"The exact source of your powers is unknown to the council, Ms. Shipton," he explained somewhat haltingly. "The binding spells that were used hadn't been tested before they were performed, and considering the unique vibrations that emanate from this island, well, the truth is they didn't know if the binding would hold if you came back here to live."

"What right did you have to bind her in the first place?" Mom demanded of him, not even close to giving up on her attack.

"It was for her own protection, uh..." I could tell he was about to say ma'am, but either he thought better of it, or my mom had stopped the words in his throat with the power of her mind. Considering it seemed I'd inherited my odd powers from my mother—which had always been a safe bet considering we didn't really know which of several handsome summer tourists had been responsible for my conception, but none of the potential candidates were warlocks—I was curious to see exactly what kind of unusual tricks my mom had up her sleeves.

The agent turned to me. "Have you experienced the return of any powers since you arrived home, Ms. Shipton?"

"Some," I said begrudgingly, knowing I probably had a glow about me only Council members could detect. If I lied to his face, he might change his mind about hauling me off.

He nodded as if he'd expected as much. I was glad I'd followed my instincts and told the truth.

"Will I have to leave?" I asked him in a voice barely above a whisper.

"No, at least not at this point. All we ask is that you keep us informed if you experience anything weird."

"Weird?" I raised an eyebrow at this thoroughly unofficial sounding term. "Define weird."

He shifted nervously, and I got the sense that he was sweating even more than would be expected of a man wearing a suit in the middle of summer. "We don't really know. This is uncharted territory."

He hadn't specifically asked if I'd been seeing spirits manifest in front of me or had slipped through a crack in time and landed in a 1920s speakeasy recently, so I decided to update my definition of weird to no longer include any of those things.

"Everything's been pretty normal," I assured him.

"Is that all you wanted?" Aunt Izzy snapped, clearly not willing to extend an olive branch for past misdeeds his agency had committed.

"Only to tell you the Shadow Council is your friend," he said it so earnestly I stifled a laugh. "We want to help you. If something unusual does happen, please come to us."

"You won't be monitoring me?" I'd half expected to have to wear a magical ankle monitor wherever I went.

The man, whom I only realized now had never identified himself by name, offered a tight-lipped smile. I knew what that meant. He wasn't going to answer because he didn't want to lie. Which meant they probably had been monitoring my activities to some extent all along. Certainly since I'd returned to the island and maybe for years. There was no telling what they really knew.

I lifted my chin, indulging in what little defiance I felt safe with. "I guess you should know everything when I do."

His expression was hard to gauge. I made a mental note never to play poker with this man.

"I'll show you the way out," Mom said, though it was completely unnecessary since he'd never come inside and was still standing on the edge of the threshold.

For the briefest of seconds, I wondered if he was a vampire. He looked like a warlock, and the air crackled around him in a way that said he was what he claimed. Then again, if he really was a vampire and didn't want us to know, we probably never would. They can be tricky that way.

"Good day, all of you." No sooner had he turned than my mother shut the door and bolted it in place.

My aunt whispered into my ear, "Do not tell them anything. You hear me?"

I swallowed, agreeing with a nod.

"Mom?" Sabrina was huddled against my leg. She hadn't done that since she was really little, and the unexpected gesture caught me by surprise.

"What is it, sweetie?" I pulled her closer.

"That guy just now. Uh…" Sabrina tilted her head to look at me, seeming suddenly very small. "Were you serious about the witch thing? Like, for real?"

"Yeah," I replied. "Like, for real."

I looked anxiously from my younger daughter to the older, tensing for whatever anxiousness would appear at this shocking news, but instead of fear, their expressions turned to pure excitement.

"Oh. My. God," Tabitha said, each word punctuated with a full stop. "This is so cool."

They grabbed onto each other, jumping and twirling around the house. All I could do was watch and laugh with relief. But it was bittersweet. They were so much like Maya and I had been at that age. So completely unaware of all the ways magic could go wrong. I prayed they would never have a reason to find out.

CHAPTER TWENTY-THREE

It was the night of the new moon, the first of August, and the start of the ancient feast of Lughnasadh, which marks the traditional beginning of the harvest season. From my arrival on the island at the summer solstice, one-eighth of the witch's year had passed. Though the summer was only half gone, there was a briskness to the air as salty breezes swept across the island and continued out to sea.

A little over a week ago, Mrs. Crenshaw had been arrested. I told the girls we're witches and had a chat with someone from the Shadow Council. So much had changed since Phil's arrest and our arrival on the island. It'd been exhausting, really.

Before every witch on the island descended upon the inn, I sprawled out on my grandmother's quilt, closing my eyes for a moment to enjoy the gentle chirp of crickets that came through my open window, along with the ever-present scent of wild rose. There was no sign of Buster this evening. Hunting was especially tricky during the new moon, and from what I'd come to know of him, I suspected he would be prowling through the woods most of the night, keen on the added challenge posed by the dark. He was that kind of cat.

"Tallie?" My aunt's voice was accompanied by a knock on my bedroom door. "Our guests are arriving. Are you coming down?"

"In a minute," I said. The door squeaked open, and Aunt Izzy held out a shimmering armful of black fabric. "What's that?"

"The dress you brought over to Brigit's shop for her to alter. She brought it back, along with a locket she said you wanted fixed." Handing over the items, my aunt turned to go. "Do hurry. The full moon celebration starts promptly at sunset."

"I'll be right there." I took the dress and locket and then glanced at the clock. It was thirty minutes to eight, and I'd been informed at least half a dozen times that day that sundown was at 8:01. I draped the dress over the chair in the corner, looping the locket through the hook on the hanger.

The metal shone like new. I wondered if Brigit had managed to get it to open finally. Glancing over my shoulder like a naughty child, I stole several precious seconds to find out. To my delight, the clasp released with gentle pressure, and the two sides swung open with ease. My breath caught in a startled gasp. Inside were two black and white photos, with two familiar faces posed in such a way that they gazed at one another when the locket was open.

On the left side was a dark-haired gentleman with a square jaw and aquiline nose, except that on closer inspection, my earlier hunch proved true. Bertie Chase most definitely had too many feminine traces to be anything but a woman disguising herself as a man.

On the right side, the photo nearly stopped my breathing altogether. The face that looked out at me was so close to being my own I had to blink a few times to make certain it wasn't a trick. But as far as I could tell, the photo was genuine, depicting a young woman who could have been my twin twenty years ago. She wore the clothing of a different era, but even in black and white, there was no mistaking that bright red hair. Shipton hair, I'd always called it, only now I knew that wasn't true. Whoever this woman happened to be, she had it, too.

"Tallie!" my aunt bellowed from the first floor.

I jumped, the locket falling against the black silk dress. "I told you I was coming!" I'll admit my tone was less respectful than it should have been, but she'd been reminding me about the importance of being on time for tonight's ritual since breakfast. Just because I hadn't practiced witchcraft since I was in high school didn't mean she had to treat me like a naughty teenager.

Only this time, she hadn't been yelling for me out of a desire to nag. When I made it to the bottom step, I saw Nora Kenworthy standing on the porch beyond the open doorway.

"You have a visitor, dear," my aunt said blandly before skirting around her to join the rest of the witches who were already assembling on the front lawn. "I've given her some lemonade while she waited."

"Hi… Nora. How… How are you?" *Real smooth, Tallie.* I was sounding more and more like a teenager with every syllable that came stuttering from my lips.

"I didn't know you were hosting a party. I can come back." Nora started to turn around.

"It's nothing, really." Just a sacred Lughnasadh ceremony, the first of its kind Tabitha and Sabrina would experience. No biggie. But despite the sun sinking lower in the west with each passing second, I couldn't send Nora away without finding out why she'd come. "Please, don't go yet."

"Are you sure?" She seemed to sense my need for her to stay, like she was reading my mind. I couldn't decide whether the prospect of Nora Kenworthy knowing my thoughts was more creepy or comforting.

"It's just some family friends. A barbecue, basically." I only left out the part where we would be casting a circle and setting intentions for the coming month to celebrate the start of the harvest season in precisely twenty-eight minutes, if my watch was correct. After that was done, though, we would definitely be having food. "What brings you around?"

She took a sip from the glass tumbler she held in her hand. "I was on my way home, and I thought I'd stop because there's something that's been keeping me up at night." Nora scuffed one tennis shoe against the painted porch floor.

"You're the doctor. If anyone can figure out the cause of your insomnia, it's probably you."

"I know the cause, but you're the only one with the cure."

"Um, okay." At this point, I wasn't sure what she was talking about. Had she come over for a pot of Aunt Izzy's calming tea? I didn't think any of the non-magicals knew about that.

"Was Bonnie the only source of confusion for you?"

"Oh." I had not expected her to put me on the spot like that. "*That's* what you wanted to talk about."

Was I stalling? Definitely. With Nora away from the island most of the week, I'd had plenty of time to think of how to deal with seeing her again and the inevitable need to discuss the Bonnie revelation and what it might mean for the future. Sadly, I had not used my time wisely. Apparently, I'd learned nothing since my school days, still relying heavily on a strategy of procrastination and winging it to get me through the toughest assignments. It wasn't working any better now than it had then.

"It's okay. I get it." Nora chugged the last of her

lemonade like it was a stiff drink before setting the glass down on the railing. "You're not interested. That's totally fine. I'm just going to go."

"Wait." I reached for Nora's hand, not willing to let her leave yet, even if her going and never speaking to me again *would* spare me from the raging flames of embarrassment threatening to set me alight. "The thing is I think I might be interested, and that's even more confusing to me than trying to figure out why you were dating a crazy woman like Sheriff Gray. I guess I never thought I would, ya know, be interested in someone like you in that way."

"You mean because I'm a woman?" There was a hint of the same reproachful look in Nora's eyes that Dana's had held the night she and Celia had gone to dinner, when I'd been accused of being homophobic. If it had hurt coming from Dana, with Nora it nearly severed me in two.

I turned to the trustiest weapon in my arsenal: sarcasm.

"No. Because you're a Kenworthy. Your cousin is a huge turd. I have to confess I'm seriously questioning my judgment right now." I started to relax as Nora laughed, and the worst of the tension drained from me. "But, as long as I'm confessing things, you're right. I've never been attracted to a woman before. It's all so new. I don't handle change well, and I've had a lot of it lately."

With the somewhat wonky return of my powers

and the close call with the Shadow Council, it was way more change than I could ever tell her about, which was another concern that gave me pause. I'd spent seventeen years with a non-magical, and look how that had turned out. Was I willing to consider doing that again?

"Okay." She studied me for a moment in total silence, until I thought I would burst out of my skin. Was that all she had to say? If so, why was she still standing there? Her lips twitched into the ghost of a smile. "So, if I asked you to dinner next week, what do you think you might say?"

"Are you asking me to dinner?" I swallowed and nearly choked on my sandpaper tongue. I glanced sharply at the yellow contents of her glass as if it held the answer I was seeking. "Or is this a hypothetical situation we're talking about? Because it kind of sounds like you're conducting a survey on the topic."

"That probably depends a lot on what your answer is." When I was still too stunned to answer, she added, "Have you ever been to LuLu's Flying Lobster Pot?"

"The place by the airport?" It was the best lobster shack on Goode Harbor Island—some would say all of Maine—and my resolve was melting like a delicious dish of rich, salty butter. "I do like lobster."

"Me too. A lot. Theirs is really good, but they're only open through Labor Day weekend."

"It'd be a shame not to have lobster there before the end of the season."

"Together? Or was that a hypothetical?" Nora arched an eyebrow, and I went all wobbly.

"Yes. Together." I grabbed the porch railing so I wouldn't fall over. "That sounds lovely."

There was some commotion outside, most likely my aunt being her suave self and reminding me that time was ticking. I wasn't sure of the time, but the sun was so low in the sky it had to be nearly 8:01.

"I should let you get to your family thing," Nora said in a breathy way that made me shiver.

"I guess so."

Nora leaned closer, her mouth aiming for a simple kiss on the cheek. Not knowing what came over me, I moved at the last second, so her lips landed on mine, soft and welcoming. Had I turned my head on purpose, or was it an accidental twitch? Even I wasn't sure.

And I didn't care.

This was hardly the time to think about motivations. I was too busy being swept away by the burst of sensation lighting up my body like a fireworks display. This wasn't my first kiss, but by the goddess, it sure felt like it. Everything was new, from Nora's delicate scent to the sweet taste of her mouth. I had never felt this way before, like a whole unknown universe was opening before me, mine to explore.

I have no idea how long the kiss lasted. It seemed both too short and like it stretched to eternity. When our lips parted, we both let out satisfied sighs at exactly the same moment. Nora blushed, and I started to giggle.

"I'll see you next week," Nora managed to say, suddenly bashful in a way I'd never imagined she could be.

"Not if I see you first." Apparently, all it took was a single kiss to make my brain malfunction like my circuit boards had been dunked in the salty water of Crescent Cove. Why did I insist on being such a moron?

"I'd like that, actually," Nora confessed, not nearly as mortified as she should have been at being excited to spend time with an idiot like me. "It's possible I have breakfast at Rosie's Diner every morning around six. Just in case you're ever up at the crack of dawn and in need of a biscuits and gravy fix."

"You're a doctor, for goodness sake. You must know that stuff will kill you. Not to mention that motorcycle you insist on riding." Now, I had turned into a public service announcement on the dangers of having fun. I had apparently not added a single ounce of smoothness where my ability to interact with someone I liked was concerned. Luckily for me, Nora looked at me like she'd never been more amused.

"Tallie, are you coming?" It was my mom, poking her head around a bush and giving me the stink eye.

"Right. That's my cue." Nora retrieved her motorcycle helmet from one of the rocking chairs, holding it for me to see, as if to show me that she took safety seriously. "See you soon, Tallie."

"Looking forward to it, Nora."

There was a heavy ache in my chest as she turned to go, and I called out to her as her foot hit the bottom porch step. "Nora, about dinner. Just let me know the night."

"Would Friday work?"

"It would." Her grin made my heart flutter.

I arrived in the front yard at three minutes past eight and was greeted by the sight of six witches I recognized and several I only vaguely remembered, all gathered around a small table set out on the grass. Dana was there with her mother, while Mira had brought both her mom and grandma, plus Marcus and Ruby, who were hanging out with my girls. Brigit was speaking to a fashionably dressed witch near a small group of witches and warlocks I had yet to meet.

As soon as they spotted me, our guests stopped chatting and moved to form a large circle around the small table with candles that served as the altar. It was my first time celebrating a holiday in twenty-five years, and I was two minutes late.

Aunt Izzy looked at her watch with a sigh. "We almost had to cast the circle without you."

With a look of chagrin, I took my place between my daughters, who were watching the entire thing with eyes wide and full of wonder. I held their hands, giving each a squeeze.

As the celebration began, I looked around the circle, taking in each and every one of the wonderful people who had become so much a part of my life in such a short time. Some old friends and new ones, too. Tears stung the corners of my eyes—happy ones, at finally being where I belonged, and the prospect of sharing a part of my life with my girls that I'd never expected I could.

Not only did I have these amazing people, but there was Nora. A woman who listened to me and cared about my thoughts. Who'd seen me at my worst, yet she still wanted to take me out to dinner. What more could I want, really?

As strange a journey as my coming home had turned out to be, something told me it was where I needed to be. I still had no idea where I was going in the long run, or what I would do when I finally arrived, but at least I could find comfort in knowing that I would be surrounded by three generations of women who would protect me and guide me on my path. It was more than I was likely to find anywhere else.

It was a peaceful night, and after the solemnities were done, we all sat out on the lawn and watched fireflies flickering in the grass while drinking sparkling lemonade. In the distance, green and purple wisps of light danced beneath the stars. It was one of the rare evenings when the aurora borealis could be seen in the sky, and I soaked it up like magic, which I truly believed it was.

"Have you had any disturbances, Tallie?" Dana asked as she plopped onto the ground beside me, criss-crossing her legs. "Any sightings of Alex or strange dreams?"

"Not a one," I answered. "Everything's been back to normal since the truth came out. I think he's gone into the light." I was a little sad I hadn't seen it happen, but as long as Alexander Tate's spirit was at peace, that was enough for me.

"That's good news," she said. "Did I see Nora here earlier?"

"You did?"

"And…?"

"We're going to dinner on Friday night. Just, you know, a friendly sort of, um…" A memory of the kiss we'd shared on the porch flashed through my mind, and I knew there was no way I could finish whatever nonsense I was trying to say in a way that anyone would believe, including myself.

"Date?" Dana leaned against me. "It's about damn time. You deserve happiness, Tallie."

There had been a time right after Phil left and I'd lost everything, when I'd honestly been convinced I would never be happy again. It seemed ludicrous to me now. Why had I been so convinced I'd been happy before?

Sure, I'd had a nice house in a leafy green suburb of Cleveland and a car that was guaranteed to start every time I turned the key instead of when it felt up to it.

I'd had friends—or at least people I had called by that name, though they'd scattered to the winds the moment news of our troubles became known.

I'd had a husband, one who ignored me, whose only expression when I spoke to him was one of annoyance that ranged from mild to vein-popping. He preferred work to being at home, and, as it turned out, stealing to earning a living. And in the end, the money had mattered more to him than his wife or kids. Was that the so-called happiness I had been clinging to for so long?

Now here I was, back home with all the people who truly mattered, in a place where magic was real and accepted. A place I could be myself and raise my daughters to do the same.

Was I happy now? Maybe not quite yet. But I was on my way, and that was a start.

It was nearly midnight when the final sparks of the fire had gone out and the last of the witches and warlocks left for home. I followed Aunt Izzy into the house, piling our used glasses and plates in the sink. "Should I wash them tonight?" I asked.

"No, they'll keep until morning. You should head up to bed and get some rest."

"I think I will," I said as I reached the back staircase and placed my foot on the first step. "I hope I remembered to turn the quilt down before I left the room, or Buster will be terribly upset."

"Okay, good night, dear," Aunt Izzy said, her fatigue making her sound more absentminded than usual. I was halfway up the stairs when I heard her ask, "Who in heaven's name is Buster?"

I chuckled, shaking my head as I continued on. Either she'd spiked her lemonade with something a little stronger than club soda, or old age was getting to her for sure if she couldn't remember the name of her own darned cat.

The first thing I noticed as I entered my room, aside from the stifling scent of roses, which I'd mostly grown accustomed to by now, was that while the quilt had indeed been turned down, Buster was not on it.

Instead, the pesky cat circled my feet as if bewitching me to follow him.

"I'm too tired for your silly games," I growled.

Ignoring my tone, or maybe reacting to it, Buster became more insistent.

"If I follow you, do you promise to let me sleep in?"

"Meow."

I crossed my arms as he stared at me. Finally, I sighed and gave in. "Fine. I'm taking you at your word."

The cat raced out the door like he'd caught a case of the zooms, and I followed as best I could as he hurried out of sight. I was down the stairs and crossing the second-floor landing when a sense of dread bubbled deep inside. A blue-green glow spilled out of the guest room like an ominous beacon.

Maybe it was all that reminiscing I'd done about my no-good ex and how poorly he'd treated me, or maybe I had reached the stage where enough was enough. Either way, my dread was replaced with a growing sense of indignation. Of all the annoyingly needy, narcissistic spirits wandering this mortal plane, how had I gotten stuck with this one? I hadn't even liked the guy when he was alive. As a ghost, he had long overstayed his welcome.

"Seriously, Mr. Tate. You need to go into the light!" I shook my finger as I charged into the room, but instead of Alex Tate, I came face-to-face with a woman. She was sitting on the edge of the bed, one hand stroking the massive, furry black cat who sat on her lap like a happy princeling.

"Buster! Who is this?" I demanded, too shocked to know what else to say.

"Hiya, Tallie," the woman said. "How's tricks?"

Time stopped as I studied every inch of her, this mysterious woman who was sitting in my bedroom, dressed in the sleeveless, black 1920s' party dress that I was certain was safely upstairs in my room right this very second. Her brilliant red hair was perfectly coiffed in classic finger waves, a narrow band of jewels encircling her forehead while the plume of a black ostrich feather framed the back of her head. From the hand that wasn't busy petting Buster, I glimpsed the locket dangling hypnotically on its silver chain. To look at her face was like looking in a mirror. I swallowed hard, my throat threatening to trap my voice inside.

"Who the hell are you?" I managed to ask. Of all the women in my family, it probably goes without saying I was the one least known for my hospitality.

"Well, isn't that a fine howdy do," the interloper said with a grunt. But then she let loose with a girlishly lilting giggle that did absolutely nothing to answer the questions that swirled in my head.

"I really must insist you tell me who you are," I demanded, "and how you got into the inn at this time of night. Also, why you're holding my cat."

"You're cat? Buster's my baby. Isn't that right?" She carried on with unintelligible baby talk, which the usually grumpy feline lapped up like a saucer of cream. When she'd finished proving her point, she said, "I'm Verity Mayfield."

"Mayfield?" Like the mysterious name I'd found in the Chesterton family crypt? Finding the nearest chair, I sank into it.

The reality of the situation became obvious as my unexpected houseguest shifted slightly, and I detected a shimmer that let me know she wasn't quite flesh and blood. At the same time, the silver ring I'd grown so accustomed to wearing, which I'd nearly forgotten about, began to emit a radiating warmth that encircled my finger.

I was as close to certain as I could be that my late-night visitor was a ghost, but if that were true, what did that make the cat?

As if sensing I was thinking of him, Buster jumped from her lap and landed on the floor, promptly curling up as if nothing out of the ordinary was going on.

My mind was reeling. "Not to be blunt, but you're dead, right?"

"Don't know." The apparition shrugged. "I guess so. I seem to be togged to the bricks and hitting on all sixes now, though."

I had absolutely no idea what any of that meant, but frankly, Verity's slang was about the least confusing thing going on at the moment.

"So, now what?" I couldn't contain an annoyed sigh at the thought that any old ghost could wander in when they wanted and disrupt me at bedtime. "Do I help you cross into the light or something?"

"The light? Oh, heavens no." She shook her head vehemently, looking aghast at the very idea of trotting off into the light. "You and I have way too much to do. There is evil afoot, you know. All sorts of calamity might befall every witch who has ever existed if we don't stop it."

"Are you shitting me?"

"Am I...?" As my words sank in, Verity burst into laughter, clapping her hands together like a delighted child on Christmas morning. "My goodness. I think I'm going to like it here."

I watched in dumbfounded silence as my new spirit friend twirled around the room.

"Meow," said Buster.

I turned to him and glared. "Don't you start with me, too."

A dizzy and breathless Verity collapsed onto the bed with another outburst of infectious giggles.

"Verity?"

The ghost struggled into an upright position, the feathers on her head decidedly askew. "Yes?"

"You were teasing about that evil and calamity stuff, right?" I offered a weak smile, crossing my fingers this was a ghost's idea of a prank.

"Oh, no. Not at all," she assured me. Then she clapped her hands again as if overcome with glee. "This is going to be so much fun!"

Fun? As far as I could tell, I'd landed myself in a world full of more trouble than I could begin to understand.

A HUGE THANK YOU!

Thanks so much for reading *Midlife is the Cat's Meow*. The adventure is only beginning for Tallie and Nora, and the rest of the residents of Crescent Cove. To stay informed about new releases in the series, keep reading for links to sign up for our newsletters.

We've cowritten 10 books now and each time, it's always an adventure. Luckily, we're best friends who go way back, and we mean *way* back. We were actually born in the same hospital nine weeks apart!

In addition to writing together, we co-own I Heart SapphFic, a website dedicated exclusively to sapphic literature. We have fresh content six days a week, and a searchable database of thousands of sapphic books in all genres that is growing every day. For the latest sapphic fiction news, you don't want to miss signing up for our newsletter.

Here is the link: http://eepurl.com/dxgunr

A HUGE THANK YOU!

As with any partnership, there's the occasional bickering, but there's a lot more laughter. We believe the books we write together are better stories because of the collaboration. Not to mention, it's less lonely writing together.

TB has published more than thirty novels, and she still finds it simply amazing people read her stories. When she hit publish on her first book back in 2013, she had no idea what would happen. It's been a wonderful journey, and she wouldn't be where she is today without your support.

If you want to stay in touch with TB, sign up for her newsletter. She'll send you a free copy of *A Woman Lost*, book 1 in the A Woman Lost series, plus the bonus chapters and *Tropical Heat* (a short story), all of which are exclusive to subscribers. And, you'll be able to enter monthly giveaways to win one of her books.

You'll also be one of the first to hear about her many misadventures, like the time she accidentally ordered thirty pounds of oranges, instead of five. To be honest, that stuff happens to TB a lot, which explains why she owns three of the exact same Nice Tits T-shirt. In case you're wondering, the shirt has pictures of the different tits of the bird variety. She loves to show off her tits to those who subscribe to her newsletter. Again, we're talking about adorable birds that she'd never be able to identify in nature, which is why she needs pictures of them on her shirt.

A HUGE THANK YOU!

Here's the link to join: https://eepurl.com/hhBhXX

And, if you want to follow Miranda, sign up for her newsletter. Subscribers will receive her first book, *Telling Lies Online*, for free. Also, she runs giveaways for paperbacks, ebooks, and audio, that her readers love. She also shares about her gardening misadventures, including her ongoing war with Japanese knotweed and regular updates on the chipmunks in her backyard. For cat fans, she shares adorable photos of her felines, who are sisters and tag-team to destroy everything in Miranda's house. Their first Christmas was a particularly trying time, and only about half of the ornaments survived. Luckily, they're really cute. Seriously, you don't want to miss out on Miranda's heartfelt and funny newsletters. She also often includes rebuttals to the wilder claims TB makes in her newsletters, so the only way to get the full story is to read both sides.

Here's the link to join: mirandamacleod.com/list

ABOUT THE AUTHORS

TB Markinson is an American who's recently returned to the US after a seven-year stint in the UK and Ireland. When she isn't writing, she's traveling the world, watching sports on the telly, visiting pubs in New England, or reading. Not necessarily in that order.

Visit TB's website (lesbianromancesbytbm.com) to say hello. On the *Lesbians Who Write* weekly podcast, she and Clare Lydon dish about the good, the bad, and the ugly of writing.

Originally from southern California, Miranda MacLeod now lives in New England and writes heartfelt romances and romantic comedies featuring witty and charmingly flawed women that you'll want to marry. Or just grab a coffee with, if that's more your thing.

Before becoming a writer, she spent way too many years in graduate school, worked in professional theater and film, and held temp jobs in just about every office building in downtown Boston. To find out about her upcoming releases, be sure to sign up for her mailing list at mirandamacleod.com.

TB and Miranda also co-own *I Heart SapphFic*, a website for authors and readers of sapphic fiction to stay up-to-date on all the latest sapphic fiction news. The duo won a Golden Crown Literary Award for *The AM Show* in 2022.

Printed in Great Britain
by Amazon